TRAIN WRECKER

ANDREW LIVINGSTON

Phrasing and reference for the life of a *Train Wrecker* is from the 1910 article in Maclean's Magazine by A. W. Rolker, accessible online at https://archive.macleans.ca/article/1907/6/1/the-railroad-wrecker-and-his-work
The Legend of the Two Sisters by Pauline Johnson as told by Chief Joe Capilano
https://www.legendsofvancouver.net/two-sisters-vancouver-bc

Cover Image: Boy on Tracks. Comanche County, Texas. April 09, 2011.
Photographer: Greg Westfall. Image has been adapted. Image Link and Licensing:
https://www.flickr.com/photos/imagesbywestfall/5617518151
https://creativecommons.org/licenses/by/2.0/deed.en
Cover design: David Prendergast
Copy editor: Amanda Karby
First Edition May 2022
ISBN: 978-1-7782317-0-4

First say to yourself what you would be;

and then do what you have to do.

Epictetus

PART I

BOY

1977–1979

1

Handy Andy

So. When my mom told my Grandpa Earl she was knocked up with me, a boy, he went straight out and bought her a mink coat and a new sports car. He told her my name. "Andy. It's going to be Andy—Handy Andy the Train Wrecker." It turned out that way, too. Except, well, my real first name's Robert, but nobody ever calls me that, and my middle name's Andy. My dad's name, my Old Man, is Robert John Livingston, but people don't call him John, they just call him "Big Bad Bob."

Grandpa Earl Livingston's first name is also Robert, and he's a "Scotch-Irish Bastard," as my Old Man likes to say. The first-born men in my family are all named Robert, and it goes all the way back in time to the first guy in Scotland, I guess, who must have been a big bad deal way back when.

Grandpa Earl and I used to have fun together. I'm way too old for it now, of course, but he used to put me up on one of his bony old knees, sitting in a chair, and he'd be laughing the whole time. "Har, har, har... It's Handy Andy... It's Handy Andy the Train Wrecker!" A couple times, I almost fell off the old fucker's leg.

The Old Man told me once that Grandpa Earl and his buddies built Vancouver from the ground up, when all you could see around was just a bunch of rocks and trees and mountains. One time, when Dad was sitting like usual, in his old chair in front of the TV, he leaned over to me like he was telling me some big secret. "Ya know what? That old bastard was a World War I Flying Ace."

I figured that's probably true. Who the hell would lie about a thing like that? One thing's for sure, that would take some balls. Flying up in the sky, all by yourself in a Bristol Sprout or Avro DH2, and dogfighting Germans with a machine gun isn't exactly everybody's kind of work, if you know what I mean. Some Saturday nights, if Mom and Dad planned a party, I'd get dropped off at Grandpa Earl's apartment in Kerrisdale.

I was sitting across from him and Gran eating supper, and for no good reason, I got the jimmy legs under the table.

"What's the matter with you, boy?" Grandpa Earl asked me, then asked my Gran, "Marion, what's the matter with the boy?" He looked back at me with a raised eyebrow. You look fine to me. Just fine." He laughed again. "Har, har, har! Well, um, Andy, now... What kinds of things *interest* you? What gets your ass up in the morning?"

"Well, sir, I like to drive in the big white truck with Dad," I lied, like an idiot. I also didn't tell him that sometimes, when the Old Man put the brakes on too hard, a Vodka bottle rolled out from under the driver's seat.

"Driving in the truck?! Har, har, har! Did you hear that, Marion? Well, I think that's just Skookum, Andy, Skookum!"

I smiled at him. I picked up my knife and fork and put them down again. I moved my dinner napkin back and forth across my legs. I imagined lots of guys probably wouldn't mind *punching* that big old nose of his, given half a chance. Gran smiled at me with her face that looked like tree bark, handing me a dish of sticky cheese casserole. I grabbed a big spoon and dropped a large clump onto my plate. We finished eating in silence, which didn't seem to bother anybody too much. Nobody in my family goes in much for palavering.

In the silence, my winker peeps got stuck on this brown cabinet on the wall. My Gran had arranged all these glass figures she collected from the old-timey days on the shelves: a boy walking a dog, a violet lady in a fancy dress, a guy with a wheelbarrow filled with flowers, a dressed-up guy with curly hair playing a funny-looking guitar for his girlfriend. I liked looking at them. They made you start thinking to yourself, "What kind of song could that guy play on that thing?" or "Where the hell is that guy pushing a wheelbarrow?"

Grandpa Earl stood up from the table and went over to sit in a chair by the window, next to a side table with an old radio on it. He turned the radio on, adjusting the dial until we heard Dick Irvin announcing the game on Hockey Night in Canada. The Flyers were playing the Montreal Canadiens at the Spectrum in Philadelphia. It damn well sounded like the Canadiens were going to win another Stanley Cup. Well, with the "blond demon" Lafleur and that "thieving giraffe" Dryden in goal, how could they screw up? Grandpa Earl sat in his chair and I laid myself out on the floor in front of him for the game. Every time Montreal scored, he closed his eyes, grimaced, and let out a whistle. He was so mad at the end of the game, he stormed off into his bedroom, shut the door, and wouldn't come out again.

Later that night, as I lay in bed in the spare room that smelled funny—like a hospital room or a dentist's office—I was still goddamn hungry. I didn't want to get up and go into the kitchen because they'd hear me and come on out and make a big deal out of it. I stared up at the ceiling and imagined all the stuff I could eat, like a giant bowl of Count Chocula, or some Hostess Ding Dongs, or maybe some Peanut Butter Ho Ho's just sitting there in the dark, all alone, behind the closed doors of the kitchen cabinets.

I closed my eyes and imagined what it would feel like if beavers and wolves and bears were running over my skin and fish were swimming in my veins. After that, I fell asleep in the dark.

2

Wrecking Trains

"Andy, get your trunks on now, we're going swimming," Grandpa Earl commanded from the door of my room in the morning. There was a pool at the complex, the Kerrisdale Mews, and Grandpa Earl liked to take me down there so I could splash around in the water while he read the paper. Gran handed me a couple of towels while I wiggled my toes at the front door and waited for him to get ready.

Grandpa Earl walked out of his bedroom wearing a goofy bathing suit which rode high up over his belly button. On his chest were patches of grey, the same grey as the fur on this old dog who sometimes follows me home from school on the railway tracks.

We walked down the hall and got into the elevator. Grandpa Earl pressed a button and we teleported down to the lobby. We walked out, pushed open the front door, and took a winding path down to the pool. It was gonna be a swell morning!

I was the first to see Old Man Donegal coming toward us. Thick veins ran up and down the bottom of his legs.

Grandpa Earl mumbled something behind me. I stopped and looked back at him; his face was as red as a fire hydrant. And then,

Jesus Christ, he yelled out, "Coward!" And then again, much louder, "You bastard!"

"What the heck?" says Donegal. "Earl Livingston?"

"You got that right. You shirker!"

Donegal passed me by and roostered his nose right up into my grandfather's face. Their eyes were only inches apart.

"Oh, for Heaven's sake Earl. I mean, give me a break. That was over fifty years ago. Fifty years! I swear you're a nutter, that's what you are! A goddamn stroppy nutter!"

Donegal turned, shook his fist at the sky, and escaped down the pool trail. We watched him go. Grandpa Earl ran his hand through his hair, smoothing it over from the front to the back.

"Some people... You know—well, Andy, I mean... It takes a certain kind. A man is the product of his choices. I mean, a man has no right to stand there and..." He trailed off, looking down at me. "Well, don't just stand there like a tree stump. Let's get going!"

When we finally arrived at the pool, I opened the gate, grabbed an old life preserver off the chain link fence, and jumped into the water. There was nobody else on the deck, not even any kids, which was just fine by me. First, I tried the front stroke. Next, I tried the backstroke. I sank down to the bottom of the pool. I held my breath for as long as I could. I shot up out of water and flopped out on the warm pavement. Grandpa Earl didn't pay any attention to me. He just lay back on one of the pool loungers and read his paper.

Grandpa Earl looked over at me. It was a while before he said anything.

"Andy. You're going to have to bring your own self up, you see. Now, I can set you straight here and there, but your character, what gets you to do right when nobody's watching—now, that's going

---

to be up to you. I want you to remember you're Handy Andy the Train Wrecker. You can be anything you want to be. Do you understand me now, son?"

When I asked my dad later about the wrangle, he told me those two were always going at it because Donegal hadn't enlisted in the Great War. Donegal had gone to university and become a veterinarian instead. Grandpa Earl was still mad about it, all these years later.

I dried myself off and we marched back to the apartment. On the way, I decided to ask, "Grandpa Earl, what's a train wrecker, anyhow?"

"Ah, OK. A wrecker's a fella who cleans up the mess when a train goes off the rails. He's like a fireman—on duty, day and night. But a fireman only covers his territory—say, Kerrisdale here—but a train wrecker's territory can cover more than a hundred or more miles of wilderness. Trains are huge, Andy—they can weigh over a hundred tons. When a locomotive leaves the track a wreck master and his crew of train wreckers must dive in and clear the tracks so the trains can start running again. Sometimes, they roll a barrel of kerosene into the wreckage, light a match, and explode the wreck, burning all the wood so the wheels and axles and bars can be cleared by the section gang."

"What happens when there are passengers on the train?"

"Oh, that's by far the worst. I met a wrecker once who told me, 'You can get used to working day and night, and you can get used to freezing and getting soaked through to the skin, but what you never get used to is seeing things that you pull from under heaps, all stoved and flattened. I've handled 'em so smashed and mashed,' he told me, 'you wouldn't know where to catch hold first.'"

9

Back at the apartment, Gran was baking cookies. I tried to get one but had no luck, given how stingy she was, having grown up in the woods in Manitoba with seven sisters and no money, "living in a mud hut" as my Old Man put it. I went and changed into dry clothes.

Standing in the kitchen, between bites of cookie, Grandpa Earl told my Gran he wanted to go down and pay a visit to one of his tenants on the Vancouver east side. "I'm taking the boy with me."

We rode the elevator down to the lower parking lot and walked over to Grandpa Earl's big Buick. He hopped in, slid across the front seat, and opened the passenger door so I could jump in. I looked at him sitting behind the big steering wheel. He was about the same size as my friend Chinsky. Maybe a bit bigger, but not by much. He started the car and revved the engine. "Now just stay put, lad. Don't move around too much. We're heading over to the warehouse. I need to take care of some business." He rolled his eyes and whistled. "How we ever ended up with those two, I'll never know."

We rolled up and out of the underground garage and began the long drive to the east side, from Kerrisdale to Commercial Drive and Venables. He steered the big machine easily. He hummed and tapped his fingers on the steering wheel while he drove. He didn't like to listen to music in the car; he preferred to make his own. We picked up speed as we headed north on Granville Street.

"This is the third bridge they've put up over False Creek, Andy, and they got it right on the last try," he told me as we crossed over. He changed lanes. We sped past a couple of long-haired hippies on motorcycles—my Old Man thought hippies were hilarious. We passed the Old Skillet Grill, the Orpheum Theatre, and the Capitol Theatre. At a red light, we pulled up behind an old camper sitting on top of a pickup truck with a sticker on the back, next to the back door. It was a salmon with an open mouth leaping high up out of the water, its silver tail curled, chasing a golden lure.

My mom told me Earl was orphaned when he was around my age. Eventually, he made his way across the country on railway cars. After the Great War, he made his way over the Rockies and settled in the Fraser Valley, with its mighty forests and mountains like sleeping giants.

At the Robson Street intersection downtown, two drunks tried to cross the street, swerving from side to side, arms over each other's backs. We turned right on Hastings and headed over to the east side. The car pulled up outside the warehouse. Over the front window was a large sign that read "Livingston Produce. est. 1929."

We got out of the car and Grandpa Earl pulled out a set of keys attached to a wire on one of his belt loops and opened one of the doors. We walked up an old staircase and Grandpa Earl knocked on a door at the top. We waited. There was no answer. He balled up his fist and tried again. *Knock-knock-knock. KNOCK-KNOCK!*

We heard a loud clunk, a clink, and finally, a topple. A booming voice yelled, "Goddamn it! I'm here already!" The door opened with a wabble and we walked into the hallway of the scuzzy apartment. A young man stood inside, shirtless and grinning. He had grey pockets in his cheeks, like tide pools on the beach at Spanish Banks.

"Good morning, Leonard," said my grandfather. "Do you mind if we come in for a few minutes?"

Leonard smiled and nodded. "Whya, sure. I don't see why not. Come right on in." He opened his hand and waved us down the hallway. At the back was a living area with two large windows which looked out over east Vancouver. Past the city, you could see the sea and the mountains. Further back, rising high up into the

11

sky, I could see the two mountain peaks folks called "the Lions."

Suddenly, this big old gal, eyes wide, came gunning for us out of the bedroom. "LEONARD! Leonard! *LENNY!* How dare youse! You goddamn motherfucker... I *WILL*... KILL... YOU! Doya hear me?!"

Leonard didn't pay her no mind. She turned on my grandfather instead. "What's the deal? What's the big deal here, Mr. Livingston? You know it's just me and Lenny left, right? Just me and him, my sweet, sweet Lenny."

Next, she turned her big fisheyes on me.

"Weeellll, what have we got here? Who's your little friend?"

I wasn't going to mention it, cause it ain't too polite, but she had these big old tits which just flopped around everywhere. I tried not to look at them, but it wasn't easy, given their size and everything. Grandpa Earl took charge of the situation.

"Well, er, you see, we, Lola... It's not so much that we don't see eye to eye, but, the bank and the power company, well these people have a different sense of time, I feel. An alternate view, so to speak."

Lenny winked at me. His eyes were cartoon crazy, like black marbles on springs. He walked over to me, bent down on one knee, and looked me right in the eye. He tugged my arm and said, "Lil' Buddy! I want to show you something... You, you want to pay attention now... Now, put yer hands up. Like this here, see."

I lifted my hands and opened my palms. He boxed me, punching my hands. First light, then hard.

"Ya gotta be tough or youse ain't gonna make it. See... This is how it is. Youse gotta be TOUGH." His voice rose. "Push that right hand! I said, fucking push that right hand! Got it? I said, you got it? Ya got it? KID! Listen, now, again..."

I was already tired of Lenny, and I'd only known him for five lousy minutes. Grandpa Earl and the big lady sat on the old couch. I looked past them again, out the big back windows. I could see the blue water of the ocean and the green pines running all the way up the back of Garibaldi Park. I thought to myself that a big place like that, I mean, just the size of it, can get inside of you and turn you inside out. Hell, even in July, those big peaks were capped in pink-white snow, like powdered sugar on the top of a doughnut.

Lenny shambled over to me again. "You wanna know something, kid? You think that old gal over there is my ma? Well, she ain't. She and me are going steady! My heart is on fire for her!" He flashed me a goofy grin.

Not long after, I heard Lola up and died. Her liver exploded one night when she was sitting on her couch watching TV. I never did see Leonard again. Grandpa Earl told me he killed a man in a street fight and vanished into the woods.

3

On the Nose, To Win

Rick Chinsky and I rode our bikes everywhere. We had these jacked up units with twenty-inch wheels, banana seats, ape handles, and sissy bars. He lived up at the top of my street, right across from the Canadian Pacific Railway tracks.

Chinsky was my first best friend. Well, there was another guy before him. His name was Philip. He died when his grandmother gave him a peanut butter cookie by mistake. I don't think about him too much, though. One day, we were building forts with tree branches in his big backyard filled with weeping willows, and the next day, we weren't. My parents screwed up telling me about it, though. I had to hear about it from some jerk at school. One thing's for sure, Phillip was a lot nicer than Chinsky. I don't remember how Chinsky and I became friends—it feels kind of like I stepped in gum one day and he got stuck on my shoe.

Most of our bike riding was spent going back and forth to school, Dr. R. E. McKechnie Elementary. Weekends, we'd go down to the banks of the Fraser River to throw rocks around and break stuff. Nobody ever bothered us down there, which is weird if you think about it, given all the kids getting snatched by weirdos. For a while, there was even some creep running around grabbing girls with a paper bag on his head, if you can believe it. Anyway, if some rock monster grabbed Chinsky and hijacked him into his Econoline van, they'd probably regret it, and fast. Chinsky was crazy. He was also lazy, had a ferret face, and looked funny, like his body might have been hammered together in an old woodshed by a drunken carpenter.

He's twelve and so am I. At least I think I'm twelve but I'm not one hundred percent sure. My parents didn't throw any birthday parties for us so it's hard to know for certain. I don't really know why. I guess my mom and the Old Man didn't go in for it. When one of the kids at school had a birthday, everybody was invited down to the Vancouver Wax Museum and out for dinner at the Old Spaghetti Factory or some other grub joint for kids. I didn't get too many invitations. I figured maybe kids were worried that I'd take over and start running things, as usual, or start wrestling guys and causing problems. But if that's what they were thinking, they had me wrong. I could be plenty polite if I set my mind to it.

When we got bored, Chinsky and I played ping pong or threw hockey cards against a wall in his basement. His old man, Ed, gambled. Often. We tagged along with him when he went to bet on the ponies at Exhibition Park. When the thoroughbreds weren't running, he'd drive us all the way out to Cloverdale to bet on *harness* races, if you can believe it. Ed usually placed ten-dollar bets. If Chinsky and I had any money, we'd get Ed to place two-dollar bets for us on exactors and trifectas. He was none too happy about it, though. Ed Chinsky was the kind of gambler who thought everyone should place bets on the nose, to win.

"Boys, only women and fools bet like you do. Always bet the winner *on the nose.*"

Chinsky's parents had run a dry goods store in northern Manitoba. When it went bust, they made their way across the Rocky Mountains to Vancouver. On the way, during a crazy night in some one-horse town in Saskatchewan, his dad won a male beauty contest, Chinsky told me. He'd been crowned "Mr. Valentino." To prove it, Chinsky once showed me a picture of his dad wearing a crown on the top of his head in his parents' bedroom. He looked young and handsome and had a winner's smile. He looked like he was ready for anything. I started teasing Chinsky about it when he was bothering me, which was practically all the time. "Hey Chinsky, what's Mr. Valentino up to tonight?" It drove him nuts. Even the guys at school picked up on it.

It took us a while, but eventually Chinsky and I figured out how to read a horse racing form. Once I got the hang of it, I ended up betting on American horses coming up to race from Santa Anita, California or Longacres, Washington State. The way I saw it, horses from those big American tracks were gaming it; they'd have lousy runs racing against class horses on competitive tracks, and when they came up to Ex Park, they'd get boxed into low-pot races with deadbeat locals, and more often than not, they'd win. I liked the names of horses. Some of them were pretty good, like "Panty Raid," or "Dancing Queen," or even "Speedy Gonzales."

If Chinsky and I weren't betting, we'd run up and down the stands picking up old tickets and stuffing them into our pockets, or eat hot dogs and drink Cokes. After the horses left the post, we'd rush down to the finish line to get a good look at the end of a race. You could see the horses coming down the stretch, fast as hell and breathing so hard you could hear it all the way up in the stands. The crowd would stand up, cheering, and the jockeys, in their bright jerseys and black boots, would keep whipping their horses so they didn't ease up until after they crossed the finish line. Every time the horses came down the stretch to the finish, this big rush would hit the crowd and they'd start cheering and you'd start cheering even if you didn't have money on a horse in the race.

After a while, I figured Ed Chinsky maybe didn't have such a great betting strategy. He couldn't even afford to fix his car. I had to slide across the back seat and get out of the passenger-side door because if you opened the one behind the driver, it wouldn't close again. Most nights, Ed was in a bad mood on the long drive home. He'd turn on the AM radio in the car and we'd listen to old guys calling in to talk shows and going off on goofy rants about the BC government, or immigrants, or anything else they might have read in the newspaper that day that might have pissed them off.

4

Not So Tough, After All

Chinsky and I hopped on our bikes and rode over to Chow's Grocery on West 57th to buy candy, play Space Invaders for a quarter a game, and find out if Chow had any firecrackers for sale. Chinsky shot ahead of me—he really was a good bike rider, and he was fast. "Slow down for Christ's sake!" I yelled at him.

He didn't hear me or pretended he didn't.

"Prick!"

When I arrived at Chow's, Chinsky's bike was splayed out on the sidewalk like he'd been in a freak accident. He always just dropped his crap anywhere and he couldn't have cared less if anything happened to it. I parked my bike and walked into the store. The first thing I heard was Chow's radio blaring, loud as hell. It sounded like some guy had his head stuck in a bucket and he was just going on and on in Mandarin or Cantonese, or whatever.

In the candy section were Pop Rocks, Zotz, Big Red Gum, Zobstoppers, Bottle Caps, Ring Pops, Fun Dips, Banana LaffyTaffy, Mike and Ikes, Razzles, and Lemonheads. All the other shelves in the store were filled with soda pop, popcorn, Campbell's soup, Ramen noodles, and dusty old cans of cat food. Chow sat on a stool at the cash desk, smirking, in front of a big collection of cigarettes: Player's Navy Cut, Rothmans, Export 'A,' Craven 'A,' Pall Mall, Marlboro, and Lucky Strike.

Chow's whole family lived in a small apartment on the second floor of the building. There was always a mean old lady hanging around, probably Chow's mom, and another guy around my age, sitting in the back behind an old bead curtain. The guy had a funny look on his face, like maybe he wasn't all there. One time, I saw him sitting on the floor in the back. He grabbed his feet, one with each hand, pulled them up behind his ears, and crossed them behind his head.

Chinsky was talking to Chow at the counter. Chow, sitting on a stool, was thin like a boy, with a large round head and swollen eyes. It wasn't going well, as usual. I walked over to the Space Invaders console, pulled out a quarter, and pushed it into the slot in front. A goofy electro-introduction jingo came out of a speaker somewhere deep in the machine.

"Just reach under the counter, Chow, and get me the good stuff from Macau. Make sure there are no duds!" Chinsky barked. Chow pulled out some Lady Fingers and dropped them on the counter. Chinsky was getting excited handling the packs, so he ended up just dropping a bunch of crumpled bills onto the counter. He grabbed six sets of Lady Fingers, tucked them down into his pants, folded his T-shirt down, and booked it out of there, mission accomplished.

Back outside, I asked Chinsky with a smirk, "So, what's Mr. Valentino up tonight?" He ignored me. He bounced a basketball between his legs in faster and faster bursts. I'd overheard a couple of girls in our class talking about being invited to a party. I fished Chinsky for details.

"So, what's up at Boom Boom's?"

"Say what?"

Bounce. Bounce. Bounce.

"Boom Boom?" He looked puzzled.

"Yah."

Bounce.

I fished some more. "Is she having a party?"

Bounce.

"Yeah, sure, whatever."

Bounce.

"Do we need to be invited?"

Bounce.

"Hell no. She loves me."

Bounce.

I rolled my eyes. I guess that meant we were going.

Boom Boom McLean's real name was Jacquie. Her mother was a single parent; she worked until at least nine o'clock every night.

A guy from our class, Piero, wandered up along the sidewalk. He pretended not to see us. It looked like there was some kind of trouble with his hair; he'd been given a home haircut: a horrible bowl cut, for guys like us, a worst-case scenario. Piero's parents immigrated to Canada from Italy. They cleaned office buildings at night with his eldest sister, Beatrice, who had great tits and a big nose.

Chinsky picked up his ball and shouted. "Hey Piero, you goddamn dirty Dago!"

This got his attention. He stopped. Secretly, I was afraid of Piero. He was tougher than you think, but I wasn't going to let Chinsky know about it. Over the years, I'd teased Piero now and again, but my heart wasn't really in it. I lacked enthusiasm, energy, verve. What I lacked was inspiration. I was a second rate bully.

I walked over and pushed Piero hard on the chest with both my hands. He tumbled back on the grass. I jumped on top of him. We locked fingers. We went back and forth for a while until he flipped me over and pinned me to the ground, face-first in the grass. He was surprisingly strong. He put his knee on my back and slowly pushed my arm up, way up, almost to the middle of my shoulders.

"OK, OK, I give… I give! What the fuck, Piero?" I murmured, staying out of Chinsky's earshot.

He let me go, releasing my arm and jumping up to his feet. "Andy, why are you always such a dick?"

"Just keep walking, penis helmet."

He walked over to his backpack, picked it up, and put the straps around his shoulders.

He ran a hand through his terrible hair and walked east up the sidewalk to his house. He didn't look back.

I turned and saw something move in the distance, along the old railway tracks that ran through our neighbourhood, Arbutus. "Hey Chinsky, check it out." I said, pointing.

He looked over. "It's Ericson," he said with relish.

What a break! Roddy Ericson was a kid in our grade. We took off after him at full throttle—oh man, when he saw us coming, he started moving! Roddy looked back over his shoulder as we gained ground on him. He swerved right. He swerved left.

"Ha! He doesn't know whether to shit or climb a tree," Chinsky said between breaths as he reached down between the tracks and picked up a heavy rock. He stopped and hurled it, hard and high, from his waist—a dirty sidewinder. Roddy was now streaking down the middle of the tracks, and the rock, suspended for a terrifying moment in space, hit him right in the back of the head. He pitched forward, tripped, tumbled down on his knees, wavered for a second, and fell flat on his face.

"Jesus Christ! Seriously?" I cried out, looking at Chinsky. After a moment, in the distance, Roddy's head popped up. He sprang to his feet and sprinted off the tracks and through the bushes. Seconds later, he disappeared.

Chinsky smiled, wiping his hands together. "My work here is done. I must get home and see my mom."

We walked back to Chow's and picked up our bikes. My bike chain was off, and I couldn't get it back on, so I was going to have to walk it home.

"See you later, pillow-biter!" Chinsky called out to me as he rode his bike backwards, his ass on the handlebars, down 57th Street toward Angus Drive. I walked my bike home.

On either side of the tracks grew huge blackberry brambles with berries as big as pinecones so I grabbed a couple of ripe ones, popped them in my mouth, and wiped the juice all over the front of my pants. At the top of Riverview Park was an old sandbox, a lonesome swing set, and a teeter-totter. As I crossed the playground, still walking my stupid bike, I heard a loud screeching behind me.

"Andrew! Andrew Livingston! Stop right there!" It was a woman. She was wearing a kitchen apron, and I could see she had large forearms and shiny black eyes, like a crow. She came up on me in a frenzy, pinched my arm, and hauled me up the street. My bike fell to the sand.

"Jeez, I mean, you just can't go running around and grab kids off the street you know," I said.

We walked up 64th Street and when we stopped in front of Roddy Ericson's lousy bungalow, I realized. *Oh man.* The old witch was his mom!

"Come on. We're going inside."

We walked through the front door, through a small living room and into a tiny kitchen. Standing next to an old refrigerator was Rod. He was scared. Next to him was his dad, a short man with a sad face. He wore a blue shirt with a bright orange decal over the pocket. I moved to stand next to them, waiting for what was going to come next. Rod's mom walked over to the kitchen counter and faced the three of us. She grabbed a handful of red hamburger meat and kneaded it between her fingers. She put the meat back in the bowl and cracked an egg into it, dropped in some chopped onions and breadcrumbs, and plunged her hands back into the mix.

"Well, well. Andrew Livingston. What 'ave youse to say for yourself? Huh? Hey? Just who do you think you are? Do you think you can just run around scaring my Roddy and everyone else, any which way you please? No, sir! Not in my neck of the woods!" She kneaded the meat again and pulled some out, making a ball in her hands and then she flattened it out into a hamburger patty. She put it aside and reached into the bowl again, now looking at Rod's dad. "Elias, do you have something to say to Mr. Livingston?"

He just shook his head. She turned on the tap in the sink. "You're not going to wriggle your way out of this one. I know your type. Yes, sir! I know boys like you, and how you twist and turn your way out of everything! I want you to make me a promise that you will leave my Roddy alone from now on, Mister L-I-V-I-N-G-S-T-O-N, from this day forward!"

She waited for me to answer with her hands now on her hips,

the water still running, in her tiny kitchen with a dirty floor and a stupid wooden cuckoo clock. I figured my best shot was to make a run for it. I turned away from her and bolted past Rod and his dad right out of the front door, up a mossy walk, down the street, and kept running until I reached safety in the shadows of the big trees of Riverview Park.

OK—well, alright, I was crying my goddamned eyes out the whole way, if you really want to know. So, there you have it. Maybe I'm not so goddamn tough after all.

5

The Park, The Sea

The green grass on the front lawn of our house was so trim, so watered, and so well-tended, it looked like it might have been radioactive, as if the Russians had dropped a nuclear bomb on the city and the result was the Old Man's lawn would glow green forever. The Old Man spent hours every weekend watering, mowing, and clipping its blades; it was an impressive lawn, an important patch. I think the Old Man spent more time working on the lawn of our house than anything else, except maybe boozing, or driving his truck. He worked as a driver for Grandpa Earl in our family business, Livingston Produce.

At first, I think he started stopping off at bars on his way back home from picking up cases of eggs at chicken farms on his truck route through British Columbia's lower mainland and Vancouver Island. Soon after, he graduated to just guzzling from bottles he kept underneath the driver's seat of his truck. When he came home in the late afternoon, he'd park the truck out front of the house and sit around drinking booze in a chair in his study.

Most of the time, he stared out the window like he was looking out at the sea. If it wasn't cold or raining, he'd take a newspaper or a dumb, dime-store crime novel and a drink out to our old wood patio. He'd turn on the radio and listen to an oldies station on AM radio, pop hits, mostly: Diana Ross and the Supremes, The Four Tops, Donovan, Smokey Robinson. He smoked a fair bit back there, too, filterless Lucky Strikes—maybe something he picked up in the Canadian Merchant Navy in the Second World War. Mom told me he ran away from home, lied about his age, and signed up when he was only sixteen. I don't know all the details; like most guys, he didn't talk about it much.

If you brought it up, he'd make a joke about hiding in a broom closet at Pearl Harbour, or not being able to smoke on the deck of a ship at night because the Germans might spot the burning cherry with a periscope, or about catching crabs one time in Australia. I read they lost one man in seven, which is a hell of a lot worse than the ratio of guys they lost in the regular forces.

So, there you have it. Maybe he was bored. Maybe he missed sailing around with his buddies all over the world, getting chased by the U-boats. One thing's for sure: he wasn't enjoying himself these days. I figured he might have been busted in the head, like a clock missing something important inside.

We watched television, every day, all the time: *All in the Family*, *The Mary Tyler Moore Show*, *Happy Days*, *Hogan's Heroes*, *Three's Company*, *Taxi*, *WKRP*, *Bob Newhart*, *Welcome Back Kotter*, *The Odd Couple*, *One Day at a Time*, *Laverne and Shirley*, *Green Acres*, *M.A.S.H*, *Beverly Hillbillies*, *Get Smart*. A magical, everlasting fountain of American comedies and game shows. One afternoon, much like all the others, we were watching an episode of *Hogan's Heroes*. The idiotic German sergeant, Shultz, takes over a WWII

American prisoner-of-war camp for a day from Colonel Klink, an even bigger half-wit.

The Old Man looked out the window. He looked back at the TV. He looked over at me. His eyes blurry yellow and half-lidded. He looked down at his shoes; he was wearing his big brown brogues, the shoes of a big man, his tough-guy shoes.

"Ha!" he snickered, looking back out the window, at the dark green trees of Riverview Park. "Asshole!" he yelled, shaking his head. He closed his eyes again and his yell turned into a mumble. "Bastard!" He fell asleep for a moment, his chin sinking down on his chest.

A sharp bark from the park, a dog, roused him.

"Come 'ere, you prick!" he hollered. "Come here and take what's coming to ya! I'll show you. I'll show *YOU!*" He shook his fist at the window.

My older sister, Darlene, who's a nightmare, told me one time he got beat up outside the pub at the Fraser Arms Hotel. I had the feeling that something like that had happened, something bad, but I never got all the facts—the hard truth, you know what I mean? The problem is, Darlene likes to stir the pot every now and again, and she doesn't always exactly give it to you straight. Anyway, nobody talks about the time Dad got beat up outside of a bar. One thing I can tell you: if it happened, and it probably did, he had it coming.

He stood up from his chair, stumbled over to me, and grabbed my arm. He shook it, hard, and smirked "Hey kid, d'ya wanna know why I married your mother? It was 'cause I had *hot nuts!*"

6

Put That in Your Pipe and Smoke It

Darlene and I had bedrooms in the basement of our house. At one time we shared a room, upstairs, with two single beds, but she bit me, so our parents split us up. Darlene had the luck of the draw, if you ask me. In her room, on her side of the basement, was a fireplace and a fake Tiki bar. I think she won out because of her age; she's at least six or seven years older than me, maybe around seventeen or eighteen, I'm not sure. She's adopted. I guess Mom and Dad didn't think they could have a baby the old-fashioned way. Ah, *hello?* Wrong. Surprise!

I think because of some big, dark secret nobody would tell me anything about, Darlene started lying all the time, drinking booze, and staying out all night. Mom and Dad went through the roof. Maybe she was just acting up—like anybody might—just to stick a poker up the Old Man's ass. I didn't really care about it too much except for all the yelling and screaming. I mean, a guy likes a little peace and quiet, and it's hard to make plans and organize yourself when everybody around you is losing their minds. Anyway, if something bad happened to her, and it probably did, I had her back.

28

She was my big sister and I loved her, so put that in your pipe and smoke it.

I needed new pants. All the pairs I owned were too small and I looked ridiculous. Ever since reading *Moby Dick*, I was obsessed with sailor pants. The ones I wanted had to have a tall waist, wide bell-bottoms, and square front pockets. I imagined myself on the foredeck of a ship, sometimes a crew member and sometimes the captain, chasing down whales, drinking rum, and having a swell time.

There was a Bootlegger Jeans store at a shopping mall in Richmond that carried them, so Mom, me, and Darlene hopped in the car and headed out there one afternoon. After we parked the car and walked through the big mall doors, I split up from Mom and Darlene and wandered around by myself, looking around. In a department store, I watched as a mother and her daughter argued about buying a new dress for a birthday party. Next, I walked over to the men's department and watched an old guy stare at a table laid out with hundreds of ties. He didn't really look all that interested; he just looked lonely as hell, all by himself, in a store with REO Speedwagon blaring down on him from speakers in the ceiling.

I walked out to the food court and watched these twins, teenage girls around Darlene's age, buy an Orange Julius and share it, drinking with one straw. I was supposed to meet Mom and Darlene after getting my jeans and I realized I was running out of time; I hadn't even found Bootlegger yet, let alone found pants, tried them on, and bought them. I found a map of the mall on a signboard with a "you are here" arrow and directions and made my way over to Bootlegger.

In the window, two mannequins were positioned as if one were blowing a kiss to the other, if you can goddamn believe it. Inside, "Hotel California" by the Eagles played on the sound system. It was a song I liked, but I didn't think a guy should have to hear it a thousand times a day. Bootlegger only carried adult sizes; I picked out a pair, the smallest, and tried them on for size. I looked ridiculous. I walked them over to a sales girl.

"Do you have these in a smaller size?"

"Sorry, cutie. They're not made for kids."

The whole thing was a nightmare. The music stopped and a voice announced over a mall loudspeaker, "Paging Mrs. Gwenda Livingston. Mrs. Gwenda Livingston, please present yourself to the mall security desk. Paging Mrs. Gwenda Livingston. Mrs. Gwenda Livingston, please come to the security desk."

Jesus, I thought to myself. *What could that be about? I hope Mom and Darlene are alright.* I raced out the door and arrived at the mall security desk, out of breath. Darlene's hands were behind her back, handcuffed. She was staring at the floor. Mom was talking to a security guard. He wore a bright red turban on his head. I couldn't stop myself from staring at it.

"In situations like these, we normally call the police," he said.

"I'm really very sorry. There must be some mistake," Mom replied.

"Oh no ma'am, there's been no mistake. We take shoplifting very seriously at the Richmond Mall. Very seriously." He reached for the phone on the desk.

"Darlene, can you please explain yourself?" Mom asked Darlene.

"I was taking it to the checkout desk, but I wanted to see what you thought, so I went out into the mall to find you, Ma," she said. "I really don't understand what's going on."

The guard put the phone down and looked at the three of us. It was like his turbaned head was a big, red machine with parts whizzing and whirring around inside as he processed all the information in front of him. It was no simple task, take my word for it.

"Well, I am going to write down your name in my book and give you a warning." He looked directly at Darlene and continued. "Young lady, we don't tolerate theft at the Richmond Mall. Stealing is a very serious crime. I shouldn't have to be the one to remind you."

I couldn't believe it! He was going to let her off. It was incredible. If it were up to me, I would have thrown the book at her. I mean, how else were you going to get her to behave herself? Some good old-fashioned Law and Order, that's how.

Well, this guy turned out OK. Maybe he felt sorry for us, or maybe he wanted us to like him. It didn't really matter in the end. Jesus, one thing's for sure: it was a good thing the Old Man hadn't been there. He would have made trouble.

Darlene also had a bad reputation in our neighbourhood. On top of all her antics, like riding around in muscle cars with older guys who looked like hoodlums and blaring music out the windows all the time, she made all the younger kids in the neighbourhood, including Chinsky and I, play a game called "Planting a Rose Garden."

There was supposed to be an element of chance to it, but really all that happened was she pinched your forearm and raked the skin with her sharp nails until you couldn't take it anymore. Most kids would start crying and run home; for days afterward, you'd see them wandering around the neighbourhood like zombies. What *really* got her into trouble though was when she started dating this heavy metal guy named Jindi.

One Saturday afternoon, not long after Darlene almost got busted for shoplifting in Richmond, Jindi pulled up to the house in his jacked-up Plymouth Barracuda. Unfortunately, the Old Man had been boozing all day and was just staring out his window, again, waiting for something to happen, as usual. Sometimes he got lucky. One morning, something did happen. He woke up, looked out the window, and saw a guy hanging by a rope from a tall Oak tree. Darlene and I saw it, too. This sad sack had jumped out of the tree in the middle of the night with a rope around his neck. When the paramedics finally cut the body down, it bounced up off the grass before falling flat on the grass. The Old Man told me not to think about it too much. He thought it was a 'long term solution to a short-term problem." But I did think about it, though. Every time I saw that tree, I thought about that guy and what might have brought him to the end of that rope, in the dead of night in a stupid park named Riverview, which didn't even have a view of the goddamn river, anyway.

Well, it was another lucky day for the Old Man. Jindi parked and got out of his car. When I heard the Old Man yelling outside, I ran upstairs to see what was happening. Dad, Jindi, Darlene, and Mom were all standing out on the front lawn in front of the whole neighbourhood.

"Get the fuck off my lawn, you goddamned Paki!" Dad screamed.

He rushed Jindi and pushed him as hard as he could. Jindi lost his balance and fell back onto the grass. He lay on the ground for a few stunned seconds before picking himself up.

Darlene screamed. "Dad! Don't!"

"Bob! Bob! Bob!" Mom yelled.

While Jindi and the Old Man circled one another, the two pugs and I watched out the front window. I have to admit, I'd never seen a real fight before, and it was exciting. Dad grabbed Jindi's shirt lapels and jerked him forward hard enough that all the buttons flew off. Jindi's face was awful—but the Old Man's, mad as hell, was worse. Darlene ran over and tried to give Jindi a hug, but he wasn't having any of it. He made a run for his car, opened the driver door, and jumped into the front seat. The Old Man stood on the lawn and watched him with his terrible eyes.

Jindi turned on the ignition, revved up the Barracuda, and stepped on the gas. He hauled off down the street, stopped with a sudden screech at the corner, and made a right hand turn on Angus Drive. After all the grey smoke drifted away from the front of the house, two streaks of burnt tire rubber were left on the pavement. They stuck around forever after that, two long black exclamation points, reminding us all of the time one of Darlene's boyfriends paid a visit to the Old Man.

7

Hobbledehoys

One thing's for sure: if you played golf, and we played whenever we got a chance, you needed a lot of balls, and balls cost money. The best hunting grounds were in a thick forest running alongside the eighteenth hole of a private, members-only club: The Marine Drive Golf and Country Club.

Getting down to Marine Drive was a big problem. It was at the bottom of a long road off Southwest Marine Drive, and we couldn't just walk down the hill and trespass without getting busted by the club marshal or course groundskeepers. Our only other option was to sneak through the yards, front and back, of one of the grand mansions sitting high on the hill above Southlands. We'd worked out a decent route passing through a cranky old widow's place. It wasn't without risk, however. One time she caught us running as fast as we could across her lawn. She busted out of the side door and told us to "Hop it, you lousy hobbledehoys, before I call the police!"

On a Saturday afternoon I followed Chinsky through a big hedge on the widow's property. As he pushed through, branches snapped back onto my arms and legs. Hard.

"Chinsky, would you take it easy?"

"Don't be such a sissy and suck it up. We're almost through," he barked back.

Once we made it through, we sprinted past the house, ducked past the pool in the back and bushwhacked down an overgrown trail. At the bottom, we slid over a muddy embankment and ran straight out through a patch of brambles into a clearing. I tried to get a rise out of Chinsky, as usual, this time by asking about his sister.

"Hey, what happened to Karla after last weekend?"

"Whaddya mean?"

"I heard the Gooch threatened to call the cops!"

His eyes bugged out. He thought I hadn't been paying attention. Karla and her stupid friend Lisa got into big trouble. Chinsky's mom, the "Gooch," busted the girls for getting drunk and finger-fucked, if you can believe it, in some strange guy's apartment in Marpole. I heard the whole thing go down from a hiding spot in Chinsky's kitchen.

"Ah, nothing. But it could have been bad. It's a crime, 'cause Karla and Lisa are minorities," he said.

"You mean 'minors.'"

"No, I don't." He continued, "I dunno. I think my dad went up there to find out what happened and sorted it out with the guy."

I nodded, gravely. "Mr. Valentino?"

He let out a slow whistle.

I added, for effect. "Damn! The Gooch was really stoked, dude. It looked like her head was going to explode!" This pissed him off. Chinsky and the Gooch had this crazy relationship. "Gooch! Gooch! Where are you, Gooch?" Chinsky would call out randomly,

35

day or night. Without fail, the Gooch would come running downstairs or into Chinsky's bedroom and lay kisses on him or stroke his hair and rub his back.

From where we were standing, I could see a big meadow, littered with wildflowers, and the ocean in the distance, beyond the winding path of the river. The waves rolled out across the water and sparkled in the sun. Across the Strait of Georgia were the islands: Valdes, Gabriola, and Vancouver.

Chinsky took off and disappeared into the trees. I followed. Without warning, I felt a hard smack on my chest.

"*Ouch!* Fuck!"

Of course, it was Chinsky. I looked up. He was standing inside a rickety old tree fort, grinning triumphantly, pleased with himself. He'd hucked a half-rotten crab apple at me—and the result? A stinking splatter on one of my favourite t-shirts.

"You deserved it, you fugly F-R-E-A-K!" he yelled down.

I ran over to the bottom of the tree to see if I could find a way to climb up to him. All I could find was an old rope dangling from a large tree branch. I grabbed the lowest knot. Chinsky ran over and started swinging his weight back and forth. I called out to him.

"Jesus, you'd better be careful, that thing doesn't look too steady..."

Without warning, a 2x4 cracked off the side and fell onto the forest floor with a dull *thud*. He shook it again. A fear-flash rippled across his face. There was another loud 'crack' and a second 2x4 broke free from the fort and fell onto the ground, this time just missing me. It was the end. The ancient fort, rotted through, came down with a thundering crash.

Chinsky hit the hard ground and somehow pulled off a crazy,

military-style safety roll. When he popped up in front of me smiling, I slapped him on the back. "Where did you learn to do that?"

We walked until we hit the forest running alongside Marine Drive's eighteenth hole. We figured, correctly, golf ball hunting would be good around Marine Drive because the members—rich folks, mostly, would slice, hook, and lumberjack their drives out of bounds on the final hole—and would be too goddamn lazy to hike up into the woods and look for them.

We split up. I scanned the bushes and trees, looking for the white flash of a golf ball.

"Found one!" Chinsky yelled.

"I found one!" I countered.

"Ha, found another one! Sucker!"

Sometimes, a brand new ball was just sitting right on the ground in front of you—as if it was just waiting there for you to walk by and pick it up. Other times, you might see a lovely, lonely one sitting on a mound of moss, or stuck up in a salmonberry bush, or even lodged in the branch of a tree. As soon as you got one, the first thing you did was wipe the ball down and check the brand to see if it was any good.

"Found one!" Chinsky yelled out again.

"Shhhh! Keep it down, wouldya?" I answered. We were damn close to the eighteenth fairway, and I could see carts and brightly coloured pants moving around on the manicured grass through the treeline.

We hunted around until it was too dark to see. In fact, it was getting so dark, we couldn't get back the way we came. We were going to have to make a run for it through the club grounds. We broke free of the forest, scrambled past the eighteenth green, crossed the parking lot, and started up the hill to Southwest Marine Drive. About halfway up, car headlights came up behind us, tearing up the road. It was old man Ferguson in his Datsun, probably on his way home, after guzzling a dozen drinks in the bar after his round.

I caught sight of him in the driver's seat. His hands were clenched hard on the steering wheel. We jumped off the shoulder of the road and into the bushes.

"Ha! That was Old Man Ferguson!" I yelled over to Chinksky once he was gone

"Well, duh. What gave you that idea? I heard he likes to FUCK!"

"Everybody likes to fuck, moron!" I said.

"Have you done it?" He asked.

"Sure. Plenty of times," I lied.

We walked the rest of the way home in silence, in the dark.

8

The Coastal Raven

The Old Man dropped us off at the McLeery public golf course the following Saturday morning. The sky was menacing; large black and grey puffers loomed over the mountains of the north shore, hiding their peaks from sight. We ignored the weather. What did it mean to us?

We pulled our skinny bags out of the back of the car and tossed them over our shoulders; inside, a putter; 3, 5, 7, and 9 irons; a driver; and a 3 wood. As we approached the pro shop, past a giant log cut half-wise and laying on the grass with a giant "McLeery Golf" painted on the side, we met Charles "Fozzy" Ferguson. He was old man Ferguson's son. He'd been nicknamed Fozzy because he looked like Fozzy Bear from the Muppets—his hair, his face, his freckles, his eyelashes—were all orange. And not just any orange either; a deep, unnatural, orange.

Sitting on a rock in a red V-neck sweater was Alvie Thompson, the club professional, who sold golf clubs on the side. He cheerfully smoked a butt and bounced a ball up and down on his putter: *tap, tap, tap, tap.*

McLeery had a club dog, a black retriever named Snatch. Snatch was terrific but she was jittery, and when she got excited, she jumped all over the tee box. Sometimes she'd try to bite the head of your club just as you were lining one up. One time she got in front of me and I hit her hind leg with my drive. She yelped and cried and limped the rest of the round. All the guys gave me the cold shoulder afterward. It was goddamn awful.

We walked out to the first tee box for our 10:35 a.m. tee-off. Fozzy was up first. He swung clean. He finished with a long first drive. It soared straight down the middle of the fairway.

Chinsky was up next. He sliced into some heavy willows off to the right of the fairway. It was my turn next. I had been developing my Zen game: you cleared your mind of anything that happened before your club hit the ball and anything you thought might happen afterward. You hit the ball *in the moment.* The only thing that mattered, the only thing that existed in time was the moment the club face hit the dimples of the ball. I pulled back my club, swung, and drove it hard. It hooked far left onto the eighteenth fairway and rolled in front of a ladies' foursome.

We put our clubs on our backs and headed down the first fairway. On the green in front were a slow foursome of old geezers. It looked like they might be gambling on their game. It wasn't going well. We stood and waited, watching them.

Chinsky, impatient, swung his club all over the place—in the air, at the trees, behind his back as a stretching tool. I could tell he was going to lose it.

"Goddamn it!" Chinsky shouted.

"Just take it easy, Chinsky."

We waited.

Chinsky yelled over at me again. "Did you see that? That guy missed his putt by six inches and now he's lining it up again? You gotta be goddamn kidding me!"

He reached into his bag, pulled out his 7 iron, a nice approach club, and lined it up behind his ball. His stance was solid: head down, shoulders straight. His club came down smooth. His ball flew onto the green, bounced, and rolled between the legs of one of the geezers as he was finishing off his putt. A beautiful shot.

It didn't go down well.

They turned on us with blank stares and wrinkled faces. As usual, Chinsky gave them both barrels. He shouted, "Get going you sad, old FUCKERS!"

A shocked silence followed.

They limped off the green. It was our turn to finish off the hole. Fozzy was up. He skulled it, hitting the upper part of his ball with the bottom of his club, forcing it to fly fast, low, and far. He landed in a deep pocket of fescue. I pitched in from the other fairway and landed on the fringe, chipped, and three putted for a two over par, six. When it was over, I counted my strokes and shouted my score to Fozz. "Five!"

By the third hole, the weather turned. Without warning, a curtain of rain came down from the sky. Out front, the geezers pulled giant umbrellas from out of their bags, scrambled for their carts, and headed back to the safety of the clubhouse.

There was no way we were quitting. McCleery didn't refund or rain-check juniors. Who knew when we'd get another chance to play? By the sixth, there wasn't a part of my body untouched by water. When we got to the eighth hole we blasted lousy balls off the tee box into the Fraser River. It was a crazy custom. We had a ten-metre elevation above the water giving our balls some carry but we had to clear the top of an old cow fence to get them out on the water. On the far side of the river bank was a log boom filled up with cut trees—a tempting target.

There was nothing in the world like the feeling of squarely hitting a ball with the head of a driver and watching it fly straight as a goddamn arrow. You can hear a well-hit ball and know it's going to be good—without even watching it fly.

After we'd finished with the boom, a long air horn blasted out from a twin screw coastal tug coming down on us from upriver. What luck! A moving target! I teed one up. I checked my stance, my left shoulder, and my left arm; I flushed the past and the future down the toilet. *I was in the moment.* I gripped my club, a PowerBilt driver, and swung. It was good and clean. The ball soared high into the air toward the rolling boat, but the high wind took it and it faded fifteen metres off her stern.

Fozzy took a turn. He calmly pushed his tee and ball into the grass. He addressed the ball, stepped back, and waited. The tug was pulling away, nearly moving out of range. Fozzy swung. He hit the ball with a crack—it sounded like a branch breaking in two—and followed through with a big finish. His ball flew high and fast. At first, it looked like maybe he was going to miss, but in the end, he caught one of her inside panels.

Bang! Bang!
Bang! Bang!

The captain, in a heavy peacoat and boots, jumped out of the wheelhouse, a red megaphone in his hand. It was bad. We were done for—even Snatch was probably going to go down. He lifted the speaker to his lips.

"Heya, kid! I said, hey there, kid! I say, yuh got a... Yuh got a helluva nice drive there!"

And that was it! Snatch barked her head off. We dropped our clubs to the ground. We laughed like hell as the old bastard went back inside his cabin. We stood on the riverbank and watched as she continued south. Painted on her stern was the name, Coastal Raven. She moved slowly down the river, bouncing happily, side to side on the waves, a few ugly old seagulls in tow.

9

Getaway Sticks

Dr. R. E. McKechnie, our elementary school, had a small outdoor pitch surrounded by a chain-link fence, a basketball court, hopscotch courts, and two old tetherball poles. We all watched the clock, waiting. *When was the bell finally going to ring?*

The hurry? British Bulldog, of course. Glorious British Bulldog! It was a game we'd picked up from older kids, who used to beat us badly, who probably picked it up from older kids, who'd beat them badly, and so on and so on back in time to who-the hell knows-when and where. The general rules were as follows: a "bulldog" was chosen; he stood in the middle of the pitch. All the players would stand at one end of the pitch in a line. The point of the game was for players to get from one end to the other (maybe one hundred metres), any way they could, without being tackled by a bulldog. If the players safely made it to one side without being tackled and turned into a bulldog, they'd line up and do it again. As more and more players got turned into bulldogs, they outnumbered the runners until only one was left standing—the winner.

We picked Patterson to be the bulldog first simply because he was wearing terrible green crochet pants his mom had knit for him. We lined up, hands on the fence, ready to charge! There was me, Dicky, Woody, Fozzy, Mean Boland, Teddy Sullivan, Gus Brown, Gerber, Mercer, and, of course, Chinsky. We heckled Patterson mercilessly, "Nice pants, Patterson!" and "Yeah, fucking GAYLORD! Ya don't have two legs, ya got two green getaway sticks!"

He tried to ignore the taunts, but I could see on his face it was getting to him. His eyes watered up; his lip quivered, he balled his hands up into tight fists—he was getting ready to turn on the taps. I could always tell. After some more of the same, "Panty-waisted Nancy-Boy!" I felt guilty and thought maybe we'd taken it too far.

I imagined his mom knitting his pants with love in her eyes, sitting in a chair all by herself—hell, maybe they were poor and couldn't even afford new pants. After all, he and his mom had moved to Vancouver from one of the Gulf Islands up the coast, where they'd lived on a floating teepee. Thankfully, Patterson called out, "British Bulldog!"

It began. I ran as fast as I could and, in all the excitement, made it to the other side without even realizing how fast I'd done it. When I turned around, I saw two guys on the ground. Patterson had gone for Gerber, the smallest guy in class. Gerber was none too happy, but he lined up next to Patterson and we got ready for another wave. After a few more runs with more guys taken out, only three of us remained: me, Dicky, and Brown.

Patterson cried out again, much louder this time. "British Bulldog!"

It was three versus six. Dicky was out in front of me, and Gerber went straight for him. Dicky yelled out "Gallipoli! Gallipoli!" as he ran. Gerber wasn't having any of it. He dove at Dicky's legs and tried tackling him, wrapping his arms around Dicky's waist and letting them slide downward, forming a tight knot, like a noose, at his ankles. Dicky kicked his legs up when he felt Gerber's tiny raccoon hands on him, bringing his knees up high and hard. Gerber lost his grip and fell to the pitch. One of Dicky's boots came down on his cheek, grinding his face into the mud. As Gerber released, he let out a wild howl, *"Ahhhhyyaaahhharrgmnnh!"* reminding me of the famous howl the Old Man let out when this ugly chinchilla Darlene adopted somehow made its way into the heating vent of his Pontiac Firebird. One morning, when the Old Man turned on the ignition and revved the engine, it squealed, shot out, and spread-eagled onto his face.

Dicky jogged the rest of the way back to the safety of the fence. He put his hands on his knees. Warm breath shot out of his nose in short bursts, like a horse at Ex Park at the end of a race. It was only Gus Brown and me left. I thought I was going to get it next, for sure. Instead, they went for Brown. He didn't stand a chance. Seven guys surrounded him. The biggest, Mean Boland, lunged forward, thrust out his knee, charley-horsing the upper calf of Brown's leg.

"Oh! Oh! *Oh*! OH MY GOD! OH OW *OW OW*." Gus caterwauled, falling to the ground on his back, cradling his leg in the air.

I'd won.

Triumphant, I raised up my hands and yelled. "YEEHAW! YEEHAW!"

The bell rang, calling us back into class. I went over to Gus and helped him out of the mud and we made the short walk back to the school together under a cold, cloud covered sun, a grey marble in the sky.

10

By Sea, Land, and Air, We Prosper

Some of the kids at McKechnie Elementary had it rough. If you lacked confidence, didn't make any effort, and simply wandered around the hallways like a ghost—or worse, froze up with nerves whenever anybody said anything to you—you were a goner. That was life. If you wanted to have fun, you made an effort.

Boom Boom McLean was having a party at her place after school, and me and Chinsky were going. We were gonna have fun. End of story.

On our way over, we stopped by Chow's and flash-guzzled some Dr. Peppers. A Dr. Pepper was about the best thing going, I figured, especially a cold one right out of the freezer. I couldn't drink enough of them.

Boom Boom's mom was a nurse who worked long hours at Vancouver General Hospital. She was French Canadian. She'd moved Jacquie out to Vancouver from Montreal to make a fresh start after a divorce and custody battle. It wasn't uncommon. Lots of people came to Vancouver to wipe the slate clean and make a new beginning. I thought, hell, maybe they should change the city's motto from "By Sea, Land, and Air, We Prosper" to "Vancouver: Leave It All Behind."

Boom Boom's House was a small ranch bungalow, like everybody else's, of course, on 58th Street in Kerrisdale. I rang the doorbell. We heard a *DING-DONG DING-DONG* inside, but nobody answered. We stood outside on the doorstep, clueless, as usual. We decided to wander around to the back. We scrambled over the fence. Safely on the other side, Chinsky put up a Shaka with his fist and yelled out, "Psyche!"

I peered through a basement window. Kids from class milled around in a recreation room, playing ping-pong and listening to records from a Clairtone. Chinsky tapped the window, hard. Next, he pulled down his pants like an idiot, reversed, and pushed a "pressed moon" against the glass. When *that* didn't get anybody's attention, he pulled out a string of Lady Fingers, lit the end, and dropped them on the ground. A loud series of fast, short, exploding bursts of gunpowder followed.

I think being around girls, or even just *potentially* being around them, in the dark, made him more problematic than usual. I must admit, I was a little nervous as well. The girls in class had been acting up. At recess, when we weren't playing British Bulldog, they pulled us into a fenced-off cubby near the jungle gym to play a kissing game. Sherri Little, the prettiest girl in our class, had already pulled me in there and smooched me.

All hell broke loose. Jacquie came out and flat out told us she wasn't going to let us in. She told me Chinsky was a "menace to society." I told her she was mistaken—he was a misunderstood genius. Man, convincing her to let us in was no small feat, let me tell you, but she agreed. I was giddy with excitement as we walked inside. I had on my favourite T-shirt: on the front was a cartoon picture of Dracula, and underneath it read, "Dracula Sucks."

Obviously, unlike Chinsky, I was cool.

Mean Boland, with a severe crew cut, and Gus Brown were taking turns playing record albums. I walked over and picked one up, Supertramp's *Crime of the Century*, and turned it over with my hands. Gerber and Woody stood together in the corner, in front of a big Canadian flag taped to the wall, giggling like idiots.

"What's so funny?" I asked them.

"We're baked," Gerber answered.

"Wuh?"

"Yeh, Woody stole a joint from his mom's purse."

Woody threw up the sign of the horns with his fist. He reached into the top pocket of his jean jacket, pulled out a pack of cigarettes, and tapped out a roach. He winked at me and said, "Have at 'er. No need to be a pussy. It's the sweet leaf."

I shrugged, took it from him, sparked a match and lit the end. The sweet, heavy smoke filled my lungs. Sometime later, or maybe not so much later, the universe began to stretch out in waves, and my body felt like a soft fabric unfurling slowly into space.

I escaped the noise and hid beneath the ping-pong table. After two unbelievably long hours, a friend of Jacquie's from some other school got down on her hands and knees, peered under the table, staring at me, as if I was a dog. I'd never seen her before. She wore thick glasses and had a few pimples sprinkled on her cheeks.

"You look like a fool," she said.

"I'm cool?"

"No."

She grinned. She had a smile that looked like the busted side mirror on my dad's truck. We kissed. Or, at least, I pretended I knew how to kiss her while she kissed me. And brother, was she ever a terrific kisser. As she lay on her back on the shag carpet, my hands found her big breasts, fast, like two sand crabs heading for the safety of the ocean on a beach.

"Yes, oh yes, oh KISS ME!" She said as I planted a massive hickey on her neck. She smelled like pimple cream and tropical flowers. "Oh, please kiss me, don't stop, don't stop, don't stop, PLEASE!"

Later, after she climbed up from under the table and left me with just a dumb smile on my face, I raced home alone on my bike: up 58th, down Angus Drive, and up 66th in the rain. My heart was on fire. I kissed a girl! I got to second base! *Second base!* I pulled a bunch of figure eights and wheelies. I saw Roddy Ericson walking home on the train tracks at the top of my street. "Hey Rod! Hey, Roddy! What up?!" I yelled and waved at him like a maniac. He stared back at me, his face a goddamn stone.

Sheesh. I thought. *I wonder what's gotten into him?*

I rolled my bike across our front lawn. A crumpled pair of pants and underwear sat alone on the neighbour's grass.

"Jesus, Bobby Jobby strikes again!" I said aloud.

Next door lived an older couple, the Wilsons. Their grandson Bobby sometimes spent the night. For some reason, he hadn't been properly toilet trained even though he was at least eight years old. If he had to shit when he was playing outside, he just let it go. He'd drop his crappy pants and underwear onto the ground, run back into his grandparent's house, and pretend nothing had happened. One time, I found two pairs on the grass, one at the back of the house and another out front.

I walked my bike around to the back of the house and hid it safely away in the driveway, behind the Old Man's muscle car, a 1969 gold Pontiac Firebird. He probably loved that thing more than anything else. Grandpa Earl bought it for him when I was four. I walked through the basement and took the stairs two at a time, nearly slipping and breaking my neck. I kicked off my shoes and took off my soggy Cowichan sweater at the top and shouted for my sister.

"Darlene! Darlene! Guess what? You won't believe it, but Bobby Jobby…"

Mom sat alone at the counter in our small kitchen, a half-eaten pork chop on a plate in front of her. Her eyes were closed. I heard the Old Man bark out from his bedroom.

"You goddamn bitch. FUCK YOU!"

Mom heard this, but not really, and after a long time of sitting there doing nothing, she suddenly screamed back at him at full volume.

"You worthless piece of *SHIT*!"

She cut a piece of pork, and stabbed it with her fork.

I needed to take a whiz. We only had one bathroom upstairs, down the hall, next to the Old Man's bedroom. I crept past Dad's door, praying he wouldn't hear me and lose his mind for no good reason. Maybe I'd get lucky; he was hard of hearing from working in the boiler rooms of merchant ships during the war. Naturally, he heard me.

"Who's *THAT*?" he yelled.

"Who do you think?" I answered, weakly. He groaned. When I'd finished, I closed the bathroom door as softly as I could. As I walked down the hall, I heard him say into the darkness.

"I wish I would die."

11

Killer Whales

I'd been lazing around the house, not doing much except sitting under a blanket and watching television. In the show playing on the TV in the Old Man's study stood a group of American castaways on a desert island. The lead moron in a white cap, Gilligan, finds a bush with magic seeds which allows anyone who eats them to be able to read people's minds. The Old Man looked over at me—I could feel his eyes on me. I ignored him.

"We're heading over to Mueller's in the morning. Go get yourself organized. We're leaving early."

Somehow, he'd got it into his head that we should make a road trip out to Lion's Bay—all the way up on Howe Sound, on the same road you drive to get to the Fitzsimmons Mountains up near Garibaldi Park—and pay a visit to his old drinking buddy, Ken Mueller. Mueller was a real character. He never spent a dime on anything, even though he had pots of money. He owned properties all over Vancouver and in "shit-hole towns" like Vernon and Trail and Hope in the British Columbia interior. Mueller had a cottage on Lion's Bay—well, actually, it was more like a miner's shack near the water with a dock where you could swim and lounge without anybody around.

In the morning, the Old Man got into his Firebird and revved its big, 350HP American-made engine. I put my backpack, towels, and swim trunks in the backseat of the car and got in. He backed slowly out of the driveway and down the lane to Angus Drive. We rolled over the west side and crossed over the Burrard St. Bridge. We passed a movie theatre; on the billboard, *MIDNIGHT EXPRESS, PRETTY BABY, DEER HUNTER, UP IN SMOKE.*

We passed through Stanley Park, broke free of the forest, crossed the Lion's Gate Suspension Bridge on our way up to the Trans-Canada Highway. We traveled through Cypress Park, past Horseshoe Bay, and finally arrived in Lion's Bay. We parked off to the side of the road, on the short shoulder, close to the trees. We hiked down the rocky path to Mueller's place in silence. Mr. Mueller told me it used to be an old cattle trail and to not complain about the hike, because in the old-timey days you could only access Lion's Bay by boat. We found some slippery wooden planks Mueller had put on the trail himself before we saw his place, which looked like it would fall over if you gave it a hard-enough push.

Mueller yelled out at us from the front steps. "Well, hiya, you two old timers! How's it going, Livi, ya bugger! You old campaigner!"

He was a big man, bigger than the Old Man, standing on his stoop wearing a Royal Navy bicorn hat. As a young man, standing on a dock in the BC wilderness, he'd been hit by the propeller of a seaplane. "The blade split me open. Hell, it can-openered me!" His left arm, shoulder, and the side of his face were deformed.

Mueller held a big drink in his hand. He offered my dad one right away. I couldn't tell if he was already three sheets to the wind;

you could never tell with these old guys; they hollered and slapped your back all the time, drunk or sober.

"Should we go down to the dock and get some sun on our faces?" asked Mueller.

He was already in his swim trunks, so Dad and I went inside, dropped our pants and changed in the kitchen. We went outside, crossed a small porch with broken planks, and trudged down a narrow path to the cottage dock which sat on the water like a stewed spider.

After we'd been sitting for a while, Mueller said to me, "That's Bowyer Island down there, Andy. Across from us, through the channel, is Gambier Island. And up there is Anvil Island. Now, Bowyer Island is named after Rear Admiral George Bowyer, who commanded the HMS Barfleur when the English stuck it up the asses of the French during the battle of the Glorious First of June."

"What are you now, Ken, a history professor?" asked the Old Man, sarcastically. Incredibly, Mueller thought this was hilarious. He shook his head and laughed. Dad mean-mugged Mueller from that point on whenever Mueller tried to make any conversation or tried to get his attention. Dad got bored and wanted to go swimming. I dropped the towel I had around my shoulders onto the deck. He looked me over.

"Ha! You goddamn sway-back! Jesus Christ, would you look at that, Ken?" he said.

"Aw c'mon, Dad, you're one to talk. Let's just get in the water."

And he was. I mean, where did he get off? He had a beer belly that stuck out like there might have been a football stuck in there.

We jumped into the bay. As I sunk, I yelled out, "JESUS CHRIST! GODDAMN, FUCK!" When I surfaced, I swam over to a large rock covered with white acorn barnacles and dried out starfish.

I lifted myself up and crawled past a swarm of black flies teeming over some stinking seaweed. I sat for a while, listening to the water lap the shore, and to some squawking gulls fighting over a dead fish.

I saw the Old Man in the water, way out, his head a small dot bobbing around in the upwelling tide. Again, and again, and again, he launched forward through the water with his big, freckled shoulders. I jumped into the water again and side-stroked out. I quickly ran into trouble. I swallowed a big gulp of saltwater. My arms started to feel very heavy. I stopped treading and kicking. I sank. Drifting slowly down into the sea, I wondered what would happen if I simply gave up and disappeared forever.

Two big hands gripped my ribs and pushed me up to the surface. It was the Old Man. I wrapped my hands around his neck. He grabbed me under the arms and used his legs to kick us back to Mueller's dock. It felt good. The Old Man was a strong swimmer; he had no trouble with the waves washing over us. It took us a long time to get back. He let me get up the ladder first and I flopped out on the deck like a dead fish.

"Would you look at that, Ken? He looks like he's dead. Ha! I had to save your ass out there today, didn't I? You need to get tougher, son, or you ain't gonna stand a chance." Mueller didn't say a word. I got up and dried myself off. I left the old boozers on the deck and hiked up to the shack. I ate a peanut butter sandwich in Mueller's tiny kitchen, lay down on the couch, and fell asleep. I don't know how long I was out.

When I woke up, Mueller was gently shaking my shoulder and the sun was going down over the bay, the clouds, an imperial red across mountains of blue.

"Andy, come on out and have a look." We walked across the

deck of the cottage. The Old Man was already out there, looking into the bay with a pair of old WWII binoculars. Out on the water was an Orca pod. I counted five whales in total. Each one dove, came up to breathe, and shot a long plume of water out of a blowhole high into the air. They dove, disappeared, came back up, and did it all over again and again. It looked like maybe the most fun thing you could do in the world.

"Well, ain't that something, Andy," Mueller said. Even the Old Man kept his trap shut. We watched the whales swim up the inlet and out of sight, toward Squamish.

It was time for us to leave.

"Well, thanks for coming out to see me all alone in the wild." Mueller told the Old Man and clapped him on the back.

"Sure, Ken, thanks. Anytime I can come out here and drink your watered-down drinks is fine by me." They looked at me.

"Ah, thanks Mr. Mueller. I really enjoyed myself. And, uh, the whales and everything…"

Mueller walked over to me and put his hands on my shoulders.

"Ah yes, the whales. They sure are something. I've seen that pod before. You know, out here in the woods with only the whales as your friends, sometimes, I forget who I am, whether I'm even alive or dead, or maybe it's more like I don't care if I'm dead. Do ya know what I mean?"

The Old Man and I walked up the now-dark trail, the trees thick, their branches heavy waterfalls of needles. Rays of light cast shadows on the rocks: bright orange, yellow, and purple. I fell into the front seat of the car and the Old Man drove us quickly through the English Properties and back down onto the narrow lanes of the Lion's Gate bridge. Getting across was tricky at best; there were three shared driving lanes, and you had to be careful to make sure you were in the correct one, indicated by a red or green signal light, based on the time of day you were on the road. Dad had no problem. He steered the car easily back to our house, even though he and Mueller had polished off at least an entire bottle of vodka. He didn't swerve, take corners too wide, or fail to brake. You might even say he was a fine drunk driver.

When we got home, it was pitch black. We tried to be quiet but as soon as we opened the door, our pugs—Darlene picked them up a few years back from a widow on Laburnum Street whose husband had taught American Literature at UBC—started yapping and spinning around between my legs. A light came on in Mom's bedroom. I walked into the kitchen to grab an apple. I found a shiny red one, pulled it out, rubbed it on my shirt, and took a large, crunchy bite.

"Nighty night, ASSHOLE!" Mom yelled at Dad after he'd closed his bedroom door. I went downstairs into my room, undressed, and turned off the light. I slipped under the covers and pulled them up over my head. In the dark, I thought about what might have happened if the Old Man hadn't cut in on my mom and her date at a sailing club dance when they first met. After that, I thought about the guy the Old Man hit and killed with Grandpa Earl's car when he was a teenager, in the middle of a snowstorm.

12

The Gooch

Chinsky was trying to organize his hockey cards. He had a big set of thick black binders filled with almost all the players in the NHL. He turned the pages, over, and over, again, and when he wanted to insert a new player, the card had to be placed in a specific order he'd devised. Every time he replaced a card, he'd have to start at the beginning of his collection and reset all the cards. It was maddening to watch.

"Have you got anything in the fridge, or any food or whatever?" I asked him. He looked up at me and then turned back to working on his card collection. I wandered up the stairs to the kitchen, shaking my head and wondering what the hell I was doing hanging around with such an idiot. I prayed I wouldn't run into the Gooch. I had a feeling she disapproved of me.

I walked down the hall, into the kitchen, and opened the fridge. Zip. Next, I opened the kitchen cabinets. Diddly-squat. I walked over to the back window to see if there were any cars in the driveway. Empty. Mr. Valentino was probably at the track, and God knows what the Gooch was doing. Whatever it was, though, you could be sure she was smoking. Man, did she smoke a lot. She smoked so much that even if she wasn't smoking, which wasn't often, she still held her right hand clenched tight, like a claw, as if there was a cigarette in it.

I walked out into the hallway and passed the Gooch's bedroom door. Inside, a female voice was singing "Rhiannon" by Fleetwood Mac. I pushed it open. Lying on the bed was Karla, Chinsky's older sister. She was wearing a bright pink tube top and her stupid diary was open in front of her. One afternoon, bored, Chinsky and I busted into her bedroom when she was at school and read it. Sister, it was filled with the most ridiculous, mean-spirited stuff you could imagine: "Marcy's breethe stinks," and "I need to get it dun," or "I smized at Jim." It was some terrifying stuff; I can tell you.

She looked up, like she'd been expecting me, and flicked the pink eraser tip of her pencil with the tip of her tongue. She had a wide face, long black hair, a smattering of freckles on her nose, and a big belly button. A red cowboy hat lay next to her on the bed. That was the worst. I mean, leaving a cowboy hat on the bed was one of the worst goddamn things you could do. It was so bad that you might as well simply commit suicide once it happened. On a side table, next to the bed, was the famous photograph of Mr. Valentino, grinning.

"Well, hiya, stranger," Karla drawled. I swear she said the most ridiculous things every time I saw her. I stared at Mr. Valentino and back at the hat and back at the picture of Mr. Valentino and back at the hat and back at Karla.

She growled at me with a sly look on her face. "*Grrrrrr.*" She reached out and grabbed one of my arms and pulled me on top of her. She pushed her tongue down my throat. I put my hands on her breasts and pushed her top down over her stomach. I reached down under her black knit tights and rubbed her blackbird with my fingers.

"Oh YAH, oh YES, aww you think you're soooo COOL, don't ya? Soooo COOL, don't ya? Don't ya, Mr. Little BIG MAN!" she taunted.

I opened my eyes. Karla's eyes, blue as sapphires, were wide open and staring into mine as I kissed her. The chimes on the back porch chimed. I closed my eyes again, as tight as I could, hoping it would stop but also hoping it would last forever.

The screen door at the front door of the house creaked open and slammed close with a THWACK! It was the Gooch. I felt it in my bones.

"Get rid of that goddamn HAT!" I yelled at Karla.

"Wha? Why? What are you saying?" Karla asked me, baffled. When I didn't answer, she slipped out from under me, jumped up off the bed, rolled up her top, and vanished out the bedroom door.

I lay back on the bed and waited. It was over—I was doomed. To tell you the truth, I was relieved. I deserved it. Obviously, I was a monster. I'd bullied Roddy too many times, I'd made my mom stay with my dad when she wanted to leave. She'd packed up our suitcases one night and lined them up at the front door. I begged her, I pleaded with her. I told her he could change. It was a big lie.

But, after a minute of lying there with Mr. Valentino smiling at me from the bedside table, I thought to myself, *Wait just a goddamn minute… It's not my fault. I'm a Prince of the Fraser Valley! Hell, I'm Handy Andy the Train Wrecker! I don't deserve to get cock-blocked by that old chain-smoker!*

I rolled off the bed, out of sight. The door opened and sure enough, it was the Gooch. She put down her purse on the bed and sat in front of her vanity mirror. She lit a cigarette. She was wearing an eye patch. Chinsky had accidently hit her in the eye with a hockey card. He'd been practicing how to spin them through the air for weeks, and he was good. One night while the Gooch was washing dishes, he fired one off at the back of her head, but she turned around suddenly and *ZAP!*

She lay her cigarette down on a small ashtray and creamed her face. I had to get out. I grabbed a sheepskin throw, pulled it over top of me, crawled across the floor, and out the door. Incredibly, I made it safely out into the hall, but ran into bad luck because Chinsky'd gotten bored, his attention span being so limited. He caught me.

"What are you doing, DIPSHIT?"

I jumped up and hit him hard in the balls with the knuckles of my right hand. He went down like a puppet and I made a run for it. I sprinted out the door, flew down the front steps, across the lawn, and tripped over Mr. Valentino's sprinkler. A flock of black starlings burst off the ground into the air and fanned out in front of me. I yelled "FUCK!" as loud as I could at the sky. I ran across the road, through a narrow path, and out onto the railway tracks. I kept on running and didn't look back.

13

Horny for Hoover

A guy my age—thirteen, a teenager—needed privacy. I put up a small hook lock on my bedroom door to keep everybody out. I had a golf set from Japan I'd bought with my own money and a growing porn collection to protect, specifically *Asian Fever* and *Biker Bitches*, which I'd found inside a broken garbage bag at the trash dump in Richmond.

In my closet were sneakers, jeans, and an *Ocean Pacific* surf T-shirt. Next to my bed was an AM/FM radio. On my bookshelf, books. One afternoon, I'd wandered up to the Marpole Library, tired of watching game shows and sitcoms with the Old Man. Way at the back, behind the librarian's desk was a small teen fiction collection. I grabbed a couple of titles, checked them out, and took them home. I started with V.C. Andrews's *Flowers in the Attic*, S.E. Hinton's *Tex*, and Stephen King's *Carrie*. I liked having them around. I liked reading them. Scratch that. *I loved reading them.* After I plowed through all the teen stuff I could find, I stumbled upon the motherlode: Herman Melville, Thomas Hardy, Joseph Conrad, Charlie Dickens, Hemingway, Jane Austin. You name it, I read it.

To get into my room, I had to go down an open staircase into Darlene's bedroom and open a door at the bottom of the stairs. Darlene's bedroom had a second door leading into a basement laundry room with an exit leading to the carport under our porch. The black pit at the bottom of the stairs scared the hell out of me. When I stood at the top, deciding whether to go down or not, a terrible fear claw would rise up and grab me by the throat. The Old Man used that staircase when he came home from work in a bad mood. Maybe that was it—I was afraid the bad mood down there was hanging around, waiting to grab me and drag me off into the black and never let me go.

One fateful afternoon, I forgot to lock my bedroom door. I was on my bed reading and Darlene was in her room. I tried to imagine what she might have been doing: rolling joints spiked with PCP, talking on the phone with one of her creepy friends, or maybe just laying on her bed, arms folded across her chest. The stereo was playing loud. Out of her big Hill PharmaTronics, the spooky Texan albino rock star, Edgar Winter, belted out "Free Ride."

Mom had left her Hoover vacuum cleaner on the floor of my room. Bored, I picked it up, turned it on, and started vacuuming the floor in my underwear. It was fun. I sucked the dust off everything: book jackets, my desk chair, even my old running shoes. While I was vacuuming, I began to think about Karla laying on her bed up the street, licking her pencil and maybe writing in her journal about me. I thought to myself, *I wonder what would happen if I put my dick into the end of the vacuum cleaner hose? I mean, would it feel good? What would happen if I changed the settings, higher or lower? How long could I keep it in there?*

Darlene turned up the stereo in the other room as loud as it could go without blowing the speakers. Mom yelled down the stairs, "Could you pleeeease turn that thing down?! I can't hear myself THINK!" Darlene ignored her. After a few more minutes, Mom yelled down the stairs again. "Please turn down the music! Goddammit, Darlene! TURN DOWN your stereo right now!"

I put the machine on its lowest setting, held the hose in my hands, and removed the nozzle. I reached into my Fruit of the Looms, pulled out my dick, and slipped it inside. It didn't feel too bad. I left it on to see what would happen. At this point, the dogs were barking, which was weird, because I usually couldn't hear them from my room. Mom called out again.

"DARLENE! PLEASE TURN THAT DOWN! RIGHT NOW!"

Without warning, Franny pushed open my door with her nose and came running into the room at full speed. She leapt up and sank her teeth into the hose. I grabbed the tube, stuck on my fully erect penis, and, panicking, tried to swing her off. First, I gave it a reverse cattleman's crack; next, a sidearm flick. I even tried a snake killer. Nothing worked. Finally, she got tired, dropped onto the ground, and made a run for the door. I followed her with my eyes. In the doorway, Mom and Darlene stared back at me.

Obviously, after that, my whole life was ruined forever.

14

Mean Boland

At home, nobody said a word. It was almost as if speaking *it* out loud, giving *it* a voice, would somehow make *it* more true and more terrible. I wish I could say the same thing about what happened at school. A couple weeks later, unbelievably, Chinsky blurted out in class that I had "fucked my mom's vacuum cleaner" when our teacher, Ken Elmer, was out of the room. The entire class of twenty-five received the news with stunned silence, followed by short fits of giggling.

Under normal circumstances, it might have been possible to retaliate with something equally outrageous; something as simple as accusing Chinsky of putting peanut butter on his balls and letting a neighbour's dog lick it off. But I didn't. I fumbled it. Badly. I started to cry. I couldn't stop myself. To be fair, nobody could have prepared themselves for something like that. I couldn't believe Chinsky had come up with something so sinister. *Did I black out and tell him in a trance or fit of regret? Could Darlene have told him? It wasn't possible. How could he have found out?*

Mr. Elmer came back into our class and continued with our

math lesson. He walked up to the blackboard and grabbed a piece of chalk,

"OK, so we're going to keep working on whole numbers. In the number 7,941, what is in the ten's place?"

Mean Boland, a poor kid with a ghost-white face and long black hair, tapped me on the shoulder. I turned around. He made a fist with his left hand and put the forefinger of his right hand in and out of it in imitation of a penis going in and out of a vacuum cleaner nozzle. He yelled out, loud enough for the entire class to hear, "Hey Livingston, I hear you're horny for Hoovers! Haha! I bet you've got the cleanest dick in the whole class! Hahahaha!"

It was all somehow made worse by him wearing a cool Pink Floyd T-shirt with a floating pig on the front. I clocked him one hard on the jaw to shut him up. His head snapped back and came slowly forward again. He slumped down over the top of his desk. His arms fell limp at his sides. I pretended nothing happened.

Well, it didn't take Elmer long to figure out something was wrong. After sizing up the situation and not getting any answers, he ordered both of us to the principal's office.

There were only two chairs in the reception area. I took one and Boland, the other. We faced each other. A portrait of Queen Elizabeth II was mounted on the wall above Boland's head. I wondered what she would think of me now, one of her loyal Commonwealth subjects—a sex pervert. It was almost too terrible to think about.

One thing was for sure: the kids in class thought it was maybe the best and worst thing in the world that had happened at the same time. As Boland and I sat and waited to see principal Pritchard, this dangerous fire Chinsky had sparked with his outburst was sucking up oxygen, leaping over streams, and spreading fast.

The door opened. Pritchard called us in and led us into his office. A photograph of Pritchard, his wife, and three children sat on a cabinet behind his desk. We sat down. Pritchard looked us over. Frankly, I didn't much like the guy. When he made announcements on the loudspeaker system, he said stuff like, "Today, because of the *inclement* weather, track and field practice is cancelled," or "Please *avail* yourself of the necessary *resources*." I mean, if you're going to say something, say it clearly. There's no point in trying to impress everybody—people are not as dumb as you think. He began the interview by asking, "So what brings you two *miscreants* into my office this morning?" We wouldn't answer him. I guess we both found the whole thing so shameful and frightening, we weren't giving anything up to anybody, especially a guy like Pritchard. After a long time, I admitted I punched Boland, but I wouldn't give a reason. Pritchard kept working on us, "So, what if one of your brothers robbed a bank? Would you tell me then? Gentlemen, your reticence is beginning to wear on me."

I had to give Boland credit—he didn't cave under pressure, and neither did I. It could also have been Pritchard messed the whole thing up. He interviewed us together; if he'd any gas in his think tank, he would have interviewed us separately.

When Pritchard realized his interview wasn't going to get him anywhere, he kicked us out of his office. I never heard from him again. I guess he just forgot about the whole thing and got on with his life.

15

A Magnificent Magnetic Field

A few weeks later, Chinsky and I were hanging around the outdoor pool at Maple Grove Park. Nobody was swimming; it was still too cold. Just a couple brat-shocked new moms killing time, between killing more time, between killing even more time sitting on the grass.

When the pool was empty in the winter, we used it as a bike jump and skateboard bowl. Infamously, one year, Mean Boland made a huge run at the pool down Yew Street on his Schwinn Stingray. He hit the concrete lip, flew a dozen glorious metres in the air, bungled the landing, and crucified his testicles on the steering shaft of his bike. He ended up in bed for five days. Afterward, his parents complained to the city, but nothing ever came of it.

We walked over to the park office and asked for a box hockey puck and two sticks. The point of box hockey was to slam a puck through holes cut in a compartmented wooden box. If you were any good, you could send a puck through your opponent's offence, defence, and goalie mouse holes with a single shot.

In our first game, Chinsky was beating me nine-to-one. "Take that ya stinky fish!" he cried as I ran back, again, to find the puck in the bushes after he'd scored, again. As I was swatting around, two girls from a grade below us at McKechnie wandered over and asked Chinsky if they could play. I'd seen one of the girls before— she was cute. Her name was Molly-something… Molly Murphy? The other girl's name was Rachel. She had a snaggle tooth that stuck out over her lower lip when she smiled at you. As for me, well, to be honest, I wasn't looking so good. Ever since Chinsky's outburst, the kids at school shunned me. It was daily torture, with no end in sight. I'd given up on the way I looked; I even stopped brushing my teeth. Most of the time, when I wasn't in school, I read books alone in my bedroom. I stopped showering. Acne plundered my neck and blackheads littered my forehead. My hair, normally feathered and fabulous, hung limp. Even creepy Darlene weighed in when I walked up the stairs one morning.

"Sheesh, you smell like a thirteen-year-old hobo. Why don't you change your shirt at least?"

I even started fantasizing about pulling off the hose of the vacuum cleaner and attaching it to the exhaust pipe of the Firebird when everybody was asleep. I'd run it through the back window of the car, slip inside, turn on the ignition, and… *Heck*, I figured, *aren't we all heading to the same place in the end? Into some kind of magnificent magnetic field out there in the universe hurtling toward an atomic, black end?* I mean, why not? With luck, maybe I'd get osmosed into a giant energy field, recycled, and shot back out into the game for a brand-new round.

Chinsky, the monster, asked Molly nonsensically, as they tapped the bottom of the box, and each other's sticks three times, "Hey, what does your dad do?"

"Who? Me? My dad's a pilot."

"You mean he flies a plane, or does he bring freighters into port on a boat?"

"Neither. He flies helicopters up the coast."

"Cool."

Rachel fired a shot from their defensive zone, through two box holes, banking once, and missed scoring on us by only a few inches. I handed my stick to Molly. She expertly fired her puck through two box holes, banking twice, and scored. "Easy peasy," she said, as she passed her stick to Chinsky, while I ran back to find the puck.

"I like your T-shirt," I told Molly when I got back. And I did. She was wearing a J.P. Patches fan club shirt, a morning show with a ridiculous, clown host from Seattle, broadcast on public television. I watched it religiously at 7:30 a.m. every morning before school. J.P. played every character on the show: Gertrude, Ketchikan the Animal Man, The Swami of Pastrami, Miss Smith, Dingbatman, Zenobia, Sturdly the Bookworm, Officer Paddy Wagon, and Charlie Can Do. My favourite was J.P.'s archenemy: Boris S. Wort, the second meanest man in the world.

Molly smiled at me and sent another one through our goal hole. When I got back with the puck, again, I asked Chinsky, "Hey dingbatman, what's the score anyhow?"

"6-1. But who's counting?"

"What does your dad do?" Molly asked me.

"Me? Mine?"

"Yah."

"He works for his dad. We own an egg factory."

Chinsky laughed. "His dad's job is to drink as much booze as he can." A crippling silence followed.

"Funny, Chinsky. Well, *his* dad's job is to lose as much money as he can gambling at the racetrack and pulling on slot machines," I mustered in reply. I slammed the puck. It bounced out of the box and rolled onto the grass. I handed my stick to Molly. "Well, it was nice seeing you guys." I walked over to the playground. Chinsky followed, calling out to me. "Hey, don't be sore. It was a joke."

I didn't really care, but I wasn't going to let Chinsky know about it. I was gonna let him suffer. I was more interested in Boom Boom McLean and her friend I'd met under the ping-pong table at the basement party, who had just arrived at the park and started up a tetherball game. I walked over to the court, trying to play it cool. The girls batted the ball between them. I waited until the point was over and said, "Well, hello there, you two rascals!"

And do you know what happened next? Jacquie let the ball drop, and they both walked over to the side of the court, picked up their backpacks, and left without saying a word.

"Sheesh. I wonder what got into them?" Chinsky mused as we walked over to the now-empty court. I grabbed the ball in my hands and, instead of starting a game, I fired it at Chinsky's head. It hit him in the face with a loud smack.

"What the hell was that for?!" he snapped back at me, rubbing his forehead, and playing it straight, even though he damn well knew he'd ruined my entire life forever.

16

Sine Timore Aut Favore

My mom was worried about me. She convinced the Old Man I needed a change—to make a fresh start. Since I already lived in Vancouver and couldn't move there from somewhere else, they agreed, without consulting me, I was to apply to the St. George's School for Boys, a boarding school in Dunbar, which also ran a day school program for locals. My aunt and uncle had sent two cousins to St. George's when they were around my age. At the time, they lived in Bella Bella on the BC coast in the middle of the Great Bear Rainforest.

The following week, I found myself sitting uncomfortably in a full classroom, writing the St. George's seventh grade entrance exam. It was supervised by a young male teacher, physically fit, wearing a tweed jacket. A no-nonsense guy. You could tell the minute you walked into the place.

The exam consisted of three tests. The first one was about the funniest kind of test I'd ever seen. On the left-hand side of the page were a set of five image boxes, each containing triangles, circles, or squares, all with lines or balls inside them. The last box was blank.

On the right-hand side, were a similar set of image boxes. You had to choose which basic shape fit into an empty one on the opposite page. You had to pay attention to what you were doing because mostly it looked like the images were designed to trick you into choosing the wrong one.

Following that, you had to read a passage of text, then answer if certain statements were true, false, or impossible to answer without more information.

In the last section, you authored an English essay. You could write about anything you wanted, so I wrote this long piece about Muhammad Ali. Everybody loved him—his appeal was universal. In the Congo, the "Rumble in The Jungle," he knocked out Joe Frazier and became world champion. Ali had famously gone "rope-a-dope," which really meant he acted like a dope on the ropes and let Frazier punch himself out over five rounds. That's when Ali let him have it. Ali was a smart fighter. He fooled Frazier. Hell, Ali wouldn't go to Vietnam to fight the Vietcong when the American government tried to make him. He told them to screw themselves.

After I finished my essay and signed it with a flourish—Andrew Robert Livingston, Esq.—I strutted up to the front of the classroom, handed it over, and sat down. On the blackboard were inspirational quotes: "A ship in harbour is safe, but that's not what ships are made for," and "No man ever steps in the same river twice, for it's not the same river and he's not the same man." I cocked my head, put my chin on my fist, and turned these over in my mind, as I imagined might be expected of a student at St. George's. I looked around at some of the other applicants. Two guys in the back row smirked and pointed behind this big kid's back, a baboon in a blazer. His name was McKracken. I found out later he'd tried to set his house on fire one lazy Sunday afternoon with his parents and his sister inside. To everyone's surprise, a few weeks afterward, the Old Man received a written invitation from the junior school headmaster, Angus Hardmeat, requesting we come see him in his office for an interview.

On the big day, the Old Man put on a tie and jacket, and we all jumped into his Firebird and drove to the Junior School campus. We arrived early. On the grounds was a single, modern, three-story building abutted by mossy cottages. It was past 3:00 p.m. After-school games were taking place: rugby practice on the east pitch and soccer on the west. We found the administrative office, walked up the stairs, and were ushered into a reception area. An old salt-and-pepper dog lay in front of the fireplace. He picked his head up when we walked in, looked us over, and laid it down again. After five minutes, Angus Hardmeat opened his office door, stepped out, and introduced himself. He invited us into his office. He wore a blue blazer and a red dragon emblazoned school tie. We sat down in three chairs arranged in front of his desk.

"Well, I'm Angus Hardmeat, Mr. and Mrs. Livingston. Welcome to St. George's School for Boys." He looked directly at me. "You must be Andrew. I welcome you. I'd like to start off by saying that we have a good bunch of boys here. Good lads. And with that, I'd very much like to keep this interview informal. Feel free to ask me anything. I usually ask a few simple questions. Does that sound straightforward?"

"Yes, sir!" the Old Man answered enthusiastically.

"Ah, ha... Well... Now, Andrew, can you tell me if you have any interests? What I mean is, what kinds of things keep you busy?"

I stared blankly back at his kind old face.

74

Mom jumped in. "He, er, he likes to read and play soccer."

"Is that true, Andrew? Do you like those things?"

"Yeah. Sure."

"Andrew's cousins, Bob and Tom Davies, graduated from St. George's in 1972," she volunteered.

"Ah, yes. I was aware of that. Fine boys. What are they up to now?"

"Well, they're doing some commercial fishing up around Clayoquot Sound."

"OK, OK. Well, we're a preparatory school, which means most of our boys go on to university. Is that what you want to do, Andy? Go to university?"

"Well, sure," I answered.

The Old Man let out a whistle. He wasn't too keen on higher education, seeing as he dropped out of high school to join the Merchant Navy. Mom shot the Old Man a look, colder than a polar bear's asshole. It rattled him. I think he was worried that if he said something stupid and screwed up my chances, she would make his life an even hotter hell than it already was.

"We have a wholesale business." Mom said.

"Yes?"

"It's here in the city."

"Of course, of course."

Mom wrung a ball of tissue in her hands repeatedly, tearing off small pieces which floated down onto the floor. Hardmeat continued. "Look—I mean, listen. Congratulations! I don't see any need to beat around the bush. Andrew's test results, especially verbal intelligence, are extraordinary. This fall we'd be delighted to welcome Andrew to St. George's." He smiled. "Do you have any questions for me, Andrew?"

"Well, yes. I, er, I do have a question."

"Speak up."

"Um, the sign on the door when you come into the building. What does it say? And I guess, what does it *mean* exactly?"

"Oh, that's our school motto, 'Sine Timore Aut Favore'". He looked me right in the eyes, winked, and said softly, "Without fear or favour."

17

Stray Cat

Time went forward, but never backward; never back, and summer finally showed her face, warm and dry, with long lovely days and everyday's-the-weekend charm.

I spent my days alone.

To get the Old Man off my back, I made a big deal out of waking up in the morning, eating breakfast, and walking out the door with a wave. Instead of golfing, hunting for balls, playing box hockey, or riding my bike, I'd head to the end of the block, make a left instead of a right, walk up and down our laneway, sneak back into the house, and go back to sleep under my bed until early afternoon. Even Chinsky, the Judas, stopped calling me.

Mom and Dad eventually figured it out; something was wrong. Their solution? Work.

Livingston Produce Inc. was founded by my Grandpa Earl. It was a wholesale egg operation with a fair-sized warehouse and processing plant. He bootstrapped the company on his own in 1929 after the stock market crashed without any help from "any goddamn bank."

In front was an office and cash counter shopped by locals, mostly Italian and Portuguese immigrants, looking to buy farm fresh eggs at a reasonable price. On top of the business were two rental apartments, host to a revolving door of colourful East Vancouver tenants (suicide, assault and battery, drug overdose). Grandpa Earl's small office was in a corner of the warehouse next to the retail cash desk. Day after day, he sat on a tall stool in front of an even taller, angled, wooden desk. He'd cut a hole in one of the walls and installed a sliding glass window so he could stick his head out and keep an eye on his employees on the processing floor. The warehouse foreman, Gord - an ex-convict who robbed a Loomis truck full of cash and got busted when he got off the plane in Brazil - ran things in the back.

In the warehouse, where the "farm fresh" eggs were processed, was a steel conveyor belt leading into a giant egg washing machine. My job, the worst, was to move cases of eggs out of walk-in fridges at the back with a hand truck and unload them in front of the processor. Next, I'd use a floating compression air device to suction up flats of eggs out of each carton, twenty-four at a time, and place them carefully onto a conveyor in order for them to be washed and graded. Most of the eggs I pulled out of cartons were caked in chicken shit. If I released the suction on the compressor too early, all of the eggs would crash onto the metal belt and crack open. When that happened, Gord would have to wash away the yolk and albumen with a hose before it hardened onto the concrete floor. After washing, the eggs continued in a single line over top of a penetrating white light into a dark hutch, where each one was individually inspected by a woman named Lucy, who had eyesight trouble, ironically.

Gord and I were pals despite the fact my grandfather owned the place. He had thick black hair he combed into a greasy ducktail and wore white T-shirts with a pack of cigarettes rolled up one arm on his shoulder. His forearms were tattooed with tumbling dice and naked women. Gord liked to call himself a "stray cat." When telling you a story, he'd say something like "this big old stray cat didn't get much sleep last night!" or "this stray cat don't kiss and tell."

At the end of my shift, nearing the end of my lousy summer, I went back to the walk-in fridge to load cartons. In a hurry to get out of there, trying to reduce my number of trips back and forth, I stacked too many cartons onto my hand truck. As I was pushing it back to the conveyor, its weight made me lose control. All of the cartons toppled over and fell onto the floor. After a terrible minute where nothing happened, egg white and yolk began to leak out of the boxes onto the floor. Gord, who'd been taking his break and smoking a butt on an overturned milk crate, saw the whole thing.

"Holy hell! Andy, whoa there! Whatchyouse think yer doing?"

"Oh crap! Gord! Oh, Christ!" I hollered. "What should I do now?"

He stomped out his butt, hustled over, and helped me overturn the boxes. We opened them up and saved as many eggs as we could. After we finished, Gord grabbed his hose and washed the yellow mess down a big drain in the middle of the floor.

"Now don't you worry, young fella. We can get this fixed up and nobody will be none the wiser. Hell, when I was working at the Coastwise Local a few years back, I was discharging Japanese oranges when the straw rope between 'em broke, and I'll be damned if about 500 oranges didn't go rolling off the pier. I damn near jumped into the water to try to save 'em, and when I looked out at the rolling waves it was like the whole Fraser was laughing at me, like I was a durn fool."

He was interrupted when the Old Man honked his horn and backed his truck into the loading bay. He'd finished his run. He turned off the engine, hopped out of the cab of the big Freightliner, and walked to the back to unlatch the back panel of the cargo box. Inside, stacked high, were cases of eggs.

The Old Man, shaking his head, passed us on his way to the bathroom at the other end of the warehouse. Gord continued, "Now that was a real job, longshoring, I can tell you. Not like this candy-ass egg picking job you've gone and got yourself." After Gord and I had finished unloading the truck, it was time to go home. The Old Man told me he'd give me a lift. On our way out, the Old Man asked Gord,

"Gordon, how's the wife?"

"She's fine, Bob, thanks for asking."

"Well, tell her I say hello and that you two should come on over to the house. We could crack a few."

"Will do. Thanks, Bob."

"Andy, let's get going."

"Hey, Dad? Can I ride in the back?"

"Why not?"

I ran across the loading bay and jumped into the cargo box. Dad jumped on the fender and pulled down the door. The latch clicked shut. In the black, I found a rope handle and held it tight with both hands. The engine shuddered as Dad pulled out into rush hour traffic on Commercial Drive.

18

Let There be Rock

Darlene's speakers blasted, blared, brayed and boomed, rain or shine, day or night. As soon as she woke up in the morning or was getting ready to go out into the night and torment older guys, she played crazy rock 'n roll as loud as possible: AC/DC, Steve Miller, Captain Hook, Bad Company, Jimi Hendrix, Bob Marley and the Wailers. One time she played "Jamming" so many times, the Old Man flipped. He screamed at her down the stairs, "Darlene! Turn that FUCKING SKINHEAD CRAP down or I'll come down there and smash that thing over your head!"

Darlene's music had a narcotic effect on me. My favourite band, AC/DC; my favourite album, *High Voltage*. Bon Scott knew exactly how I felt. I was now part of one big, ugly, happy, dirty AC/DC family. I would never be alone again.

One morning, as I was leafing through the *Vancouver Province* newspaper, in the entertainment section, right next to a stupid Dolly Parton interview, I stumbled across a small black-and-white ad.

POWERAGE WORLD TOUR
AC/DC
AEROSMITH
Pacific National Exhibition
Tuesday 25 July 1978
8:00 p.m.

I couldn't believe it. I reread it three times. *Was it some kind of a mirage?* My favourite band was coming to Vancouver! Mom would never let me go alone. I was going to have to get some tickets and a comrade in arms. Asking Chinsky was out of the question. *Who did I know who loved rock n' roll, could afford a ticket, and whose parents couldn't care less where they went or who they were with?* Fozzy Ferguson. Fozzy loved rock and roll, had plenty of money from gambling and petty crime, and smoked weed. He was the perfect candidate. I called Fozzy on the phone, putting my finger into the rotary dial seven times after looking up his dad's name in the phone book. It rang three times before Old Man Ferguson answered.

"Hey-low?"

"Hello, sir. May I please converse with Charles, if convenient?"

There was a long silence on the other end of the line. He bellowed.

"Charles! Charles! Pick up the goddamn phone!"

"Hullo?" Fozzy answered.

I got straight to the point.

"Say, Fozzy, how would you like to go to see AC/DC at the PNE next week?"

"Who is this?

"It's Andy. Andrew Livingston."

"AC/DC?

"Yah! AC-fucking-DC!"

"OK."

"Right on. I'll buy the tickets at Sam the Record Man and you can pay me back."

19

The Thunder From Down Under

The night of the concert gusted in like a big sou'wester rolling all the way up from Oakland, California, where AC/DC played the night before. The Old Man sat in his chair, pounding vodka on the rocks and smoking Lucky Strikes. He yelled at the TV while watching a parade of American morons compete against each other for prizes based on their knowledge of the retail prices of consumer goods, things like a Master luggage lock or Cinnamon Toast Crunch cereal. *The Price is Right* was one of his favourite shows.

"It's $8.50, you stupid BITCH!"

I picked up the phone in the kitchen and dialled Fozzy's number, inserting my finger, again, seven times into the rotary dial. He picked up on the first ring this time.

"So, what time do you want to catch the bus to see the show!?"

"I dunno."

"Do you have any spare cash?"

"Sure."

"What time do you have to be home?"

"I dunno."

"I scored a big fat *J-O-I-N-T*." I whispered into the receiver.

"Uh huh."

Unfortunately, Fozzy's mom, Alice, met this declaration with more interest than Fozzy. She'd been listening in on the call from a second phone in her bedroom. Apparently, she tapped all his phone calls. At warp speed, I found myself sitting in my family living room (never used for anything, not even entertaining, the couch in plastic), sitting across from Alice Ferguson, my mom, and a very bored looking Fozzy. He knew I'd sunk myself. All he was going to do was sleepwalk his way through the whole thing.

"So, what do you think of our situation?" Mrs. Ferguson asked me. "You must know drugs are wrong. Have you considered their effect on your brain?"

I didn't have an answer for her. My mom jumped in. "Well, have you? Andrew? Andrew, Alice asked you a question. Do you know how serious this is? You could go to prison!" She spelled it out for me, "P-R-I-S-O-N."

"Um, it was only one... Ah, nevermind," I said.

Everything was going sideways and fast. There was only one option left if we were going to still make it to the concert. We had less than fifteen minutes to catch our bus. I begged for mercy. It was the only way out.

"Listen, I'm really very sorry. I don't know what I was thinking. *Please* forgive me."

"Well, where did you get it?" Mom asked.

"I bought it from a hippie on the Granville Mall. I made a terrible mistake."

I looked over at Fozzy. He smirked. I looked back at Mrs. Ferguson. She said to my mom, "Well, Gwenda. What do you think?"

In the end, they let us go.

Fozzy and I bounced along in silence on the Arbutus bus as it charged south to Hastings Street, where we were going to have to transfer and get on another bus.

I nudged him. "Dude, that was heinous. Why do you think they let us go? I'd never have guessed we'd get out of there in a million years."

"Don't sweat it. They wimped out. It was a classic stalemate. If they didn't let us go, we'd have made their lives miserable."

"Well, maybe…"

"Do you think they have pizza at the stadium?" he asked, changing the subject. The old bus rattled and wheezed until coming to a stop at our transfer. We got out, waited fifteen minutes, and boarded a new bus packed with headbangers. At Clark Drive, we heard a loud *clunk* from under the bus. The driver pulled over.

"Everybody out!" he hollered and opened the doors. The bus had broken down. We'd made it far enough that I could see the old wooden roller-coaster on the grounds of the PNE.

We ran as fast as we could, weaving our way through the crowd on the sidewalk. I crashed into some guy's back and couldn't get past; Fozzy came to a halt next to me.

"What's happening? Keep on truckin!" he yelled.

"I can't," I answered. Five males, shirtless, all with long hair down their backs, blocked our way. They were punching and kicking passersby, male and female, old and young, at random. The leader—well, at least he sure looked like the leader—was wasted out of his mind. Another one, maybe even more wasted, punched a girl Darlene's age, and gazed up into the sky. Something was spooking him. He moved his head around, wildly, as if an invisible Pterodactyl was attacking his face. The others ran through the crowd shrieking. They grabbed a bystander, threw him to the ground and formed a loose semicircle. Each stomped on him, in turn.

Finally, this tough-looking old bird stepped out of the crowd. He walked over, waving his arms and yelling, "Why don'tcha takeah fucking hike, you goddamn arseholes!" The biggest one walked over to him, swung wide, and hit him in the temple. It was a *damn* hard throw. He fell down, face-first, on the asphalt. Fozzy yelled out, "Oh my God. I think he's dead!"

It was too much for us. We cut and ran. At the stadium entrance we stopped, caught our breath, and smoked two cigarettes Fozzy had stolen from his old man. I handed my ticket to the security guard and sprinted to GATE B, SECTION 10, where two seats waited for us in the dark arena. We sat down. It was the tail end of Aerosmith's backup set. Steve Tyler and his band were so wasted they could barely play their instruments. They played, or at least I think they played, "Walk this Way" and "Sweet Emotion." Making matters worse, feedback from the lead microphone created some kind of positive gain loop, overloading the system. A meathead in front of us (in shock and on a date) shook his head, and muttered, "Jesus Christ! Would you look at that? They're piss-drunk is all. Piss-drunk."

When it was over, nobody cheered.

After about forty five minutes, a chant rose up, loud enough to send shivers into the massive cloud of smoke hovering in the middle of the stadium. "AC/DC!" It took on a life of its own, and in the end, *everybody in the stadium was screaming, AC/DC! AC/DC! AC/DC!* At long last, the lights went out. A spotlight shone onto the middle of the stage. Bon Scott stepped into it, a shining electric guitar in his hands. He kicked off the set with "Live Wire." Girls pulled out their hair and screamed. Head bangers, banged. Thrashers, thrashed. I looked over at Fozzy. His face was frozen in fear.

"The Thunder From Down Under" delivered over two hours of the most punishing, heaven-sent, rock 'n roll I'd ever heard. The apex of the show was when Angus Young, on lead guitar and wearing a prep school uniform, straddled Bon Scott's shoulders and waded into the crowd. The rest of the set list was "Love at First Feel," "Problem Child," "High Voltage," "Night Prowler," and "Dirty Deeds Done Dirt Cheap." The show ended. A colossal roar of applause followed the band off the stage. The lights came on and we made our way, satisfied, elated, exhausted, toward the stadium exit doors. Fozzy grabbed a slice of Hawaiian pizza at a concession stand. Holding it in his hand, he tripped and pitched forward into the back of a troop of heavy metal baboons. A greaseball with a head shaped like a rugby ball turned his head and shouted, "Why don't you watch where yer going, ya fucking Tangerine Tit!"

We watched as he walked out of the stadium. Stuck fast on the back of his motorcycle jacket was Fozzy's slice. Mom picked us at the corner of Renfrew and McGill. We drove home in silence. After dropping Fozzy off at home, Mom pulled the car over to the curb and turned off the ignition. We sat in silence until she turned to me and said quietly,

"So, where did you really get it?"

"Get what?" I asked, my eardrums still hissing from the concert.

"The marijuana cigarette."

"Aw, come on, Mom, give me a break. We went over this already."

"Well, we went over it, but I don't believe you bought it on a street corner. You're not getting off that easy."

I was damn tired and she wasn't going to give up. Under the fluorescent glare of a streetlight at the corner of Laburnum and Angus Drive, I ratted out my big sister.

"It was Darlene. Darlene gave me the joint."

I never heard about it again, but every now and again it bothers me, the snitch part, because Darlene never would have dropped the dime on me.

PART II

ADOLESCENT

1979–1981

20

Queequeg

The intensity of sunlight reaching the earth's surface waned, and the fall arrived; it was time for a new wardrobe and a fresh start. My days as a lanky, hopeless, chip-tooth, pot-smoking, good-for-nothing, cry-baby, rat-fink bully had come to an end. I bought a St. George's school uniform at Hill's of Kerrisdale: two pairs of grey flannel pants, two white button-down collared shirts, one blue blazer with a school crest on the chest pocket, two school ties, and a pair of brown Clarks Wallabees.

"Well, Joan, of course we're excited about making a change for Andrew. I mean, why don't you see if he can apply?" I overheard Mom chatting to a friend on the phone. "You mean his grades? Uh huh. Yes, well, it does cost a fair amount." She paused. "Well, I can't see that being a problem. Why don't you get his father to pay for it?" And finally, "It's not a fancy school, Joan."

Getting to school every morning by 8:00 was an ordeal. St. George's was at least thirty-seven city blocks from my house. If you didn't have a car, getting from point A to point B in Vancouver was, in no particular order, boring, exhausting, frustrating, and time-consuming. The worst part about getting to St. George's was that every morning, on top of getting to a pre-arranged pickup spot on Southwest Marine Drive at 7:30 (Mom had found a younger kid, Woodward, commuting in with his dad from Richmond) or catching one of three buses if Woodward wasn't available, I had to wear a clean white shirt, gray flannel trousers, and a tie around my neck.

Every morning, the guys at St. George's played an old schoolyard game called Conkers before the bell rang for morning chapel. If you wanted to play, you needed your own Conker— basically, a horse chestnut with a string through the middle. Two players, standing opposite one another, Conker in-hand, would, in turn, attempt to wound or shatter their opponent's Conker by swinging their own Conker at their opponent's. A Conker not cracking or shattering through an offensive strike or defensive hit was declared the winner.

Probably the best part was that you could ruin a guy's entire day by destroying his Conker. The thing was, the more times your Conker won, the more attachment you felt for it. The hardest Conkers won matches, and there were three ways to improve your Conker's luck. The first was to bake your Conker in the oven. The second was to boil it in vinegar. The last, frowned upon, was to paint it with your mom's nail polish.

"Hey, Livingston! Hey, Handy Andy! Let's give it a go! Boner's thirsty for new blood!" Boner was Chris Talbot's Conker. He called out to me, swinging Boner in front of him as I was leaning against a wall of the school, minding my own business. Talbot was on a roll; I'd watched him destroy three Conkers already. The last of them belonged to Franklin Woosencraft. After Boner shattered

Woosencraft's Conker, Woosencraft, frozen with grief, stared at his empty string for a full five minutes, chestnut shards scattered at his feet.

I slowly pulled out my Conker from my blazer pocket and hung it opposite Boner, nut to nut. Instead of an old shoelace, Talbot had threaded Boner with a piece of shipping twine. Boner's shiny coat blinked in the morning sun. Had Talbot brushed him with lacquer or varnish?

"Ha! Would you look at that! What's its name? It looks like you pulled him out of your butthole!"

"Queequeg," I murmured. Talbot rucked up his face at the enigma. The illiterate fool!

"Come on Queequeg! Let's have a go!" he yelled. A crowd formed. Talbot cracked Queequeg three times with Boner, fast, in succession. Queequeg split in two and fell apart on the pavement. Talbot lifted one of his big shoes and stomped on his remains, shouting, "Stampies! Stampies! Ha ha!"

The bell rang. Talbot carefully wiped Boner off with a tissue and slipped him into the side pocket of his blazer.

It didn't take long to get into the rhythm at St. George's. I found I didn't miss my old life at all. I was so busy with clubs and sports and homework that there wasn't any time to worry about anything else. St. George's was big on goal setting: handwritten notes, calendars, coaching, reminders. It worked for me. One thing I hadn't anticipated: the academic work. It was no joke. There were some smart kids at St. George's. Many came from all over the world, and others had won scholarships to attend. Most of the teaching masters, masculine, self-confident men, didn't take any crap from the students, and the expectation was academic excellence.

One morning, the head boy of the Junior School, John Carmichael, announced the winner of the school's short story competition. The title was "Appleby's Magnificent Machine," and the author was a scholarship student in my homeroom class named Yevtushenkov. Yevtushenkov walked up to the podium and shook hands with Carmichael. Behind them hung a Canadian flag, the provincial flag of British Columbia, and a Union Jack, or as the Old Man called it, "the butcher's apron."

As soon as the award service was over, I ran to the box outside Hardmeat's office to get a copy of *The St. George's Explorer Record*, where the "Magnificent Machine" had been published. I found Yevtushenkov's story and read it quickly. It was great; not only great, it was funny and honest. It was daring. It had imagination. Hell, it was *moving*.

As my bus, the Dunbar Express, bounced me home that night, I thought to myself, *I don't think many of the kids at my old school could even read something like that, let alone write it.*

Over the course of the year, I signed up for, and made, a good number of A-level squads: English rugby, soccer, badminton, long jump, and cross-country running. I joined the drama and boxing clubs. I was enjoying myself, strangely enough.

21

McKracken

In the eighth grade, we moved up to the St. George's Senior School campus. The Senior School facilities, four blocks west of the Junior School, were modern, with an enormous swimming pool, games facilities and grounds, and a full teaching faculty across all disciplines, including photography, theatre, computer science, and typing (if you can believe it), all of which was superintended by Headmaster Robert Theodore Pillicock, a fifty-one-year-old recreational hang-glider with a PhD in mathematics.

At St. George's, if you held your own on a pitch, or in academic competition, you got a free pass—freedom from having a garbage can overturned on your head, eating lunch alone in the cafeteria, getting a "gonchie," or suffering endless, unmentionable, taunts from the pimple-faced masses.

John McKracken—the arsonist, 'Kracky" to his few friends—jammed a baseball bat into the spokes of the front wheel of my new life. We hated each other. With some guys, if you had a problem, it was probably because you didn't understand one another. You hadn't "walked a mile in their shoes." The problem with McKracken and I was that we understood perfectly.

McKracken was a big guy with hairy knuckles, a pitted chin, the cunning of a rat, and an enormous penis. He played A-level rugby and was born in Ireland. The McKracken penis was a marvel of the locker room, a giant one-eyed monster in a bird's nest of black pubic hair.

Energetic, optimistic, and ready-for-anything, I rounded a corner on my way to the school cafeteria and happened upon McKracken as he was reaching up to put something into his locker. Without giving it any thought, I snuck up behind him. I reversed a clenched palm over the top of my shoulder, raised my elbow, and put my mouth to his ear, and whispered, "Top o' the morning to yer, Kracky."

I threw an elbow down hard where the cervical meets the thoracic vertebrae on his spinal column. He gasped, pitching forward. Before he could retaliate, I fell back and disappeared. At the end of the school day, as I was reaching for the handle of the south exit door of the main building, I heard a loud bellow from behind, "LIVINGSTON!" Of course, it was McKracken.

The big vengeful fuck came right at me. I couldn't get out of his way in time. He put a foot expertly behind one of my ankles, pushed, and I dropped to the ground. As I floundered, he grabbed my ankles; one in each hand. He began pulling me backwards, a reverse wheelbarrow, —first slow, and next, fast. "McKracken!" I yelled. "I'm burning!"

A horrible grin crossed his face. Soon enough, the heavy friction generated between my pants and the carpet burned the cloth of my pants; next, off came the skin on my ass. I wailed and flailed. I tried to kick him off me, but he was too strong; he held my feet tight, in an iron grip. I was able to flip over onto my chest. He dragged me to the end of the hallway.

An eager crowd gathered round. I tore myself free and jumped up. We faced one another. He lunged at me, wrapped his arm around my neck, and put me in a guillotine choke. I couldn't breathe. Desperate, I reached down, easily found his big balls, and squeezed. His grip around my neck soon faltered; I increased the pressure. He let out a wild, shuddering, howl. We rolled into a classroom doorway. Suddenly, I heard our names called out.

"LIVINGSTON!"

"MCKRACKEN!"

It was Headmaster Pillicock. He stood above us, trembling with rage. I found out later standing behind him was a senior official in the Iranian government and his wife. They were on a tour of the school, trying to find a safe place to board their son, Babak Ramezani, while back at home religious fundamentalists set their country on fire. Pillicock separated us and pointed at the exit doors. McKracken and I stood up, dusted ourselves off, and walked out. Brother, it wasn't over, though. There were going to be consequences. There was no point in trying to make a case for yourself. In disciplinary matters, everybody knew it: Pillicock played the man—not the ball.

On my way home, I waited half an hour for the number ten Dunbar bus. I was a mess. Blood was all over my pants. I sat down next to a kid I recognized from the Junior School. He took one look at me, squeezed past my legs, and took a seat up front near the driver. I made it home after two bus transfers and a long walk across the park.

Most nights, when I came home, the Old Man was watching

his sitcoms or game shows in his study, but not tonight. I walked down the hall, threw down my backpack, and stepped into the kitchen. Franny and Zooey, the pugs, were at my heels, Mom was sitting at the kitchen counter. Her bathrobe was open. Her left eye was swollen and black.

"Mom? Jesus, are you alright? What happened? Did you fall?" She wouldn't hear me.

I sat down next to her. "Mom!" I stood up and put my hands up under her arms. I managed to drag her into her bedroom, lay her down on the bed, and pull a blanket over top of her. I closed the door and looked down the hall; Dad's bedroom door was closed. The lights were off.

Jesus. Did he belt her one? I wondered. *Should I call the police...? No. I'm only a kid. What the hell did I know?*

I walked to the top of the stairs, got down on my hands and knees and played with Franny and Zooey, trying to give myself time to think. Each of them, in turn, lay on their backs on the floor: itching, scratching, biting, rolling, kissing. After a while I descended the stairs. I hadn't seen Darlene in a week. I opened my bedroom door, took off my tie, unbuttoned my shirt, and took off my socks. I threw my pants into the trash.

I lay down on my bed and listened to CFUN on my AM radio—"One of These Nights," "Boogie Wonderland," "The Logical Song," "My Sharona," "I Don't Like Mondays"—until I fell asleep.

22

Pillicock to the Rescue

I picked up, or he picked me up—do we ever really know?—a new friend: David D'Aubert. D'Aubert, my new pal, buddy, chum, was a great-looking kid. He had blonde, curly hair and the eyes of a baby fawn. One good look at D'Aubert and you might say to yourself, *Jesus, even the ears on this guy are beautiful.*

We hit it off on the track and field team. I'd been running since I was a kid, at McKechnie. Our homeroom teacher in the sixth grade, Ken Elmer, who sent Mean Boland and I to the principal's office, was a local legend. He ran for Canada in the men's 1,500-metre race in the 1972 Munich Olympics—you know, the Olympics where eight Palestianian Black September terrorists murdered eleven Israeli athletes? Elmer, a world-class athlete, turned me on to running; I won a 5,000-metre BC provincial championship. Brother, I had endurance. D'Aubert and I trained together. In the woods, on the track, anywhere.

We hit it off so well I invited him over to my house after school. We hung around in my room and listened to the radio and when we got tired of that, we went into the study and watched TV with the Old Man. On the screen, a television advertising executive, Les Nessman, was trying to organize a promotion. His plan was to drop forty-five live turkeys onto the parking lot of a Cincinnati, Ohio shopping mall. I changed the channel. A clever Black kid named Arnold and his older brother, Willis, argued with their adoptive father, Mr. Drummond, a white millionaire. I flipped the channel again. A funny-looking teacher, Mr. Kotter, stands in front of his class, the "Sweathogs," in Brooklyn and asks a question. A skinny moron in the back, Arnold Horshack, raised his hand and screamed, "Ooh! Ooh! Ooh! I got it, I got it!" I turned the TV off. The Old Man got up, grabbed his car keys, and headed off to the liquor store.

We went into the kitchen. I turned on the electric burner. I sprayed a frying pan with PAM, buttered four Wonder Bread slices, cut some cheddar cheese, and fried up two grilled cheese sandwiches. I prepared place settings for the two of us: two knives, two forks, two paper napkins, and served up the chow. We ate and finished off with two glasses of milk. D'Aubert smiled at me affectionately afterward, a white milk moustache on his upper lip.

After washing the dishes, I opened the cupboard. Instead of putting the can of PAM away on the shelf, I played around with it. I tossed it up in the air. I read the instructions out loud to D'Aubert: "Use only as directed. FLAMMABLE. Do not spray on heated surfaces, heated pots or pans, or near open flame. Never spray directly into the oven or the can may burst. Contents under pressure. Do not puncture or incinerate. Do not expose yourself to heat. Keep out of reach of children. Intentional misuse by deliberately concentrating or inhaling can be harmful or fatal. PAM is a product of Arthur Meyerhof."

Can in-hand, I pulled open a drawer. Inside, I found a plastic bag. I opened it and shot some PAM inside. I lifted it up and inhaled. After a few seconds, my face flushed with warm heat. After a few more seconds, my head turned into a boiling kettle. Unable to breathe, I panicked, dropped the bag on the floor, and rushed to the sink. I turned on the cold water. I put my entire head under the faucet. I could breathe again. I towelled my face with a dishcloth. D'Aubert, incredulous, stared. I picked the bag up off the floor, sprayed some more PAM into it, and handed it to him. "Oh. Hey. I really don't think I should, I've never…"

"Awh. C'mon. What's the worst that could happen?"

"I could die."

"What's the second worst thing that could happen?"

Not long after the PAM experiment, Headmaster Pillicock, wearing grey flannels, a black blazer, and a school tie paraded into our homeroom class before our regular teaching master, Dr. Ho, arrived. He addressed the class.

"Boys," he began. "I want to speak to you this morning about the changes your body is going through. You are going to experience changes you might not understand…"

He had my full attention. I was obsessed with my body; I was maturing much later than all the other guys in our grade. My voice was high-pitched and feminine. I had the body of a twelve year old. I didn't need to shave my face. Already, a few of the guys in our grade had five o'clock shadows! The new Iranian kid, Ramezan, could already buy booze at the liquor store without getting asked for ID.

Pillicock wasted little time and got straight to the point. "Boys, you *are* going to ejaculate semen from your penis, you *are* going to grow hair on your face, and you will need to shave every day." He stroked his chin. "Your voices will change and grow deeper. You will become a man. Rest assured."

What a break! I thought. *Pillicock wouldn't lie about something like that!* A tremendous weight, as if I'd been trapped under a car, lifted. Pillicock, in a fit of hysterical strength, had set me free. How noble, how reasonable, how rational of him! I was going to be able to cum, grow body hair, and talk like a man someday, and someday soon. It was a biological imperative. *I had Pillicock's word on it!*

"If any of you boys have any questions, please feel free to come and see me in my office." He turned and walked out the door. I felt a hard stab in the ribs. It was McKracken.

"That's right, Pillicock." He snickered. "Right, right. Well Livingston, have you got your period yet?"

23

Pencil Pusher

After the Night of the Black Eye, Mom and Darlene disappeared for long periods of time without any explanation. Mom took temporary secretarial jobs in offices as far away as possible—Port Moody, Coquitlam, White Rock. Darlene slept on a friend's couch.

You could hardly blame them. The Old Man and I spent more and more time together, like two lead actors in a bad sitcom: *The Stiff and Me! Lush Life! The Souser and the Kid!*

Somebody was in the study, jibber-jabbering with the Old Man. Study? More like a lair, a burrow, or a cave. It might have been my Uncle Frank, but I didn't see his pickup parked out front. I poked my head in through the doorway. Sitting opposite the Old Man on the couch, was our neighbour, Rex Wilson. Dad peered at me through a shroud of cigarette smoke. On the table in front of them lay an open pack of Player's Navy Cut, a giant ashtray, and two drinks.

"Ah, hiya kid. Say hello to Rex from next door. You remember Rex, don'tcha?" Dad said.

"Hello, Mr. Wilson."

Rex nodded, lifted his drink, and tipped it at me before taking a swig. Dad laughed. "Rex's taking the day off work today. He's a bean counter! Ha, ha! You know, a pencil pusher!"

I closed the door. I walked back into the kitchen and made myself a peanut butter and raspberry jam sandwich on Wonder Bread. I went downstairs to look for my missing issue of *Screw*. I'd already checked everywhere, maybe a dozen times. On the cover was an illustration of a girl with her legs spread open, pointing at a blinking button between her legs. In print, beneath her, "Mork and Mindy's Sex Life," "Hot Sex in Hot Tubs," "Orgy Etiquette," and "Sex Secrets of an Amputee." I searched for almost half an hour: under my bed, behind a special ceiling tile, tucked inside an album cover. I walked back up the stairs, slowly, step by step. I walked down the hall and opened the door of the study.

"Dad, what the…"

Rex lay on the floor, his forehead hard-pressed against the carpet floor. Zooey sped inside and licked one of his ears. Rex mumbled. It was impossible to make out what he was saying. The Old Man couldn't keep his mouth shut. "Jesus Christ, Rex!" he yelled. "What the hell is wrong with you? Why can't you get up?'

"Dad! Stop it!" I interrupted. "Don't you worry, Mr. Wilson. I'll get Mrs. Wilson!"

I sprinted down the hall, out the door, and down the back stairs. I ran down our driveway and across the lane to the Wilson's rancher. Mrs. Wilson opened the door wearing a kitchen apron, her hair in a severe bun. "Um, good afternoon, Madam, I'm Andrew Livingston."

"I know who you are."

"Everything's fine… But ahh, you see… It's that we need you

to come over and get Rex. He can't get up." She pushed me aside.

To be honest, I didn't feel like watching what was going to happen next, so I crossed the laneway, sat down, and waited. Sometime later, the screen door flew open and the Wilsons stumbled out together onto the landing. Rex's eyes were closed. Mrs. Wilson said nothing. She helped Rex down the stairs.

"Kate," he said, repeatedly. "My dearest Kate, Kate, Kate."

Mrs. Wilson opened our gate and crossed the lane into their backyard. On the way to the back door of their house, Rex slipped and nearly fell into their koi pond. It had been installed a few years back, but they couldn't keep any fish because Fozzy kept stealing them in the middle of the night.

When I went back into the burrow, the Old Man was kicking back. He'd enjoyed himself. It looked like he'd even poured himself a fresh drink.

"That old bugger must be on some kind of medication," he told me, shaking his head. "Ha! Bean Counters!"

The Old Man had endurance, you had to give him that. He lit cigarette after cigarette. His eyes, now half-lidded, looked out the window at the park. He snickered. He cursed. He let out a long whistle. I played with Franny and Zoey on the floor for a while before going downstairs into my room and laying down on my bed.

24

Butkus

At St. George's, we assembled twice a week for *typing class*, if you can believe it, pounding out Q W E R T Y Monday and Thursday mornings at 9:30 sharp, in a special classroom lined with typewriting stations. The teacher was an ancient Scot named Ms. Hickenbottom. I sat next to Franklin Woosencraft. One afternoon, I glanced over at his page. On it, he'd typed,

> All work and no play makes Jack a dull boy
> All work and no play makes Jack a dull boy
> All work and no play makes Jack a dull boy

I recognized it immediately. It was from *The Shining* by Stanley Kubrick. Well, it was based on a Stephen King novel adapted for the big screen and directed by Kubrick. Jack Nicholson plays Jack Torrance, a struggling bum of a dad who goes crazy while trying to write a novel at a haunted Colorado resort in the middle of the winter. Before he tries to axe-murder his wife and dies frozen in a snowbank, all he can type is "All work and no play makes Jack a dull boy" endlessly, line after line, page after page.

I appreciated it. It took balls to submit something like that to Hickenbottom with a straight face. I decided, at that moment, I was going to befriend Woosencraft. Woosey was beautiful like D'Aubert, only taller, with short, curly hair, brown skin, and full lips, like a girl. I stopped typing and turned to him,

"Hey, Woosey, I like your assignment. Do you plan to hand that thing in?"

"Sure. Why not?" he said with a smile.

We started hanging out.

We sat together in the cafeteria at lunch, we walked to the bus stop together, we called each other on the phone. One weekend, he invited me to his house in West Vancouver to sleep over. Mom drove me over in the car. We found the house in the British Properties and pulled into the driveway. It was enormous. It might have had three wings and a four-car garage. We could see Burrard Inlet, downtown Vancouver, and all the way over to Vancouver Island from the driveway.

I knocked on the front door and Woosey answered. He introduced me to his mom and his younger sister, Emily, when I stepped into the foyer. His mom had the face of a fashion model.

Mrs. Woosencraft told me to put my backpack on a bench while she took me on a house tour. In the big backyard, a bunch of construction equipment was scattered everywhere: a mini digger, an excavator, and a bulldozer. As we walked around the soon-to-be luxury pool—a giant hole in the ground, she told me, "Well you see, Andrew, Franklin's father is building an addition to the house. He's a psychiatrist, don'tcha know, and he needs privacy to run his practice. Emily and I wanted a swimming pool, and Franklin wanted a hot tub, so everybody's getting what they want. We're almost finished. Right, Emily?"

Emily, in a dress, holding a Raggedy Ann doll, with a thin face, blue eyes, and short bangs cut above her eyebrows, smiled at me, clearly self-conscious. It looked like a big job to me.

"Almost finished?" I asked her.

She ignored the question. Because of all the construction, a tarp covered half of the rear of the house. Making matters worse, the whole place was freezing cold. Later, when Woosey and I played *Blackjack* and *Music Machine* on his Merlin, I could see my breath whenever I said anything. I jumped into a sleeping bag and wouldn't come out. Even the family dog, an oversized German Shepherd named Otto, couldn't stand it. He howled the whole afternoon until it was time for dinner. Mrs. Woosencraft called us down to the big dining room. We sat down at a long, formal, table.

"Andrew, what would you like to drink?" Mrs. Woosencraft asked me. Over her shoulder, in the distance, shone the candescent lights of downtown Vancouver, the reflection of the buildings shimmering on the water, and car headlights moving across the Lion's Gate bridge.

"Ah, er, water. No, Coke. Water," I answered.

"Well, what is it going to be? One or the other?"

"I don't know."

It was going to be a long night. She brought me both. Woosey smiled.

"Franklin," Dr. Woosencraft asked. "Did you remember to walk Otto this afternoon?"

"Oh, sure Dad." Woosey lied. "Andy and I took him over to Hadden Park. We saw the Coulthards' dog, you know, ah, what was his name again, Andy?" Everybody at the table turned to me.

"What? Oh yah, the dog... Butkus?"

"Yes, that's it. Butkus!" Woosey exclaimed, satisfied.

Dr. Woosencraft said nothing for the rest of the dinner. He watched me with his handsome, chiselled, American-movie-star face as I tried to figure out what to do with all the forks and knives lined up in front of me. In the end, I grabbed the ones closest to my plate and just cut up everything in sight and put each piece into my mouth.

When it was over, I figured if all rich folks did was sit silently at a dining room table and pass a big invisible medicine ball filled with tension around, I'd rather watch the *Mary Tyler Moore Show* or *Laverne and Shirley* and eat dinner in front of the TV with the Old Man any day of the week.

The following morning, we went into Woosey's backyard and started fooling around with all the tools laying around the place. We crushed rocks with a sledgehammer; we hurled an axe into the trunk of a tree and took a branch off with a hacksaw. Mr. Woosencraft walked out before lunch, glowering, and asked us to help him move a ladder from the side of the house to the rear so he could work on preparing for the installation of some new windows on the second floor. As we trailed his dad, Woosey goofed off. He yoo-hoo'ed, he crowed, he shouted "Don't mention the war!" from a skit in a stupid English TV show we watched every Thursday night called *Fawlty Towers*. He *goose stepped* while putting his forefinger across his upper lip, pretending to be Adolph Hitler.

Under Mr. Woosencraft's steady glare, we dragged the ladder, upright, toward the back of the house. The goddamn thing was top-heavy, and it wobbled, dangerously. Woosey lost his grip first. The ladder and I waltzed around a few more steps until I too finally lost hold. The ladder fell, at full force, into the centre of a pile of neatly stacked Spanish pool tiles and bounced into the empty hole where the pool was supposed to go.

Woosey and I gazed at the wreckage. Standing next to what might be his luxury in-ground pool one day—Mr. Woosencraft went off the deep end.

"You IDIOTS... You FUCKING CLOWNS!" he sputtered. "How dare you! How *dare* you!" His eyes, combusting, looked first at me, and then to Woosey.

Incredibly, he lunged at me, missed, slid, and fell to the ground. Next, he got up and chased Woosey. After a turn around the yard, he caught him by the ear. He dragged him back toward the house. When they mounted the steps, Woosey spun free and made a run for the side gate. I followed. Fast.

We ran up the driveway, slipping through the gate. We ran for a full five minutes or more and made it to the Trans-Canada highway. We waited for a big 24-wheeler to pass, sprinted across four lanes, and headed through some brush, toward Lost Lake. Woosey led us to a giant tree stump. It had a crack in the middle, big enough for us to wiggle through. On the ground, inside the stump's hollow were a couple of Old-Style Pilsner cans and a used condom. Woosey sat with his back against the wall and closed his eyes.

About an hour later, he woke up and made a stupid joke I'm not going to even bother to repeat, and we wandered outside. We hiked through the forest. After about twenty minutes, we broke free of the trees and found a good spot to sit down on the grass and look out over Burrard Inlet and the lower mainland. Deep on the horizon to the south, in Washington state, stood the ominous live volcano, Mount Baker.

A windsurfing class zigzagged, or zagzigged, across surging waves in front of Jericho Beach. At least half a dozen sailboats, a few power boats, and a Chinese freighter rolled under the shadow of the Lion's Gate Bridge on their way out to the Strait of Georgia, and from there, who knows? The whole Pacific Ocean was in front of you.

"Jeez, Woosey, I wonder if we could make our way down there and stowaway on one of those boats. I bet soon we'd wake up and find ourselves somewhere you couldn't believe. Maybe Russia, Japan, New Guinea, Australia, Antarctica…"

Woosey started blubbering. I watched the boats while he emptied himself out.

"Jeez, Woosey, I'm sorry. I am. You should try not to think about it too much." I exhaled. "Sheesh, you should meet my Old Man. He's about the biggest bastard you've ever met. They're all like that, one way or another."

He wiped his eyes with his bare forearm and smiled at me. He puckered up his big, fat, girly lips and spat two huge loogies into the bushes. *HAWWKTTOK*, and again, *THAWWWUTUHK*.

Without anything else to say, I looked down at my new Nike runners and turned the right one up to see its black, waffle-iron sole. I'd never seen anything like it on any other kind of runner. A coach down in Oregon named Bill Bowerman had invented them in his kitchen.

We walked slowly back to his house in silence. I guess what happened next, or rather, what happened over the next couple of weeks, shouldn't come as a big surprise.

25

A Ruby Slipper

The freeze D'Aubert put on me after I huffed PAM in my kitchen, thawed. It might have had something to do with our shared interest in track and field. After school, sometimes we were the only two guys out there, practising. I supposed D'Aubert made up his mind, maybe sometime between a lonely javelin throw or a desolate shot put. *"Ah, forget about it, Livingston's not such a bad sort, I guess? I should give him a second chance."* After that, we ran laps, we hurdled over hurdles; we high, long and triple, jumped. Heck, we even *pole vaulted.*

The only other student around was John Dogg, a local legend at age sixteen, a Senior A-rugby fly half, who kicked balls endlessly into the early evening until it was almost too dark to see. Over and over, he'd dig the point end of his ball into the grass. Again and again, he'd take three or four long reverse goose steps backward over the grass, lope forward, and send one through the uprights.

From the school exit doors in the distance, Woosey, of all people, burst out onto the field, waving his arms. On the side pitch, Dogg stopped mid-approach, scowled, and retreated to repeat his ball address. Woosey whooped at us, as he ran.

"Guys! Hey guys! Get a load of this!" He was wearing his full-dress uniform: blue blazer, rep tie, grey flannels. Panting, out of breath, he put one hand on each of our shoulders when he reached us.

"I have a couple of poppers for you two clowns."

His tie was unbuttoned; his fly, open. Both, of course, were minor dress code offences. He slipped his hand into the side pocket of his school blazer and pulled out two red pills. They sat on the middle of his palm like jellybeans.

"What are those?" D'Aubert's asked, his eyes widening.

"They're called speeders. You swallow them. I grabbed a bunch from the cabinet in my dad's office. They're prescription-only. And now, I'm prescribing 'em to you!" He giggled. "These buggers will make you run ten times faster, and ten times as far as you do now. All the best professional athletes take them—Gretzky, Abdul Jabbar, Larry Bird."

D'Aubert's eyes narrowed. I laughed, nervously.

Woosey guffawed. "What are you guys anyway? Don't you have any balls?"

"Fuck you, Woosey," I said as I reached into his palm, pinched the capsule between my fingers, and lifted it up under my nose. I sniffed it.

"Ah, screw it."

I dropped the pill into my mouth and swallowed it. D'Aubert snatched the other one and did the same. After several seconds, D'Aubert's eyes bugged out of his head like somebody had shoved a stick up his ass.

Panicking, I blurted out, "Jesus Christ, Woosey, what have you done?"

D'Aubert put his hands on his throat, spun around, and fell to the ground, his arms flailing. He flipped over onto his back and sang. "Party people! Party people! Get funky! Ha Ha! I got you two fucking pussies soooo goood... That was awesome! Andy, you looked like you were going to have kittens!" He jumped up off the ground, finger-gunned us, and crowed. I punched him hard on the shoulder, at the joint, where I had learned from McKracken, it hurt the most.

"You're a bastard D'Aubert!"

"Yah, really. What a *cunt*," added Woosey.

We sat down on the grass, waiting for our new superpower to kick in, our free speed, watching Dogg kick balls until D'Aubert's mom drove up honking the horn of her red Morris Mini. D'Aubert looked over at his mom's ridiculous toy car, back at us, and then back at the car again.

"Oh crap, what time is it?" he asked me.

"It's 4:30 or something. What's the matter?"

"I've got to get my wisdom teeth out in half an hour!"

He bolted across the fresh-cut grass dodging Dogg's balls, opened the car door, and folded himself up into the passenger seat of the mini. His mom kissed him on the cheek and handed him a milkshake. Seeing us encamped on the grass, she smiled and waved.

I smiled back at her. She was lovely. D'Aubert invited me over to his house once, before I inhaled poisonous cooking oil spray, and she spent the whole time with her beautiful bare legs up on the couch reading European fashion magazines, drinking wine at 3:30 in the afternoon, and smoking thin, gold-wrapped Russian cigarettes.

We watched as the car bumped and lurched up the hill. Dogg lined one up and sent a spinning zeppelin through the centre of the uprights.

I wasn't feeling anything, so I said goodbye to Woosey and

headed home. I trudged to the bus stop and waited about fifteen minutes until an old whale of a bus came barrelling down the street and pulled to a stop next to me. The first warning sign appeared when I tried to get up the stairs—my feet were as heavy as concrete blocks. I stomped all the way to the back of the bus and sat down. After a few minutes, I closed my eyes.

The next time I opened them, sitting next to me was an old geezer with tangled grey hair; in front of him, sat two Musqueam women, arguing. Outside was a playground with kids running around after school, one of them holding a sword high up over his head. I closed my eyes, again.

"Say, kid! Kid! It's the end of the line. You need to get off the bus." A new driver now stood in front of me, shaking my shoulders with beefy hands. I got to my feet and staggered down the aisle to the exit doors. The driver helped me down the stairs.

"Say. Where are we, anyway?" I gasped.

"Burnaby Transit Centre."

I found a pay phone inside the bus terminal and called home. After several rings, my mom answered. She agreed to pick me up. I sat on a bench and waited. When Mom finally arrived, I told her I'd been "studying so hard at school and everything that I must have fallen asleep on the bus."

"Oh, don't worry about it, Andy," she told me. "I'm so proud of how hard you've been working."

I found out later that Woosey's "speed" pills had a street name: "Ruby Slippers." The clinical name was Secobarbital, a barbiturate prescribed to treat insomnia.

Everything fell apart when the St. George's physical education master, Ted Wilkinson—who, unlike most gym teachers, wasn't an idiot—caught Woosey passing out more pills at his locker to a guy from the A class, Thomas Ibbotson. Ibbotson, clever, entrepreneurial, and rebellious, had quickly set up a sophisticated distribution network for Woosey. Woosey would steal pills from a locked cabinet in his dad's home office, smuggle them to school in his backpack, and hide the stash in his school locker. If a guy wanted some pills, Ibbotson would get the hand off from Woosey and tuck the pills into a ridiculous cowboy hat he'd started to wear around for the purpose of dealing drugs. When a customer wanted a popper, Ibbotson gave him the hat to "try on for size."

Wilkinson, suspicious, ambushed Woosey at his locker. He caught him red-handed with three mixed bags of Captain Codys, Red Devils, and Black Beauties. Wilkinson pocketed the evidence, put Woosey in a wrist lock, and dragged him down to Pillicock's office. On the way, Woosey tried to talk him out of it. Wilkinson wouldn't budge.

Woosey panicked and broke free of Wilkinson's hold, bolted out the emergency exit doors, setting off the school fire alarm system. He flew across the parking lot, crossed the street, and disappeared into the dark forest of the University Endowment Lands. He ran all the way to the Camoson bog, where he hid for two days in the base of a hemlock tree.

He survived alone with no food or water. Cold and hungry, and wearing only his school uniform, he wandered into Dunbar and stole a motorcycle outside a Subway sandwich shop and drove it to the Granville Island Marina. Next, he jumped into a speedboat and locked the captain, a local car dealership owner, in the boat's head, and battled across the inside passage for several hours on his way to Vancouver Island.

He nearly made it.

Before he could find a safe place to dock the boat, he was boarded by a Canadian Coast Guard patrol boat.

When I heard all about the bust from Ibbotson, I knew we were all goners. It was only a matter of time. I didn't bother hanging my hopes on Woosey doing the right thing, like keeping his trap shut and taking the fall himself. And, you know what? I was right. Woosey finked out every last one of us, even idiot bit players like D'Aubert and I, the Rosencrantz and Guildenstern of the story.

26

Totem Pole of Pain

A week after Woosey's capture and arrest, I sat in Dr. Charbonneau's BC history class. His lecture topic: the Chinook jargon.

"The Chinook jargon, or simply, the 'Hudson Bay language' was a trade language that evolved between the native peoples and local settlers of the Pacific Northwest. Usage peaked from 1850 to 1900 but then declined because of World War I, the Spanish Flu epidemic, and the residential school system," he explained.

Charbonneau was classically handsome, early middle-age, with grey hair rolling back his head in small, elegant waves. He walked over to the board, picked up a piece of white chalk, and turned to face the class.

"In the late nineteenth century," he began, "the native tribes of the Pacific Northwest and the, primarily, Scotch Irish settlers, cooperated in trade and in almost all facets of daily life. They developed a shared language, a pidgin trade language, the Chinook jargon, which forms part of our multicultural shared heritage. Let's have a look at some of the words still in use—of course, only in remote communities and villages—today." In white chalk he wrote three words on the board: SKOOKUM, KLOOTCH, MUCKAMUCK.

"'Skookum' has multiple meanings. Now, it can mean either 'grand' or 'big,' or at the same time 'OK.' Next, 'Klootch,' or 'Klootchman,' means 'female.' A female woman, or a female something. Finally, we come to 'MuckaMuck,' or 'Mucky Muck.' Now, this could mean 'eating and living well.' For example," he continued, smiling, "Headmaster Pillicock is a 'high Mucky Muck.'"

He was interrupted by a short knock on the door.

"Well, speaking of a 'Klootch,' here is Ms. Williams now." Pillicock's middle-aged secretary walked into the classroom.

"Yes, Ms. Williams?"

"Andrew Livingston to see Headmaster Pillicock, if you please."

Here it was. The End. Pillicock was coming for me.

I stood up and stepped away from my desk. Fingers trembling, I put my binder into my backpack. I walked up to the front of the room and out the door, followed by Ms. Williams.

"Please sit down here until I let you know it's time to go in," she said, pointing to the chairs outside Pillicock's office. All week guys had been called in to see Pillicock and then disappeared on suspensions. I sat and waited, wondering what was going to happen next.

"Mr. Livingston, you can go in now," Ms. Williams told me from behind a big IBM Selectric typewriter.

Inside, Pillicock sat behind his desk. He held his hands up in a triangle in front of him, finger to finger, thumb to thumb. On the wall were framed degrees from UBC, Cambridge, and Princeton.

The big desk suited him. He was a large man in stature, intellect, and ego. Anything smaller, he would have risked looking ridiculous.

He peered at me through the heavy lenses of his glasses— so thick, in fact, he was mocked behind his back for looking like a famous Disney cartoon character.

"Good afternoon, Mr. Livingston. Sit down."

Behind him, through large glass windows, the Senior A rugby squad moved across the pitch like a giant beach crab.

"Do you know why we're sitting here today?"

"No sir," I lied.

He kept his eyes on mine. A heavy silence followed my answer.

"So. You took Franklin's pills?"

"Well, sir, one pill. He gave me one pill."

I continued.

"Er, actually, he told me it was a speed pill. He lied and told me it would make me run faster…that I could win races. Independent school races. I think he's lying to you, too. He didn't say it was wrong. I mean, we didn't think we were doing anything wrong, so…"

"I've spoken to your mother this morning."

"Yes, sir?" *Great! What luck! Maybe there's a chance I'm getting off…?*

The question vanished as quickly as it had appeared. Pillicock popped it, like the balloon it was.

"She agreed you deserve to be punished, if I felt it necessary. I feel it's necessary. Please take off your blazer and lay it on the couch and put your hands on the top of this chair."

He took off his blazer. He rolled up his shirtsleeves and walked over to a large closet, opened it, and pulled out a long bamboo cane. I stood up and walked over to the chair. I bent over. I wondered, *how many other guys have been in this exact same position? McKracken, for certain. Had Pillicock even heard what I'd said about Woosey lying*

to us…? Did he even care? Maybe everybody at St. George gets caned…
Maybe it was some kind of rite of passage or badge of honour. Maybe it
didn't really matter if you were innocent or guilty.

I felt Pillicock's cold hand move down the back of my pants.
He was feeling my ass to make sure I hadn't padded it. He took a
step back.

I heard it, a *swoosh*, displacing the air on its terrible mission,
before it hit. You don't expect it—without warning, a shocking
spasm is the only thing you know, the only thing that *matters*. The
cane's firebolt shot across my ass and *through* my ass, all the way to
my balls and down my legs to my ankles. The son-of-a-bitch even
counted out the strokes.

ONE
TWO
THREE
FOUR
FIVE
SIX

The result: a Totem Pole of Pain. When it was over, he wiped the
cane off with a towel. He carefully placed it back into the closet. I
wondered if that thing had a Chinook Jargon name: Rod of
Sorrows? The Sinister Minister? He walked over to his chair, sat
down, and sighed. I wanted to get out of there. I made a bargain
with myself: *OK, that only happens once. If he ever comes at you again,*
break his fucking neck and light out for the woods, like Lenny.

Pillicock observed me.

"You've been placed on suspension until December 5th."

"All right."

"And one more thing, Mr. Livingston... You become your friends. I'd like you to reflect on that during your suspension. You can go now."

"Thank you, sir."

As I walked out, past Ms. Williams, one thing I can tell you: he thought he was bigger than me. *Well, sorry, buster, but you're dead wrong! This world is my idea. I'm bigger than you by a thousand miles.*

I limped back to my locker, my ass on fire. I slid out of one of the side doors of the school. Dogg was out on the pitch again. He ignored me as he walked up behind another ball. When I reached the end of the field and left the school grounds, he kicked it: a long one, a lovely spinning zeppelin that moved slowly through the air. It flew straight through the centre of the uprights and bounced, helter-skelter, on the far side of the posts before coming to a stop on the grass.

27

Cracked

I walked along Commercial Drive to a Subway Sandwich shop across from Livingston Produce. The streets were filled with people, mostly Portuguese or Italians getting on with their daily lives. I passed the Turistano Travel Agency, the Bufton Flower Shop, and Do Couto's Dry Cleaners. On my way back, on the opposite side of the street: European Glass; Miceli's Plumbing; Electrical, and Hardware; and Enda B. Fashion.

In total, nine guys were caned and suspended by Pillicock. Woosencraft was expelled, naturally. In addition to my school suspension, my parents punished me by making me work at the warehouse every day for a week while I wasn't attending class.

The routine was straightforward: I worked from 8:00 a.m. to 3:00 p.m. At the end of my shift, I was allowed to take five dollars from the till and buy myself something to eat. I didn't really mind working much. It helped take my mind off things and Gord was a happy-go-lucky co-worker. Every day, he told me a joke or a story to cheer me up.

Nobody said much except for Grandpa Earl, who asked me into

his tiny office, closed the window to the warehouse floor, and said, "Say anything you like, or say nothing at all." I ended up giving him the whole story. He sat at his big desk and looked at me, processing everything I was telling him, trying to put all the pieces of my story together. I must admit, I got confused a couple of times and had to start again from the beginning. I didn't tell him about getting whipped by a bamboo cane for some reason. Maybe I was ashamed or maybe I figured he probably knew already.

He didn't say anything when I finished. He got up off his stool, straightened his tie, and opened the door for me. I felt lousy about that, I can tell you. In the end, I gave up trying to make myself understood.

I figured Pillicock closed the book on the whole thing when it was finished. It was simply another disciplinary episode on his long list. But it wasn't finished for me, not by a long shot. The problem was, Pillicock thought the game he was playing was math or physics. But it wasn't. It was botanical. The seed he planted with his long stick was a weed. A brain weed with some gnarly roots.

The night before I was scheduled to go back to St. George's, Mom called me into the kitchen where she'd finished eating her dinner alone. "Andy, I've spoken to Mrs. Woosencraft. Franklin is staying at uh, a place where he can get some rest. It's up near Oak Street, about fifteen minutes by car. I'd like us to go up and pay a visit to him."

"Aw, Mom, seriously? Do we have to?"

"We have to."

We drove up there that night. Mom parked the car and we walked to the front entrance of a two-story concrete building. We presented ourselves at a nursing station and were told to take an elevator up to the second floor. I was hoping to hear screaming—guys chained in cages— moaning, chains rattling, a purgatory—but the place was empty. In fact, it looked comfortable. We stepped into the elevator and I pressed the button for the second floor. We rode up in silence. I looked down at the top of my feet. My awesome Nikes looked terrible. I'd worn them all week working at Livingston Produce and they were splattered with chicken shit and dirt from all the eggs I'd processed.

We stepped out of the elevator. In front of us, a long room with a dozen white beds.

Woosey was the only patient in the ward. He wore blue hospital scrubs and sat up in his bed, drinking a milkshake through a straw. He was excited to see us. He must have been lonely, up there all by himself.

Mom and I pulled up two small stools. I handed him a stack of *Mad* and *Cracked* magazines I had bought for him—with my own Livingston Produce money—at Chow's.

"Hey, Woosey." I smiled at him.

"It's awful nice of you guys to come and see me." Woosey said and smiled. He looked down at his hands, folded across his lap, and said,

"Ah. You know. I'm real sorry about everything..."

At this point, I saw he had long bandages taped from his wrists to the top of his forearms. *Jesus*, I thought, *he's tried to kill himself, on top of everything else.* He put the straw in his mouth and sucked on his milkshake, the three of us sitting in a sort of uneasy silence for a few moments. Mom cleared her throat.

"So, how are your mom and dad?"

"Oh, ya know. They were upset, ya know, but my dad—well, he's cooled off now..." he trailed off. I think the whole thing was getting on Mom's nerves. She said, a little too enthusiastically,

"Oh, now, that's wonderful!"

"So, what did you do when you were living in the woods?" I asked.

"Oh, ya know. It was cold at first but it got easier after I found a big tree trunk in the bog that became my base of operations." He perked up at this. "I found some old newspapers and rolled them up around my arms and legs under my uniform, and that helped with the cold a bit. Man, was it freezing. I can tell you, my only friends were the pine trees. Most nights, I only had the moon to keep me company. I had a lot of time to think things over." I couldn't help myself from asking,

"Did you, uh... Were you handcuffed?"

"Oh, sure. When the Coast Guard guys jumped on the boat— you want to know the funny thing? I mean, it's hilarious! The name of the boat was *No Worries*, if you can believe it. She had these big twin Evinrude 250s at the back. Hahaha! Don'tcha think that's ironic? Hahaha!" He kept on laughing and laughing, and I have to admit, I did think it was funny, but not as funny as he found it. It took him a while to settle down.

"So, what's going to happen to you? I mean, where are you going to go to school?"

"Ah, my parents are going to send me over to one of the boarding schools on Vancouver Island. I think maybe Brentwood College. I haven't met with the headmaster yet, so it ain't fixed. We're all going to take the ferry over as soon as they let me out of here." I looked up at the fading yellow paint on the ceiling.

"Oh."

We sat in awkward silence until Mom piped up again.

"Well, that's wonderful news, Franklin! Vancouver Island!" Thankfully, the nurse came in and told us it was Woosey's bedtime.

"Well, thanks for making the trip to see me and everything, Andy." Woosey smiled. He seemed relieved.

"Sure thing."

On the way out, I took one last look at Woosey sitting on his bed. He was sucking on his straw again and had flipped open one of the magazines. *Cracked.* I grinned. *Now, that's ironic.*

"What's so funny?" Mom asked as we stood in the elevator. She pushed the button for the ground floor. As we walked toward the car, the cold light of the Child and Adolescent Psychiatric Emergency Unit's entrance softened. On the way home, I thought to myself that maybe Woosey wasn't such a bad guy after all, except for maybe being a rat and spilling his guts out to Pillicock in the end. All the pressure must have gotten to him. Maybe it wasn't even all that sudden; maybe it had been building up day after day, year after year, until it finally erupted. It could've probably happened to anybody.

28

Buy the Ticket, Take the Ride

Spring emerged, phantasmagorically, spreading its multicoloured wings like the Haida Firebird on the trunk lock of the Old Man's '69 Pontiac.

When I started school the week after visiting Woosey in the hospital, all the guys involved in the drug bust, including D'Aubert and I, had become overnight sensations. All the younger kids, and even students in the senior classes, were interested in us. Guys who never even bothered to say "hello" now wanted to sit with me at lunch in the cafeteria. Hell, even McKracken stopped marauding me for a couple of weeks. I think it was probably all the excitement. People need variety in their lives. Heck, you had illegal drugs, a dramatic escape and flight from justice, an attempted suicide, whippings, suspensions, expulsion—I mean, come on. You've got to admit, a scandal like that doesn't come along every day.

Afterward, I tried to rally D'Aubert for some fun stuff a couple of times: go-kart track racing, shopping for records at Sam the Record Man downtown, playing Pac Man, Defender, Frogger, Missile Command, at the Richmond Arcade. I had no luck.

Being on the receiving end of a bamboo cane and a suspension didn't sit well with him. He ignored my calls and avoided me at school. In effect, he put the freeze on me for a second time. With Woosey gone off to boarding school on Vancouver Island, I was, effectively, two friends short.

So, I fell back in with Fozzy; my orange crutch. Fozzy came at a cost, however. He had baggage. He'd call me up at all hours of the day or night, not caring if he woke up the Old Man, to see if I wanted to smoke weed and commit petty crimes, like going after the Cunningham's fishpond in the middle of the night (as if), or break into one of the mansions on Southwest Marine Drive—on the hunt for booze or easy-to-carry valuables.

One night, the phone rang as the Old Man and I watched *Wheel of Fortune* on TV. Vanna White spun a huge carnival wheel painted with winning cash amounts—also bankrupt, turn, and free spin. It was Fozzy. I picked the phone up in the basement so I wouldn't have to worry about Mom hearing everything I said.

"So, do ya wanna come to the Magee dance?"

"What for?"

"Whaddya mean 'what for?'"

I was quiet.

"Oh man, do I have to spell it out for you? You might get lucky for once!"

I considered this. I'd only been with one girl, Chinsky's sister Karla, and even then, not really, because the Gooch cock-blocked me.

"The tickets are ten bucks, but I can get you one for nine. You have to decide tonight because the dance is tomorrow. It starts at 8:00 p.m."

Of course. *Of course.* He was getting my ticket for free.

"Let me call you back."

To be honest, I was worried about my appearance. I thought I looked terrible—I was too skinny, I had a chipped front tooth from when Chinsky threw a rock at me on the train tracks a few years back, and I had all these lousy freckles on my face. If you saw me, you might have thought I'd just got back from trying to push a pickup truck out of mud. My hair was a big problem. I couldn't simply walk up and get a quick razor clip-job from the old Greek boozer in Marpole. It takes a lot of willpower to make up your mind to get a haircut. After a couple of minutes of staring at myself in the mirror, I relented. I called up Fozzy. He picked up on the first ring.

"Yeh?"

"Aw, hell. Why not? I'll go. Let's meet up at your place beforehand."

Fozzy went to the local public high school, Magee, on West 49th in Kerrisdale. It was a big, west-side school, originally called King George V High School, a much better name, in my opinion. The Fergusons lived in a two-story bungalow about fifteen minutes up the hill from Riverview Park, across the tracks.

Fozzy told me that his parents were going out to the Marine Drive Golf Club for dinner—hers, food; his, booze, and to come over when I was ready. I pulled on my jeans, carefully laced up my runners, and threw on my favourite Ocean Pacific T-shirt. There was a giant "OP" on the front with a silhouette of an African kid looking out over the savannah. The top of the "O" was a multicoloured sun, divided into different sunset-coloured stripes, from yellow at the top to a deep red at the bottom.

I opened Mom's bedroom door and told her I was going out and wouldn't be home until after midnight. She didn't ask where I was going, and I didn't tell her. Ever since Pillicock's whipping, I'd shut up about everything to everybody, especially adults and my parents. I was on my own. It was going to be easier that way.

I walked through the park and sat down on the swing set and spun around for a while even though I was too big for it. I stood up and walked over to the seesaw, sitting on one end, the other an empty plank, pointing high up into the gloomy sky. I looked back at the row of bungalows on our street, practically all the same size and shape, running all the way up the street and ending at the railroad tracks.

When Darlene and I were a lot younger, my parents bought a new Sears washing machine, and they saved the big empty box so we could fool around inside of it. After abandoning it as a fort—Darlene was a marauding Squamish, I was a wounded Haida—we ended up putting it on our Radio Flyer wagon. One afternoon we decided to pull it up to the top of the hill in front of our house. Darlene had an idea.

"Listen, let's have some fun. You get into the wagon." I jumped in and sat down. "Now, I'm going to put this box over the top."

"I can't see anything! Everything's black!" I told her as she stabbed the box at eye level with her fingers. She tore a round hole in the cardboard; it was big enough to allow me to see down the hill in front of the wagon, but not much. She pushed the box, hard, from behind.

"Darlene! Wait! I can't steer this thing!" I accelerated down the hill, fast. I gripped the handle. Through the eyehole in the box, I could see cars on Angus Drive, moving quickly in front of me at the intersection. I decided, in a flash, my only chance of survival was to veer hard right over the curb. With any luck, I'd land safely on the grass of the park.

About ten metres before I reached Angus Drive, I swung left, forcing the front wheels to go hard right. I hit the curb. I flew through the air, still in the box, yelling "AYAYAYYYYY!" I landed on the grass and gazed up at the afternoon sun, a yellow starfish in the sky.

I looked around for Darlene. She was still up at the top. *She didn't even run alongside me to make sure I was safe!* I picked myself up, shook my arms, and kicked my legs. All of my limbs worked perfectly. I hadn't hurt myself! Not only did I not hurt myself, I was exhilarated. I felt awesome! I put the box back on the wagon and dragged it back up the hill.

"OK Darlene! I did it! Now it's your turn! It's fantastic! It's like you don't know what's going to happen, but you do it anyway. Once you try it, you won't be afraid."

"Ah, I don't think so. I'm not feeling it."

"What? It was your idea! Get in! I'll push you. I'll even run alongside to make sure you don't crash into a car on Angus Drive."

"No, thanks."

She wimped out. There are two kinds of people in the world: those who will get in a box on a wagon at the top of a hill, and those who won't.

I jumped off the seesaw and walked up 64th street. I ambled up Adera Street, found Fozzy's house, and knocked on the door.

After a long wait, Fozzy slowly opened the door and stuck out his head. His face was as red as a pack of Chow's firecrackers.

"Jesus Christ! Fozzy, you look like you stuck your face in a blast furnace. You can't go out looking like that. Does your mom have any Visine in the bathroom?"

He let me in. While he was in the bathroom, I went downstairs and snooped around in Old Man Ferguson's pub. Incredibly, Fozzy's Dad had built an authentic English pub in the basement of his house—all the way down to the wood panelling, stools and bar, dart board, towels, portraits of the King and Queen, the whole nine yards. There was a big glass bowl on the bar filled with matchbooks from all over the world. I loved to dig my hand deep down into the jar and see what I could pull out; Club Moulin Rouge, New Orleans, The Ringside Club, Houston, The Carlingwood Restaurant, Ottawa, and That's Entertainment! The Fraser Arms Hotel, Vancouver BC.

I went back upstairs and talked Fozzy into letting me get something to eat. In a kitchen cupboard we found the Mother Lode: Keebler Fudge Magic Middles, Pepperidge Farms Star Wars Cookies, Apple Pop Tarts, Super Pretzels, Fruit Roll-Ups, Pepperoni Hot Pockets, Famous Amos Chocolate Chip Cookies, and Gold Mine Bubble Gum. We washed it all down with a half dozen cans of Tahitian Treat.

We didn't say one word to each other the whole time. That was one thing I liked about Fozzy: silence between us wasn't awkward. We could spend entire afternoons together without speaking. Another thing I liked was how Fozzy had just about as much freedom, maybe even more, as I did. Mr. Ferguson was always working, playing golf, or concentrating on boozing, and Mrs.

Ferguson didn't care where Fozzy was or what he was doing. For the most part, we both did whatever we wanted, whenever we wanted.

By the time we finished our junk food fest, it was time to go. We grabbed our matching jean jackets and walked down to the train tracks, made a right, and headed north to Magee. We moved easily over the wooden sleepers, jumping back and forth between the rails. The trains had stopped running along the line for some time, or if they were still running, it was usually in the middle of the night, when everybody was asleep.

"You got to meet my man, Chris Kaholo. Dude, he is hilarious." Fozzy told me as we approached a small group in the distance, standing on the corner in the dark. "He's a real surfer and everything. He's got a bitchin' board, I've seen it. It's called the Celestial Wave. It's got a moon on it and everything."

"Watch out, radical dudes!" Fozzy called out as the welcome smell of weed crept up my nose. He slapped one of them on the back and introduced me as his "pal from St. George's."

"Whoohoo!" said a tall guy, sarcastically, dressed in a ridiculous shirt, cut into a square with a zipper diagonally across the front.

"*Fan-cee*," added another, holding a skateboard and wearing bright, multi-coloured confetti-splattered pants.

We had stumbled into the middle of some kind of argument. Chris Kaholo, tall, good looking with long black hair, was yelling at some guy with a Neanderthal brow.

"You can't fucking take something that's not yours, Frankie. You sleazy greaser!"

"I didn't mean anything. Christ, it was a mistake! It slipped into my pocket!"

"I doubt it, you motherfucking MAGPIE!" Kaholo snapped.

"I'm really sorry, Johnny. Please."

"Ah, forget about it," Kaholo said and tousled Frankie's hair.

After that, everybody relaxed. In the short time we stood on the corner, I gathered Chris Kaholo was originally from Hawai'i, surfed, and could play guitar.

"My brother was back home and brought back a gram of Maui Wowie. It's old school, don'tcha know? All the greatest surfers smoke it: Lopez, Tomson, Rabbit Bartholomew... It creeps at first and then, *POW!* It blows your head clean off your shoulders!"

He pulled a thick joint out of his pocket, licked up and down its sides, and fired it up using a black Zippo lighter. He inhaled a huge hit, and watching him, I thought *holy shit, this guy sure isn't afraid of the future! He's buying a TICKET and taking the RIDE!*

When he was done, he handed it to me. I finished it, exhaled, and dropped the roach on the pavement. Within seconds, my lungs made their feelings known. I coughed. I hacked. I retched. I spat onto the sidewalk. *HAUCH-THOO.*

"Nice Bogart. Sheesh," Fozzy said.

"Forget it, Fozzy, you're high enough already." I told him.

As we walked along the sidewalk in a pack, Frankie pushed me off to one side and I stepped in a giant puddle. Adding insult to injury, we passed Chinsky, hanging out with a bunch of nerds, waiting to go in.

The Magee building was made of dark, stone brick, with turrets like a castle. We found three girls standing at the bottom of the stairs, waiting for us. They passed a menthol cigarette between them.

"Hullo, you fine-looking ladies," Kaholo greeted them.

"Hullo yourself. Do you have our tickets?"

"Yes ma'am, I do indeed."

Kaholo reached into his breast pocket. "This one's for you, Terrible Tammy. And this one's for Wicked Wanda. And this one, this one's for you, Bodacious Brenda."

Out of Brenda's mouth, slowly, appeared a large, pink bubble of chewing gum. Kaholo popped it with an outstretched finger.

All three girls had festooned their eyes with alternating shades of shadow: bright pink, dark purple, and shiny blue. Brenda's blonde hair was a giant whale-spout ponytail, Tammy's was hot-rolled cotton candy, and Wanda wore hers in a spectacular, permed fe-mullet. They were groupies. Kaholo was the lead singer in a fledgling rock band called Hot Nuts. Giant rectangle earrings hung off the sides of their heads. Brenda and Tammy went to Point Grey High School, also on the west side of the city, and Wanda went to Magee.

"Let's get inside, dick-draggers," Kaholo said to me and Fozzy.

We walked through the front doors and were confronted by what looked like the school principal, wearing a jacket and tie, and a short man with thick glasses, probably a teacher, standing beside him.

"Kewl" Kaholo said to me under his breath, reeking of weed. "This is going to be a walk in the park. It's McLintock and the Birdman." He handed his ticket to the man with the tie. "Good evening, Principal McLintock, sir. How are you this fine night?"

"Well, good evening, Mr. Kaholo. It's going well. Almost a full house. How are you boys tonight?"

"Well sir, we're very much looking forward to an evening of mild refreshments and entertainment."

And that was it—he stepped aside, and we walked right in.

29

Esse Quam Videri

I gave Fozzy a slap on the back as we walked down the hall. *Sheesh, what a dump!* I said to myself as we walked over the dirty linoleum floor and passed trash bins overflowing with garbage and vandalized lockers. The whole place smelled like rotten fruit, soaked in Mr. Clean, and dusted with Borax.

Fozzy pushed open the door to the school gym. All was dark, except for the glittering of a silver disco ball turning slowly, sending bright light particles across a small crowd of teens bending, twisting, and gyrating on the dance floor. The DJ, dressed as Spock from Star Trek, stood behind a mixing board underneath a basketball net. Blondie's "Call Me" blasted from two black obelisks on the floor.

Straight out of the gate, Fozzy, Kaholo, and all three girls ditched me.

I sat on the bleachers, alone, listening to Queen's "Crazy Little Thing Called Love," The Pretenders' "Brass in Pocket," and "Heartache Tonight" by the Eagles. I took a walk. In the hallway, I stooped over to take a drink from a water fountain, like some kind of giant bird. When I raised my head, standing in front of me was Molly Murphy from Maple Grove Park. She was wearing a Kiss T-shirt. Gene Simmons, Ace Frehley, Paul Stanley, and Peter Criss gazed back at me. Simmons's tongue, a long unsheathed dog's penis, dropped down past his chin.

"Andy? what are you doing here?" she asked with a smile.

"Oh, Hi. Hey there. Oh yeah, Molly—I forgot you went to Magee. Um, the Fozzy—I mean Charles, Charles Ferguson invited me. Do you know him? He's this fugly orange guy..."

"Sure, I know him. Well, I know about him. Well, where is everybody?"

"Ah, inside. I was on my way back."

"Oh."

"Ya."

"Well, I should get back. I mean, they're probably waiting and everything..."

"Sure." She paused, then said quietly, "Hey Andy?"

"Uh huh?"

"It's good to see you."

"It's good to see you too, Molly. Killer T-shirt—it rawks!"

An awkward silence fell—I axed it with one of my enthusiastic wolf-howls, "*Ahhhh Whoooo!*"

Molly flashed me a funny expression.

Jeez, girls are so weird. I waved goodbye and walked back to the gym.

I scrambled back up onto the bleachers, sat down, and stretched out my legs. DJ Spock dropped "Emotional Rescue" by the Rolling Stones onto his turntable. On the dance floor, some brave souls tried out some new dance moves: the Electric Slide, the Robot, the

Moonwalk. I put on my Wayfarers—inside, at night, like a complete idiot. At the end of the song, he put his mouth to his microphone and raised his hand by his side. He split his ring and index finger into a "V."

"You might wanna grab someone special out there. This is the last song of the night. Live long and prosper!"

He put on "Stairway to Heaven" by Led Zeppelin.

Out of the crowd on the dance floor appeared Brenda, right in front of me, smiling. She pointed at me, and then she pointed to the middle of the dance floor. I checked behind me to see if Kaholo or Fozzy were back there, goofing off and trying to catch me up in a mean practical joke. The seats were empty. I pointed at my chest. *Me?* Brenda nodded. *Yes. You.*

I stumbled back down over a long bench, fully tripped, and only partially recovered. Brenda tried to help me. She made a grab for my arm and missed. I righted myself and took off my stupid sunglasses.

We stepped out onto the gym floor. I looked down. Next to Brenda's fantastic red cowboy boots was the Magee lion, the school mascot, painted on the gym floor. Beneath the lion, was the school motto: *Esse Quam Videri.*

I reached out and pulled Brenda close. We looked into each other's eyes. I could feel her hands on my back. She lay her head down on my shoulder. I felt like I was an asteroid that had been cracked in half in space and I'd been drifting around forever since, until now. When I held Brenda, it was like I'd found the other half, the lost half, the missing intergalactic space half, and we fit perfectly.

I closed my eyes, hoping it would never end.

When I opened them again, over Brenda's shoulder I saw

Wanda making out with Kaholo, hot and heavy—or was it heavy and hot? Eight minutes and two glorious seconds after "Stairway to Heaven" had started, it was over. The fluorescent gym lights came on.

DJ Spock thanked everyone, "For coming on out, eh?"

Bodacious Brenda Brady! I said to myself. It was impossible. How had she settled on *me*? I was ridiculous.

"OK, kids, the party's over. Drive safe and be safe! Goodnight. Goodnight! Goodnight!" said the Birdman, appearing out of nowhere and walking to the middle of the magical dance floor, now a boring old basketball court again. Tammy waved to us from the side, came over, and pulled Brenda away from me—the little bitch.

"Your night's over too, Poindexter," Tammy said.

I watched the two of them leave, a wooden smile carved on my face. Brenda looked back, fake frowned, and smiled. Wanda pulled her deeper into the crowd, and she disappeared. Everybody was grabbing their jackets and making for exit doors. On my way out, I asked Principal McLintock, who stood at the door, about the Magee school motto.

"You mean '*Esse Quam Videri*?' It means, 'To be rather than seem to be.'"

How did I get home? Did I walk? Did it matter? Did *anything* matter, now that Brenda and I were together? I walked home on alternate streets, I ventured strange paths. I didn't go home, I *journeyed* home. I was a pilgrim, a man of destiny. I was a Champlain! A Frontenac! A man of action. At one point, on the tracks, I crossed paths with a lone coyote. He stared at me, eyes shining in the dark, and I stared right back. *That's right, buddy. It's me. Handy Andy the Train Wrecker!*

When I arrived home, I opened the door and stepped inside as quietly as I could. The pugs came charging out of the Old Man's study.

"*Shhhhh*, be quiet!" I hissed. "You'll wake up the Old Man and we'll all be sorry."

I pulled off my runners and tiptoed down the hall, crept down the stairs, and stepped into the bathroom. I turned on the light. I put toothpaste on my toothbrush and glanced up at the mirror, seeing myself for the first time in hours.

"Ha! You *airhead*!" I hollered at the glass. "You coward! You fool! She *likes* me! Goddamnit, Brenda Brady likes me!"

Smiling, I opened my mouth and brushed my tongue. *Take that, tongue!* Satisfied, I walked into my bedroom, took off my shirt and let it fall onto the floor. I jumped out of my pants and underwear, old-school style, kiddie style, Bobby Jobby style. Still grinning like an idiot, I hopped into bed and fell asleep.

I dreamt.

It was cold. *Very* cold. I was running through the woods, the forest thick with branches and underbrush. I was wearing a strange get-up: tall, black lace-up boots, a cap, and a heavy Mackinaw jacket. I saw a light in the distance, beyond the treeline—a fire, maybe—and I kept running and running toward it, as fast as I could. When I broke away from the trees I came upon a wreck of twisted steel and iron.

A train wreck.

The locomotive lay on its back next to a rushing creek, smashed and broken trees laid out in a row behind it. A dozen railway cars were on the ground in its wake, including a toppled wood-carrying car with the inscription CP 374 on the side in large gold letters, logs scattered everywhere. Beyond that, at least five cars were also on their sides. I ran down the tracks, down the embankment, and made my way to one of the windows of the locomotive. Inside, a decapitated body lay lifeless on the floor—now ceiling—of the interior.

I heard a cry for help from one of the cars. I leapt off the locomotive and made my way to the back, cutting a path through the wreckage. I heard the cry a second time. It was coming from the lead passenger train. I jumped onto the side of the car and stomped on the window with my boot, shattering the glass. It was hard to breathe. Smoke burned my eyes. Inside, bodies were everywhere. I lifted up an overturned seat. Underneath was Brenda. I lifted her up. As I carried her in my arms, I couldn't tell where I stopped and where she began.

I woke up with a start.

In the morning, as I wrestled with my school tie in the kitchen, the Old Man sat at the counter and wolfed down a plate of eggs, bacon, and toast. Mom stood at the kitchen sink, looking out the window.

"Mom. Dad. I have something to tell you," I said.

The Old Man grunted. Mom stopped scrubbing, lifted her hands out of the sink, and turned to me, expectantly.

"I'd like to transfer to Magee in the fall. I'm done at Saints."

The Old Man nodded his head, slowly.

"Are you sure that's for the best Andy?" Mom asked.

"Indeed, Mom, I do. I do think it's for the best."

30

May Athena Smile on You

My final year at St. George's played host to three Life-Changing Events. First, the big referee in the sky blew the final whistle on Grandpa Earl Livingston. He suffered a fatal stroke, standing and reading a newspaper, while riding the East Hastings bus on his way to work. A pre-twentieth-century death, if you will; one where you dropped dead on your way to work, at work, or after working.

Next, Darlene threw in the towel and moved out of the house to live with a forty-five-year-old real estate agent from Burnaby, giving me sovereignty over the entire basement. Last, the Old Man got fired from his job. That's right, fired from the company his dad founded during the Great Depression. You might have thought Death was the worst of those outcomes, the saddest, the most terrible, but you'd be wrong. It was the Old Man's drama wreaking the most havoc, settling in like a geological era: the Hadean, the Archean, the Proterozoic, the Phanerozoic, and the Time After Dad Got Fired from the Company His Father Founded.

Grandpa Earl Livingston's driver's licence was revoked after he developed cataracts in both eyes. Not being able to drive threw him for his first real loop. He blamed the government, the police, even his doctor. After the stroke hit him, he hit the floor of the bus on his way to Livingston Produce and never regained consciousness. There wasn't a funeral. Mom organized an awkward family gathering in our small living room, attended only by a few family members, my gran, and a pastor nobody had laid eyes on before.

I didn't really feel much, I guess. If you had asked me how I felt about anything except Brenda, I'd have a hard time giving you a straight answer. I knew one thing, though: I was going to miss him. He'd always been a big booster of mine. It meant something. Encouragement goes a long way. A helluva long way.

Not too long after Grandpa Earl died, without giving much thought to the consequences, my parents sold Livingston Produce, lock, stock, and barrel. The business, the client list, the warehouse, the apartments, the Old Man's truck, the egg-washing machine, everything, to an East Indian businessman, Mr. Mahboob Argarwal of Bangalore, India. All the staff were kept, including Gord and the Old Man. As you can probably guess, the whole thing was a terrible idea. In the end, we split the modest proceeds with my aunt in Kelowna and her six kids, our cousins, who were, if you can believe it, even wilder than me and Darlene.

I'm not sure exactly how we spent our half of the money, except that soon after we got a new Sony Betamax video tape cassette player, a new wide-screen television set, an AMC Eagle 4x4 luxury station wagon, and 50,000, penny stock, common shares of the Fortune Island Gold Mining Corporation, registered to a post office box address in Hope, British Columbia that the Old Man bought one afternoon from Chinsky's dad in the bar of the Fraser Arms Hotel.

As for Darlene, she up and left one afternoon, taking her turntable, amplifier, and all her vinyl albums in milk crates with her in what might have once been a 1977 Dodge Tradesman van, now transformed into a miraculous "shaggin' wagon." The sides were spray-painted with a mural of a towering, half-naked warrior, *The Spirit Warrior*, holding a war hammer across his chest. Inside was a wooden hexagon steering wheel, green shag carpeting, and a good-sized bed. A handmade, willow-hoop dreamcatcher with eagle feathers hung from the rear-view mirror.

"You take care, lil' brother!" she called out to me from the back of the van before slamming the door shut. Her new, moustached boyfriend fired up a butt, turned on the van ignition, and drove away. It wasn't as dramatic an exit as Jindi's, but of course, the circumstances were different altogether.

While all this was going on, I fantasized about Brenda and the kind of life we were going to lead once I quit St. George's and enrolled in Magee in the fall. In my imagination, we were going steady already. Magee had a good rugby squad—legendary. It would be no problem for me to make the squad as fly-half. Brenda could come over from Point Grey, bundled in a warm wool sweater, and watch the team play after school on fall afternoons. Or maybe we'd hang out at my house, now that I had the entire basement to myself. The possibilities seemed endless.

The trick was going to be to try to stay alive and keep out of Pillicock's way until the end of the school term. Over the summer, I'd get a job. In September, when I started at Magee, all my problems would be solved. Brenda would be my girlfriend. We'd take on the world together: vigilantes, outlaws, nomads, riding on the plains of Love.

A couple of days later, the phone rang, and I picked it up. It was Fozzy.

"Uh, Brenda wants to get together with you," he mumbled.

"What?! When? With who? Bodacious Brenda?! Fuck off!"

"It's not a joke. Tammy told me at school yesterday."

"Yesterday? Why are you calling me now? Yesterday!"

"Uh huh."

I processed all this information quickly, in a lightning flash, like a robot or an automaton.

"Tell her I'll meet her in front of the MacMillan Planetarium at 1:45 this Sunday before the Pink Floyd laser light show. And Fozzy, thanks. Uh, do you want to come with us?" I added tentatively.

"No."

Fozzy was useless.

Saturday afternoon, I decided I wanted to buy Brenda a gift. I took the bus downtown to the Granville Mall. I figured there'd be plenty of places to find something she'd like, given the mall was several blocks long with a Sam the Record Man, a Hudson's Bay department store, and half a dozen head shops selling bongs, comics, and jewelry all run by guys who were into bongs, comics, and jewelry.

I waited at the bus stop at 65th and Angus. Finally, a big, new blue and silver unit made the turn, came down the hill, and came to a jarring stop in front of me, tossing everyone inside it forward a couple feet. I jumped up the stairs and put my money into the coin collector next to the driver, made my way to the back, and we soon charged downtown, past 47th, 49th, West King Edward, through Shaughnessy, where a good number of the guys from St. George's lived in big stone mansions.

148

We passed Broadway, 4th Ave., and crossed the Granville Street Bridge. The driver called out "Seymour!" as the bus came to a stop. I stood up, headed to the front and hopped down the stairs, planting my feet on the wet sidewalk.

I walked down the strip toward the Hudson's Bay department store. I passed a street preacher on the corner, standing on top of a milk crate, yelling at the top of his lungs. He was dressed in black and wore beat-up old shoes. On his neck he wore a white priest's collar. Long brown dreadlocks fell down his back. Nobody paid any attention to him.

"Money can't buy you happiness! Stop fooling yourselves! Praise God, Hallelujah! Look around! Do your eyes see the Glorious Cathedral of Sky above us? The Majesty of the Forests? How about Poseidon's Glory? The Unfathomable Ocean and its Glorious Multitudes? I believe in Jesus! Praise be to God! Can you hear the susurrations of the Pipe of Pan in the wind? Do you scorn the love of the Great Lord of the Glen? Well, friends—prepare yourselves, dear travellers, for the tearing apart! Your cries will echo across the ages! For all eternity!"

I stopped and listened. He wasn't half-bad. I figured he must be some kind of a pantheist; he believed everything was magic—*that there was magic in everything*, and not only one big, omniscient, vengeful God in the sky with a chip on his shoulder. I agreed with him. On the sidewalk in front of him lay a sad old merchant seaman's cap with a few coins scattered inside. I reached into my pocket and pulled out a dollar bill. I threw it in. He smiled and said, "May Athena smile on you."

I walked on, waiting for something else to happen or for me to happen to something. At a crosswalk, waiting for the light to change, an old coffin-dodger stumbled out in front of me. It was clear she sure as hell wasn't going to make it to the other side before the light turned green. I ran out, took her arm, and hustled her across before a big truck almost flattened us out in the middle of the road.

"Oh, my... Oh, my..." she started, out of breath. I put my index finger over my lips. *There's no need to say anything. It was my pleasure.*

I walked south to Seymour Street and passed a greasy spoon. Inside, trapped in a highchair, a baby made faces at passersby out the window. I don't really know much about babies, but there was something about this one I liked, so I started doing a crazy dance in front of her to try to make her laugh. She got going pretty good too until her mom saw me and turned her highchair around.

I kept walking. I passed the Penthouse nightclub where some homeless guy in an old overcoat and cowboy boots jacked off against a wall. He was staring at old black-and-white photos posted next to the door of dancers with beehive hairdos in lingerie.

I ran all the way over to Granville Street. The first place I tried was a head shop called Nirvana selling bongs and rolling papers and all the crap potheads needed to smoke weed.

There was a long glass cabinet near the front of the store, inside: vintage bongs with Tiki heads, totem poles, Apogee bongs, Zig Zag and JOB rolling papers, long glass pipes, a leather rolling pouch, and Clippys for roaches. Next to the cabinet was a rack of magazines and books, including *High Times* magazines, *Weed: The User's Guide, Fabulous Freak Brothers* comics, and *The Psychedelic Killer Weed Colouring Book.*

On the back wall, over cracks and water stains, hung posters of Cheryl Tiegs in a pink neon bathing suit, Olivia Newton John wearing a headband on the beach, and Farrah Fawcett posing in a red bathing suit. None of them really did too much for me, to tell you the truth. The girl for me was Tatum O'Neal. I loved everything she did: *Paper Moon*, *The Bad News Bears*, even *Little Darlings*. I wrote her a long letter once and mailed it to Hollywood. I never heard back.

The proprietor, a grizzled old guy in a black leather vest and Gandalf wizard-beard, kept his eyes on me the whole time I was there from a stool behind the counter. I stumbled on a display case with silver jewelry by local native artists. Inside: a sparkling starfish necklace, a silver dolphin bracelet, a raven ring, a frog ring, bear earrings, and a killer whale pendant on a long chain. *That's the one,* I thought. *Brenda will love that one.* I lifted it out and turned it over. The whale was coming out of the water, its back arched in a perfect semi-circle. It had a tall, curved, thorn-shaped dorsal fin and a split tail. I remembered the family of killer whales we had seen off Mueller's dock. It was perfect. Orcas were the outlaws of the ocean! The owner called out. "Hey kid, can I help you out with something today?" I reached into my back pocket and pulled out two sawbucks. It was all the money I had left, except for some change I was going to need to get back home. I walked over and put the bills on the counter. Gandalf Wizard-Beard looked at me, and down at the shiny pendant I carefully set next to the bills. "Why, that's a fine piece you've picked out! This must be for somebody special."

"Yes, sir!" I answered.

"Well, uh, this whale here is an apex predator. Did you know that? The Haida believe they're manifestations of their clan ancestors, who live in human form in undersea villages."

He boxed it up for me.

31

Shine On, You Crazy Diamond

Sunday afternoon arrived. The big day—date day. *Brenda Day.* I asked Mom to drive me to the MacMillan Planetarium. I told her I was going to meet some friends from school to see the Pink Floyd laser light show. I didn't say anything about the girls—Brenda, or Tammy, or Wanda.

On the way down, in the car, I told my mom without warning, "I hate Dad."

She pulled the car over to the side of the road and looked at me.

"Sorry? What's that?"

"I hate the Old Man. And I'm pretty sure he hates me."

"Don't be silly. Your father loves you very much."

"No. He doesn't."

We sat with this for a while; just the three of us: she, me, and the Thing I Said.

Finally, she spoke, as she pulled the car back out into traffic. "Andrew. I know you don't believe me, but your father loves you with all his heart."

"OK, Mom."

I had to hand it to her, she had no problem living with a lie like that. It wasn't going to wash with me, though.

The show was set to start at 2:00 and I was already running late. I didn't correctly calculate how long it would take to drive almost sixty blocks north. It would have been terrible to screw up the rendezvous.

"Mom, can you please hurry it up? I don't want to miss the show! I'm meeting Fozzy and Chinsky in a few minutes!" I lied.

"I don't understand why you still hang around with Charles Ferguson."

"Mom!"

"There's something funny about him."

"C'mon Mom, there's something funny about everybody. Can you drop me off here? I don't want to let them see you driving me." Her face darkened and she pulled the car over. I ran two blocks to Vanier Park, the site of the MacMillan Planetarium. Standing out front, claws high in the air, stood an enormous metallic statue; a silver crab, Karkinos. There was no sign of the girls. Giant clouds passed overhead, relieved themselves of water, buckets, rivers, whole Pacific Oceans of precipitation, before taking flight and lifting themselves over the mountains of the north shore.

I killed time—well, actually, I wasted time—sitting on a bench. I gaped out through a huge arch, the Gate to the Northwest Passage, overlooking Burrard Inlet. *What if this is all a bad joke? What if Fozzy had placed some kind of cunning bet with Kaholo that I could be tricked? A date with Brenda at the planetarium?* The idea of the date seemed more outrageous and far-fetched the more I thought it over. I slipped my hand into my front pocket and fingered Brenda's orca pendant for good luck. By the time all three girls jumped out of Brenda's dad's pickup, holding their jackets over their heads, laughing and smiling, I'd convinced myself Fozzy had played a fantastic con, leaving me alone and humiliated

The four of us walked through the glass doors of the planetarium and lined up to buy tickets. Brenda was gorgeous, alive—a girl! I had no idea what to say to her. I went to an all-boys school and hadn't spoken to any girls other than my sister, Darlene, and even then, only in efficient, machine-gun-like bursts. Tammy asked me as politely as she could—gently, even,

"Uhm, Andy… Andrew? Well, you're quiet this afternoon. Have youse been to one of these shows before?"

"No," I sputtered. "I've seen the space show with my school, but not Pink Floyd. I mean, I like the band and everything—that is, I think they're great. Er, *Dark Side of the Moon* is obviously better than *Animals*, but *The Wall* is great, too, except for all the British prep school angst and revenge fantasy."

I bought a ticket for Brenda using the money I earned working at the warehouse, while Tammy and Wanda bought their own. After I handed her the ticket, she put it in her pocket. She reached for my hand. I took it, and we made a run for the planetarium doors.Inside, a couple of lunatics were tripping out on acid. They wandered around screaming at each other.

"Tyler, Tyler! Holy fuck! Look at the stars! I can't fucking believe it. I'm at the centre of the galaxy! Tyler, oh fuck! The top of my head feels like a fucking Roman candle!"

After a few minutes, an angry, pimple-faced usher basically blinded them with a flashlight, and they scurried off to their seats.

I was the first to find our seats, four together across the third row. The girls giggled as they shuffled around. I noticed Tammy gave Brenda a gentle push in the dark. In a flash, she slid down into the seat right next to me.

As we sat and waited for the show to start, Brenda asked Tammy, "So, what's the deal with your mom and sister? Every time I'm at your house, they're fighting about something."

"No kidding. I've no idea. Well, wait, that's not true. They're the same person in different bodies."

"No kidding?"

"Sure. My sister is going to be my mom within five years. She'll be married to some 'Steady Eddie' like my dad, a couple of snappers at her feet, living in a house with a white picket fence around it."

A couple of ushers pushed the wheelchairs of two unlucky bastards into a section reserved for the handicapped. From several rows behind us came a terrible cry:

"Die, cripples!"

Everyone heard it. I turned my head around. Even though it was dark, I saw the monster who said it, crouched down in his seat, laughing and stuffing popcorn into his mouth: Henry Tunselman, a Magee student. The whole thing was so outrageous, so shocking, the crowd had no choice but to ignore it. From the speakers, in surround sound, "Shine On, You Crazy Diamond" flooded the planetarium, followed by "Dark Side of the Moon" from the album of the same name. Laser lighting shot across our faces while the music played. On the ceiling, a phantasmagoric blend of swirling planets, stars, and asteroids. A CFUN DJ introduced the show, "Well, I sure hope you folks are all *comfortably numb,* heh, heh, if you know what I mean?"

About three-quarters of the way through, between "Wish You

155

Were Here" and "Breathe," I reasoned Brenda would be wanting me to make some kind of move on her. Why else would she be sitting in a dark planetarium next to me? Why else would she have painted her face that very morning with seductive purple eyeshadow and put on bright red, cherry lipstick? I put my hand on her knee and turned my face to her. She took her eyes off the fake stars on the ceiling, turned to me, and closed her eyes. We kissed.

On the speakers, the sound of an acoustic guitar.

Minutes later, I lost control of the situation—or, well, maybe myself. My right hand prowled up under Brenda's sweater, over her warm belly button, on its way to her breasts. She brushed my hand away. Somehow, thinking this was a game girls play all the time, I pushed my hand back under her sweater. This time, she broke free of our kiss, on her face: disappointment, anger, and wrath.

She slapped me. Hard. Not only did it hurt like hell; the sound was terrible.

I turned away from her, frozen, and stared straight up at simulated constellations on the planetarium ceiling: Orion, Andromeda, Cassiopeia. Next, a giant crab appeared—Cancer, rich in open clusters and double stars. The crab sent by Hera to defeat Heracles.

When the show was over, lights shot out everywhere in a dramatic, frenzied, finale. Brenda's seat was empty. She was long gone and so were Wanda and Tammy; all three of them had bolted before the end of the show.

I walked out of the planetarium, the brooding mountains of the north shore shrouded in bands of dark cloud behind me, crossed the street, and walked up to 4th Avenue. I took a seat on a bench under a bus shelter. Three southbound buses stopped and opened their doors for me. I didn't board any of them. I just sat and watched the traffic.

I took the fourth bus. It was empty; I was alone, except for the driver. I disembarked at 49th and walked along Angus Drive toward my house. I fooled around on the sidewalk, putting off going home. I jumped on and off the curb, into traffic and back again. A big dump truck came barrelling down on me at blistering speed. I could have easily jumped back to the safety of the curb, but I didn't.

The driver slammed his brakes. The truck, its large chrome grill grinning like a maniac, came to a groaning halt, six inches from my face. The driver yanked open the door, jumped down to the pavement, came around to the front of the rig, and stabbed my chest with his finger. He was Sikh, and wore a beautiful purple dastar on his head. "GAH! You're a… Youse a… You're a, a, a *maniac*, a disgrace!" He spat the words into my face. "You're fooking looky to be alive!" He walked back to the cab, got in, and drove away. When I got home, Zooey greeted me at the door. As she licked my face, I put Brenda's Orca pendant on her dog collar.

I thought it looked pretty good.

32

Paper Boy, Paper Man

A compound word, like "windshield" or "fireman," takes two things and turns them into one, resulting in another thing altogether. Wind and shield. Fire and man. An idle, unemployed man is one thing: an alcoholic, another. If you put them together, if you compounded them, you got another thing entirely, and in this case, you got the Old Man: both sets of problems, combined. He was spiralling out of control. When my parents sold Livingston Produce, they didn't think to bargain for an employment contract for Dad, so within a few weeks, Mahboob reduced his pay to minimum wage. After a few more weeks, when Dad didn't quit, he fired him.

It didn't help that the Old Man kept up his bad habits. He only worked when he wanted, he drank on the job, stopping at bars on the way home after picking up eggs at chicken farms, and he took money from the till whenever he was short. Absent work, he simply sat in his chair for hours, from morning until night, muttering to himself, "Jesus Christ, eight dollars an hour? Eight fucking dollars?" He terrorized the pugs. He yelled at them, he'd give them a kick in the ass, he'd even put a clothespin on their tails and laugh when they spun around in circles, trying to bite them off.

He spent time looking in the classified section of the morning newspaper, the *Vancouver Province*. He circled positions, a handyman or a bus driver, suitable for men without high school diplomas. Mom took to working long hours in far-off suburban offices in New Westminster or Port Coquitlam. Working late with a long commute kept her away from the house.

Eventually, he landed a job at Southam News delivering the *Province*. Publishers had stopped using kids on bikes to deliver papers, now opting for adults with cars. They could pick up papers at a central distribution point and cover more ground in half the time.

He was an awful delivery man.

Sometimes, I tagged along to help him out. He'd get out of his beloved Firebird, open the trunk, and hurl a paper at a customer's doorstep. More often than not, he missed, and the paper would soar into a bush or back hedge. When he finished his route, he always had too many papers left over, and instead of finding out where he'd missed a delivery and returning, he dumped them in a garbage can next to the playground at the top of Riverview Park.

Mom seemed to pick up on the idea that, if she told people Dad had retired on the proceeds of the sale of Livingston Produce, we wouldn't lose any social status. Juggling this giant lie on top of everything else was no easy feat. But before it got better, it got worse.

One morning, before the sun was up, Dad came down into my bedroom and shook me awake. He'd been up all night, drinking. He had bad news. He needed my help. We got in the Firebird and drove out to the distribution centre and picked up the morning papers. On the way back, he veered all over the road.

"Dad! Maybe go a little slower and pull over to the side here for a minute… This is crazy!"

"Just let me… I need to… Just let me… I need to do my job!" he barked back at me.

Fortunately, it was so early in the morning that there was nobody on the road. At Granville and 67th, he pulled over. We grabbed papers out of the trunk and dropped them off, one by one, in front of retail stores and into apartment vestibules.

Dad pitched on the sidewalk like a sailor on the deck of a ship. He was struggling. At one point, his weight pushed him forward, well ahead of his feet, and he staggered toward the large glass window of Tad's Sporting Goods. At the last minute, I grabbed the back of his jacket; he spun and fell to the ground.

"Dad, this is crazy." I told him. "Let's go home and finish up later." He ignored me.

The day star began to rise in the distance, casting shadows onto the sidewalk. A car pulled over to the curb next to us. The driver's door opened and a clean-cut young man, mid-thirties, hair cut short, with a thick moustache, popped out and strode purposefully toward us.

"Don't trash the 'stache!" I said to myself, thinking he was out of earshot.

"What did you say to me, kid?" The Old Man was back on his feet. "Good morning, gentlemen, I work for the Southam Newspaper Corporation." He glanced at the Old Man. Neither of them said anything. He turned to me. "Uh, er… Look here, son. Your father's been drinking."

PART III

YOUTH

1981–1983

33

A Fully Fledged Monster

In the same way people moved to Vancouver to leave the past behind, I made a fresh start, a new beginning, in the tenth grade at Magee. I presented myself on the first day in the gymnasium, where Brenda and I had fondled our way through "Stairway to Heaven," wearing a yellow mariner's jacket, blue jeans, my favourite T-shirt, and Nike running shoes. Unlike St. George's class registration, orderly and hierarchical by grade point average, Magee's registration was a free-for-all where all students gathered on the gym floor on a certain day at a certain time. Each student was expected to take their name card to various subject booths, manned by teachers, and register. The result: a disorganized brawl, a melee, where all the most popular courses, either easy or taught by lazy teachers, developed long lines and filled up early.

When I arrived, I sat down cross-legged on the floor in the L section, a long row of students (with girls!) with last names A–K in front, and M–Z (with more girls!) behind me. After a few minutes, the principal, Mr. McLintock, exasperated, announced class registration would begin in ten minutes. I looked over my shoulder and saw my old pal David Patterson from McKechnie. I stood up and walked over to him.

"Hey, David. It's me. Andrew Livingston. How the hell are ya?" I clapped him on the back enthusiastically.

"Hey, there."

He'd matured since we'd last seen one another. He was handsome and laid-back in his back-to-school Levi's, bright polo, and leather boat shoes. He barely resembled the scrawny Poindexter in homemade knit pants we'd terrorized on the playing field in elementary school. Recognizing me, he narrowed his eyes.

"You're going to find things have changed quite a bit, Livingston."

"Yah, well, you know, hah. You can't put your foot in the same river twice, ya know, David?"

He didn't answer. He turned his head and started talking and laughing with a kid in front of him, another "P" surname maybe, I wouldn't know. We weren't introduced.

I turned and looked behind me. A giant sat with his legs crossed on the floor.

"Hiya, my name's Andy."

He glared at me.

"I'm new here. I went to a different school last year." I said and smiled.

He said nothing. I turned around. *Sheesh. What kind of place is this anyway?*

"Hans. My name's Hans." I heard the giant say softly behind me as Principal McLintock walked out and stood over the Magee lion on the floor. He lifted a whistle to his lips, hanging from a chain around his neck, and blew.

Excited, I leapt up and ran as fast as I could straight to the English table. *First in line, yes*! I handed over my card to the young teacher, Ms. Buchwald, and returned the bright smile she flashed me as she wrote down my name.

I felt a heavy hand grip my shoulder and pull me backward, away from Ms. Buchwald's registration table. When I regained my balance, in full view of my new classmates, I was face to face with Principal McLintock. I looked into his furious black eyes.

"What is your name?" he asked.

Without waiting for an answer, he snatched my registration card. Behind us, students flew, raced, and quick-stepped to registration tables: French, Physics, Geography, Mathematics, Photography... Photography? *That looks good.* I would have to remember to...

"Well, Mr. L-I-V-I-N-G-S-T-O-N, you were told to *walk* and not *run*! Running is against the rules! Do you understand me?"

"Yes sir, I understand you. Completely."

"You will sit out the rest of this registration. If you can't behave like the other students, you will not have the privilege of *participating* with them."

I navigated my way over to the bleachers and sat down. It wasn't a good start to my high school career—it was, in fact, a very bad one. My registration was completed by McLintock's secretary who, ignorant of my interests, talents, or abilities, included shop and physics on my timetable.

My locker, down a short flight of stairs, off the west side entrance of the school, was located, by chance, next to the locker of the most beautiful girl in the tenth grade, Heather Babbington. Most of the girls at Magee wore baggy sweatpants or colourful leggings, sweat-tops, and headbands. Heather wasn't the exception. However, even camouflaged, it was plain as day: Heather's body was magnificent. A paradise, an Elysium, a cosmic trick, and for me, daily torture.

Another bit of bad luck was her constant companion and boyfriend, Mike Ferriera. A tall, muscular Portuguese with fashion magazine-good looks, Ferriera played on the Senior A rugby team. He hung around her, and therefore, my locker, every chance he could. It seemed whenever I needed to switch out my textbooks, grab a snack or gym kit, Ferriera was there, omnipresent. Over time, Ferriera, Babbington, and I developed a comedic routine. I'd pretend not to pay any attention to what they were doing, but regardless, Ferriera would punch me in the shoulder.

It went something like this:

"Oh sweetie, are you going to give me a ride home this afternoon?" Heather would ask him. Pout. Frown. Wink.

"I can't, baby, I have rugby practice until five," he'd respond.

He'd put his hand up. She'd put up hers. Their fingers would intertwine.

"Aw, but you promised. You always do thwat,"

"Do thwat, baby?"

"Break your promises to me."

On and on it'd go.

My first impression was that Ferriera was deeply insecure in the relationship. He lived with his twice-divorced father in a two-bedroom apartment somewhere in Vancouver's east end. Through some quirk of fate, or a glitch in the system (take your pick) he woke up one morning and found himself dating the hottest girl at Magee. I think he sensed his fairy tale was going to end soon—he was going to graduate in the spring. He was self-conscious in his manner, a little sideways. A second-rater as far as bullies go, he wasn't in the same league as a McKracken. Although, to be fair, nobody was in McKracken's league—McKracken was world-class.

As for Heather, who knew? She had three more years before she graduated. She was naive, gullible, innocent, and beautiful. Hell, she might even have had a few good years in front of her before she turned into a fully-fledged monster.

34

The Lions of Vancouver

Sabotaged by Principal McLintock at registration, I found myself enrolled, of all places, in shop class. We assembled twice each week in the school basement. The instructor, Jim McBride, was an angry, hulking Scot without a hair on his head. McBride had given up any teaching ambition, if he ever had any, and settled on simmering rage. I could see how it happened; almost all the morons in class spent their class time trying to figure out how to make a satisfactory hash pipe. Initially, after the bell rang, they'd pretend to make parts for assignments like the arm of a chair or the leg of a stool. However, as soon as McBride's back was turned, pipe prototypes popped up out of nowhere, into the arms of the lathes and under the drills.

Almost every class, after McBride's short introduction, I snuck into a storage room you could access through a door at the back of the workshop and, sitting on a countertop under a long fluorescent light, I'd read Russian novels. Having started with Gogol on the recommendation of the Marpole Public Library librarian, I was now halfway through Tolstoy's *Anna Karenina*.

One morning, before class, a fight exploded as we waited for McBride to open the shop doors. Two students in the tenth grade, Abraham Huang and Gus Brown, faced off against one another for no reason other than Brown had decided he was going to give Huang a lesson in race relations. Huang was well-built, an excellent athlete, and a Hong Kong immigrant. His family owned a small BC hotel chain. Brown, by comparison, was also muscular and a good athlete. His father owned an auto repair shop at the foot of Southwest Marine Drive, south of the Fraser Arms Hotel, where the Old Man got his ass kicked and, some years later, bought worthless shares in a gold mining company from Chinsky's dad.

The fight was an awful thing to watch. It started with a not-so-good-natured shove and escalated into a contest of two-fisted face hammering when Brown called Huang a "Rice Hopper." The pummelling lasted for much longer than anyone wanted or expected. In the end, there wasn't a clear winner; all four fists, and two faces, were splattered with dark red blood.

The saddest thing, though, was the look in Huang's eyes, mono-lidded and stinging with shame. He was a going to be a "Chink," a "Slope," and a "Spade Face" to the popular white kids at Magee, and nothing else, no matter how hard he tried or how much he accomplished. It was heart-wrenching. Huang made a run for it down the empty hallway. I watched him go.

I followed the others into the workshop. McBride began class by demonstrating how to turn a spindle on a lathe (take a blank, line up the headstock and the tailstock, align your tool rest…), then quickly retreated to the safety of his desk at the front of the workshop. I quickly slipped out the back door, book-in-hand, to the storage room.

After about ten minutes, the storage door burst open. It was McBride. He hurled himself into the small space, his shiny chrome-dome glistening under the bright fluorescent light. He came up empty-handed. There was nothing to find—no illegal drugs or gay sex. Simply an anguished bookworm sitting on a table, stuck on a Russian train station with Anna Karenina. Disappointed, he said nothing. He unclenched his fists and went back into the shop.

I turned my eyes back onto the pages of my magnificent book.

From there, things went from bad to worse. Weeks later, sitting in physics class, bored out of my mind, and not enjoying myself, I felt a sharp pain in my knee.

"*Ouch!* What the…"

Tom Papadopoulos, punk rocker, class clown, and self-declared nihilist, sat next to me wearing an idiot's grin, mohawk haircut, and black *Teenage Head* T-Shirt. He'd stabbed me with his Dixon Ticonderoga pencil. He bared his teeth at me and growled.

"Jesus Christ, Papadopoulos, get a grip on yourself!"

I went back to drawing a giant Van Halen logo on the front cover of my notebook. At the back of class, Kaholo and his pals from Hot Nuts joked around and goofed off, their feet on their desks, talking and doing everything they could to avoid learning about the laws of time and space. I looked back at them with envy. I had fun with Kaholo before the school dance, but he ignored me now. I couldn't really blame him. He probably got all the gory details of my planetarium date from Wanda. *He did what? Oh my God! What did Brenda do?* It was too awful to think about.

The truth was, I really wanted to hang out with them. I felt I was being miscast. I was misunderstood. I was a *real* rock and roller—a burnout, a wastoid. I could grow my hair as long as I wanted, I could smoke, drink, and stay out all night. Granted, I couldn't sing, play the guitar or the drums, but I could learn! How hard could it be?

They even had Wanda! Wicked Wanda, with her permed, fe-mulleted hair, was the most famous of the Hot Nuts groupies. Fozzy told me she'd done the broken lawn chair with at least half a dozen guys—in pool houses, in basement recreation rooms, in the art class dark room, even on the railway tracks. It was saintly. *Wanda's such a saint*, I thought nodding my head slowly, watching Mr. Rasmussen, overweight, bald, and undersexed, scribble formulas in white chalk on the blackboard.

$$v=d/t$$
velocity equals displacement/time
$$g=10 \ m/s^2$$
Gravity: acceleration of a free-falling object is 10 m/s²
(m/s² or N/kg)

Each day, before and after class, Rasmussen wasted endless amounts of time trying to sniff out high school gossip from anyone he could—who was dating who, who was popular or unpopular, teachers the kids liked, or disliked. He was especially interested in the popular girls: Stacy Scott, Heather Babbington, and Sherri Carlyle. The truth was, he probably wanted to fuck them. We all did. Rasmussen moved on to laser theory, even though it had nothing to do with the tenth-grade curriculum.

"A laser is, uh, a device that emits light through, uh, a process of optimal amplification, based on stimulated emission of electromagnetic radiation."

Maybe I was completely bored out of my mind, or confused, or sex-obsessed, or all three, but when Rasmussen said, "stimulated emission," I started giggling and couldn't stop. I covered my mouth. I plugged my nose. I even pulled my hair. Nothing worked. After a while, Rasmussen stopped mid-sentence.

"Mr. Livingston—uh, do you need to take a minute to collect yourself outside?"

Silence.

Suddenly, a thunderbolt was hurled from the back of the class. Frankie Arges, burnout and founding member of the Hot Nuts (bass guitar), yelled out in a voice chock full of his entire wretched, stupid, life, "What a *fucking LOSER!*"

Talk about velocity equals displacement over time. The class fell silent. I turned to Tom Papadopoulos. He stared straight ahead at the blackboard.

The next day I passed Teddy Sullivan in the hallway, one of the old gang from McKechnie. We knew each other well. We rode bikes in Maple Grove Park together, played British Bulldog, and spun the bottle with Boom Boom McLean. The bastard, dressed in a pink Polo shirt turned up at the collar and clam-digger Khakis, looked right through me, without even a nod. *OK. So that's how it's going to be. Well, fuck you too, Narbo.*

I continued walking to geography class. Arriving late, I accidentally slammed into somebody in a crowd waiting at the door. A steel pencil case hit the floor with a clank and scattered its contents everywhere. Out of nowhere, Frankie Arges appeared and bull-horned, loud enough for everyone to hear.

"Pick up all that crap, you spaz!"

I got down on my hands and knees and scrambled to pick everything up. Some idiots even found it funny. Arges's foot stomped down hard on a plastic protractor, cracking it.

"Look at that! What a nerd! What a loser!" He cackled.

I stood up and faced him.

"Fuck you, Livingston. I'll Bruce Lee your stupid skinny ass!" he barked at me.

"The hell you will, Arges."

He spat into my face. Before I could react, our teacher, Mr. Jannsen, opened the door, scowled, and said,

"Good afternoon, Mr. Arges. Good afternoon, Mr. Livingston. Would you like to come in and join the class?" He ushered us in with a wave of his hand.

"Meet me in front of the chink's grocery tomorrow after school," Arges said to me as he went through the door. I sat down at my desk as Mr. Jannsen stood at the blackboard. On it was a sketch of two large mountain peaks, one slightly taller than the other, followed by a long descent to a mountain lake.

"Anybody know what these are?" he asked. "You could see them every day if you crossed the Lion's Gate Bridge or went swimming in Lion's Bay in Howe Sound. And by the way, that's a hint." A hand popped up at the back of the class.

"OK. In the back there."

"The Lions? I mean, the Lion mountains?"

"Good. Or, I should say, not bad." He cleared his throat.

"They *are* called the Lions. However, I prefer 'The Twin Sisters.' I'm going to tell you why. The Sisters are composed of hornblende diorite, the oldest plutonic rock on the west coast of Canada. Who can tell me about plutonic rock?" He waited. Nothing.

"Anyone, anyone? All right. Plutonic rocks are crystalline igneous rocks formed by the consolidation of molten rock or magma below the surface of the earth. Therefore, they get their name, 'Plutonic,' from Pluto, the Roman god of the underworld." Someone in the back yawned.

"The Squamish people called them the 'Twin Sisters.' They were transformed by the Sky Brothers after twin Squamish sisters had married with Haida twins, and it led to the end of a terrible war between the tribes." He picked up a book and read it aloud.

"'And on the mountain crest, the chief's daughters can be seen, wrapped in the suns, the snows, the stars of all seasons, for they have stood in this high place for thousands of years and will stand for thousands of years to come, guarding the peace of the Pacific Coast and the quiet of the Capilano Canyon.'"

He put the book back down on his desk but continued his lecture. "In 1890, an ignorant United Empire loyalist, Judge John Hamilton Gray, had them renamed 'The Lions' because they reminded him of the giant stone lions of Trafalgar Square in London. So, there you have it: the story of the Twin Sisters. I think it tells you everything you need to know about the relationship between Canada's Indigenous people and ourselves." He set down his chalk with a satisfied smile, facing us a final time. "That's right, folks, I'm talking about you and me."

Jeez, I thought. *This guy Janssen wasn't like the other teachers at Magee.* I remembered seeing those big peaks out the back window of Dolores and Lenny's apartment window when I was a kid. The bell shrieked again announcing the end of class. I waited around awhile so I wouldn't have to run into Arges or his buddies on the way back to my locker.

35

The End of Days

That night, at home in the laundry room, I did dozens of pull ups and sit ups, thinking, like an idiot, I might somehow tilt the balance of the fight with Arges in my favour in less than twenty-four hours. I pushed myself up and down on the concrete floor. I was angry. Fair enough, I'd screwed up my life by changing schools, but it wasn't as if I hadn't tried to at least think it through. Pillicock's whipping wouldn't have been our last encounter. I was a loose screw, and he would have to screw me right back in, and tight.

But now, somehow, I'd managed to come loose even further, almost completely. Even the burnouts had it in for me now. Laying with my back on the cold floor, exhaling, alone, I made a vow to myself: it was time to be seen.

I stood up and took my shirt off. I walked into the bathroom and studied myself in the mirror. My abdomen muscles looked like rows of boat rope—I was in good shape. I went back into the laundry room and did more crunches. I tried to imagine myself in five, ten, or even fifteen years, but I came up blank. My arms trembled. My forearms burned. I pushed myself, up and down, down and up.

Before I called it a night, I heard the Old Man's big brogues stomping on the floor upstairs and the door to his bedroom slam shut with a heavy thud. The dogs closed their eyes. The kettle on the stove, the stools in the kitchen, the mattresses on the beds, the chair in the study, even the glasses in the cupboard—everything in the house let out a collective sigh of relief.

In the morning, I went upstairs into the kitchen, grabbed an apple from the fridge, and made my way to the study to check on the Old Man. He was reading the morning paper, the headline, "Drillers Work to Sever Lion's Gate Bridge Foot." Zooey was sitting on a stool, gazing at the rain, through the front window. I pulled my hoodie over my head, crossed the park to the bus stop, and waited.

At school, word had spread fast. I wandered from class to class condemned, marked for destruction. I began to imagine myself losing, and badly. *I wonder what school I could attend next—Point Grey? Kitsilano?* I walked up the stairs to the second floor bathroom, sat down on a toilet in one of the stalls, and I closed the door. I heard a couple of kids come in to take a piss.

"Frankie Arges is going to kill Andrew Livingston after school in front of Chow's!" one of them cackled.

"Ha, there's a fight? Schweet! Arges is badass. He's going to tear off Livingston's head and fuck his skull!"

I kicked open the stall door and confronted the two, tiny Hell-Serfs.

"Jesus Christ, guys! Try to cut me some slack. I'm freaking out here! You heard me. Fuck off out of here!"

They bolted out the door, one after the other. I walked over to the sink, turned on the tap, filled my hands with cool water, and splashed it over my face. Of all people, Chinsky was waiting for me at my locker after class. Heather and Ferriera weren't around.

"So do you think Arges might stab you?" he asked me.

"Do you think I could get out of it, like, escape somehow?"

"Not a chance."

I lifted my arm and gave him a half-hearted fist bump.

The clock on the wall said 11:15. At lunch, I joined the cafeteria line up in the school café. Two Pakistani women with black hair nets served up greasy French fries, the most popular thing on the menu. I bought a Pop Shoppe pop, walked over to an empty table, sat down, and unwrapped a peanut butter and jelly sandwich my mom had made me the night before.

I looked up at the clock: 1:55. I had one more class to go, History. I walked out of the cafeteria, down the hall to my classroom, and took my seat next to Papadopoulos. The teacher, Mr. Munro, was an ex-hippie in his late forties with long hair and a narrow face like a stick of rhubarb. He sat at the front of the class. Without turning his face from the window, he began his lecture.

"OK guys let's start where we left off last class. What do we know about John Deighton? 'Gassy Jack,' the founder of Vancouver's Gastown."

He read aloud from a book on his desk.

"'Deighton's Native wife died. Before she passed, she arranged for Deighton to marry her twelve-year-old niece Quahail-ya, also known as Madeline, or Matrine. In 1871, she gave birth to Richard Mason Deighton. Jack's brother, Tom Deighton, and his wife took over his business in 1873. Jack returned to working the steamship that plied the Fraser River, this time as a captain of the steamer *Onward*. However, after a family quarrel a few months later, Jack resumed management of a saloon and operated it until he became ill and died at the age of forty-four on May 23, 1875. He is interred at the Fraser Cemetery in New Westminster, British Columbia.'"

As Munro closed the book, Papadopoulos nudged me in the ribs. He wanted to tell me something. Neurons looked to be springing to life between his temples. "Well, did ya hear that, Andy? Vancouver, our fair city, the wonder of the Pacific Northwest, was founded by a drunken rock monster."

"Fuck Vancouver," I replied.

"Right On!" said Papadopoulos.

The bell shrieked at last, and I made my way to the bathroom, again. I walked over to one of the urinals. As I scrambled to find my fear-shrunken penis and pull it out through my fly, I saw that some clown had freshly scribbled, at eye level, in large black letters on the subway-tiled wall:

LIVINGSTONES
DED

Doomed! I was *doomed!* I raced back to the safety of my locker. Waiting for me, his arms crossed, was Ferriera.

"Are we ready to rumble?" he asked me, excited. He was planning to *shepherd* me to the fight. "It's GO, GO, GO time!" he yelled to the empty lockers around us.

"What's your damage Ferriera?" said a voice behind me. It was Chinsky. "Why don't you head on over to Chow's? We'll meet you there."

"Not so fast," said Ferriera.

"Don't worry, I'll make sure this stick of dynamite shows up," said Chinsky, putting his arm around my shoulders.

Ferriera thought this over. "OK, OK. but no funny business. I expect to see both of youse outside the chink's in less than five minutes."

He walked off, up the stairs, and out the doors.

Chinsky sized me up, trying to be reassuring. "Now, don't you worry 'bout a thing. I'll be right there when Arges stabs you and we'll have plenty of time to get you to VGH before you bleed out."

"That's hilarious."

"No, seriously. You got nuffin' to worry about. I've thought it all over, I've worked it out. Remember the 1976 Philadelphia Flyers? Bobby Clarke and Reggie Leach? The guys who beat the undefeated Red Army team? Well, like those guys, reverse Arges's jacket up over his head so his arms are trapped, and then BOOM, crack his nut, old-school hockey style."

I shrugged.

We walked out the doors together and along the tracks, the same ones we walked as kids, all the way to Chow's. A small crowd had gathered in the front of the store. As we approached, they turned toward us at the same time, like a school of startled fish.

I knew everyone there: the two little bastards from the bathroom, Roddy Ericson, Patrick Dickinson, Sullivan, Mean Boland, Patterson, Kaholo, and Fozzy. Two of the school's biggest loners, even bigger loners than me, Dolbeck and Harrison, stood at the back, towering over everyone, dressed in long black coats. Dolbeck was holding a giant black cello case on wheels. *You could probably fit a human body in there*, I thought. *My body.* The excitement proved too much for some of the younger kids. They screamed.

"Fuck him up, Arges!"

"Yah, get that oogley freak!"

"Cut him bad, Frankie!"

The crowd opened around us in a loose semi-circle. I had read a book on the art of boxing once. The author proposed the idea that footwork was the secret to winning a fight. I shuffled my feet. I zig-zagged. I flim-flammed.

He came straight for me.

He hit me with a couple of weak punches. The first, bounced off my shoulder, and the second, my neck. I put him into a clinch. It was at that moment I decided to take Chinksy's advice. I reached up under his arms, grabbed his jacket from the bottom, and pulled it all the way up over his shoulders. Deprived of both sight and the use of his arms simultaneously, he kicked his legs out, maniacally, panicking, and lost his balance. As he warbled, I pulled back my right arm and punched him hard, twice, in the face. It felt good. I was fast. He went down. I quickly jumped on top of him, straddled his chest, and threw a flurry of punches at his face, his ears, his forehead, anywhere. Blood exploded out of his nose. I stopped and looked at my hands. My knuckles were covered in dark red blood; Arges' blood.

"Stop! Enough! *Enough*! You FUCKING PSYCHO!" Arges cried.

"Have you had enough?"

"Ya," he sputtered.

"I didn't hear you." A grin spread across my face.

"Yes. Yes, fuck. I've had enough, by Christ!"

I climbed off him. He lay there on the ground, curled up on his side like a sleeping baby. I kind of felt bad. I guess the tough guy act was a big put on, a sham, a Potemkin show. I brushed myself off. Everybody was watching me, wondering what I was going to do next. Honestly, I didn't even know myself. So, I made a run for it back to school. All eyes watched me go.

As I crossed Maple street, I passed Molly Murphy. She was walking to the bus stop with her girlfriends. Well, OK. There was something else. In case you think I'm just showing off and turning my life around by winning a fight— as I crossed the street, I was bawling my eyes out. I can't explain it.

"Hey!" Molly called out to me. I didn't answer.

"Hey!" she said again. "Andrew, is that you? Are you OK? Do you need any help?"

"No. Thank you," I said; and added, in Canadian, "I'm sorry!"

I kept on running. I couldn't let anybody see me like that, especially not a bunch of stupid girls. Fozzy caught up with me on the tracks after the fight.

"Oh man, have you been crying? Damn. Anyway, that fight was crazy! Did you hear all the kids from Maple Grove yelling and screaming?! Jesus. Your face, man, I mean the look on your face. It was... It was, well... *Vile.*" I glowered at him.

"Oh, come on, Fozzy. What did you expect? I was scared out of my mind. I thought I was going to get *stabbed.*"

"Well, you didn't. Anyway, I've been thinking about you."

"Yeah?"

"You have your driver's licence now, right?"

"I should have an adult driving with me in the car."

"And your dad lets you use his Firebird?"

"Yeah...?"

"Well, I need a car. We need a car. I've been growing my own weed and I need some seeds, some new seeds, and a guy I know told me I could drop by his house and shake a few off the plants he's growing in his backyard. Saturday's a good day, right? Drive by my house and pick me up, around four. I've timed everything out."

So here it was. Again. Like a spider in the dark, Fozzy had spun a web. I was going to fly right into it.

"I'll get back to you."

Saturday came along, and I didn't have anybody to talk to, let alone anything to do. I stared out the window all morning at Riverview Park until the sun was high over the trees. I grabbed the keys to the Firebird.

"I need it back by six!" the Old Man yelled from the study. An American corporal sat at a desk dressed as Cleopatra during the Korean War on the TV set. A spiral of blue smoke coiled around the Old Man's head, hanging in the air.

As I pulled up in front of Fozzy's house, the front door opened, and he bolted out. I reached over and opened the big passenger door for him. He reeked like nicotine and weed, both acrid and sweet at the same time.

"What's up wit chu, boy?" he asked me, grinning from ear to ear. He wrung his hands together and stamped his feet against the floorboards.

"Oh, you know Fozzy. Playing it straight as usual."

"Well, I am psyched dude, psyched!"

I pulled the Firebird out onto Granville street and headed north. "Alright, well, where are we going?"

"There's this guy—this clown, ya know. He lives on West 43rd! What a joke."

I pushed the button on the cassette deck and Neil Young wailed out of the speakers. By coincidence, I had discovered Neil Young, the Clash, and Jimi Hendrix almost all at the same time. A once in a lifetime rock 'n roll trifecta.

"Fozzy, what happened to your dad? My mom saw him at the

corner store, and she said he looked bad."

"Yah. My stepbrother paid him a visit the other night."

"I didn't know you had a stepbrother. What the hell happened?" I turned the music down.

"Well, you've never met him. His name's Arthur. He's got all kinds of problems—he's a head case. He was living in a shotgun shack in Red Lake, Ontario for a few years and then he moved to Prince Rupert, working the mines and the docks. He came back looking for money. My dad told him to take a hike. He asked a couple more times, but Dad kept saying no. Arthur rang his bell for him. I was hiding behind the front curtain."

"Sheesh, I…" I shook my head. "I don't know what to tell you. I'm so sorry."

"Don't be sorry. The old hammerhead had it coming. He's got twenty-seven stitches in his head and now he won't come out of his study. The place hasn't been this quiet for years! Nobody hassles me, not even my mom. I sit in my room and hit my pipe most of the time. I haven't been to school for at least a week. Good riddance, I say."

We kept on driving. I turned at 49th. "Fozzy, why do you like weed so much anyway?"

"Fuck man, I dunno, I love it!" He clapped his hands together. "Getting high, getting wasted," and then, "Getting trippy. My buds, I like 'em sticky! And, hey pal, don't you forget, you turned me on, way back when."

Of course, this was a shocking lie. *Was it?* I thought as we drove up Angus Drive. Fozzy started singing "The Joker" by the Steve Miller Band in the passenger seat. We approached the turn for the laneway behind 43rd. Most of the garages, clapboard, looked like they were either rotting out, sunk, soaked or all three. I stopped the car.

"No—no, man, take it down, take it down further," Fozzy told me. I inched up about twenty meters. "Here."

He opened the car door, stepped out, and pushed it closed. The door latch clicked, ominously. I watched him move down the lane in the rear-view mirror. He slid along the fence and criss-crossed to the other side and back again, as if he was an escaped convict, trying to avoid a roaming prison spotlight.

I closed my eyes. My mind was racing. How could Fozzy blame me for his weed obsession? Was it a criminal act to steal to marijuana plants from a drug dealer who was growing them illegally? If I was caught with marijuana in the car but argued that it was Fozzy who was in possession of the plants, could I be busted?

We weren't too far from Elm Park where Fozzy and I played soccer on Saturday mornings for the Southwest Marine Dolphins when we were kids. We even beat the Kerrisdale Roadrunners one year, captained by the legendary John Dogg, 1–nil, to win the BC Lower Mainland Championship. Some of the Roadrunners were in tears at the result. It was a magnificent, underdog victory.

Now, we were stealing weed from drug dealers. After a long fifteen minutes, I heard someone behind the car. Fozzy pounded on the trunk. I could see him in the rear view, holding a giant, green, Pacific-rainforest-sized marijuana plant.

"Ah, fuck it!" he yelled. He ran up to the side of the car and threw the plant into the backseat through the open window, jumping in after it.

"Get moving!" he yelled, inches from my face, breathing hard. I reached for the rear view and angled it for a good view behind the car. A beer-bellied biker holding a black shovel was sprinting behind the Firebird and catching up fast. I froze.

"Put the pedal to the metal!" Fozzy yelled at me.

He reached down past my leg and pushed the Firebird's gas pedal to the floor with his hand. The big engine came to life, and we rocketed forward. I struggled with the steering wheel as gravel spun off the rear tires and fired pinwheels of rocks back into the biker's face. He dropped the shovel. As we took off down the lane, I kept my eyes on the mirror. He kept getting smaller and smaller, until finally, the speck of him disappeared.

Fozzy was in a state of hyper-excitement.

"Holy, holy, holy!" He high-fived me. He hugged me. Hell, he kissed me. The sweet, myrcene smell of the buds took over the Firebird. Eventually our heart rates slowed, and we drove in silence. By the time we made it back to Fozzy's place, in my mind, "a heaven or hell" as Milton cautioned, I'd made it through an entire trial for drug possession and had already spent two years in juvenile prison.

Fozzy made me drive around to the back of his house so he could sneak the plant into the basement. Before he stepped out of the car, I took a deep breath.

"Fozzy, I'm really sorry, but I'm done with this."

"How's that?"

"I mean… I know we've been friends a long time and everything, but this isn't for me. None of it's for me."

"What's your damage? They really did a number on you at that fancy private school." He rolled his eyes. "Well, OK. It's been schweet. Wayz out!" He grabbed the stem of the plant, shook the dirt from the roots, and disappeared. I turned on the car radio. "Roxy Roller" by Sweeney Todd blared out of the speakers. *What an awful song.* I thought to myself. *How long are these local BC hits going to last, anyway?* The Chilliwacks, the Troopers, the Payolas, the Loverboys... Who could say? Maybe they'd just move around like pinballs, up and down, back and forth, bouncing between the big coast mountains, Vancouver Island, and the 49th Parallel until the end of days.

36

Fearful Symmetry

Having cast off any claim to the stolen marijuana plant and, effectively, Fozzy, I began a physical self-improvement program the following week. I reasoned mental improvements would naturally follow. Adjacent to the Magee gym was a small fitness centre. Inside were a few barbells, a bench press, treadmill, and Nautilus machine. The only other student who seemed to use it, other than me, was one of the creepy loners, Dolbeck.

Over time, I developed a workout routine. I began with my forearms and biceps, moved on to my abs, quads, delts, and finished with my calves. I ran on the treadmill. Day after day, usually after school, Dolbeck and I worked out in silence.

Dolbeck suffered terrible acne. On his face was a great field of it, a WWI battlefield. He was tall, about six foot four inches, with enormous feet.

One late afternoon, to my surprise, with the light of a gloomy northern sun shining through the dingy window blinds, he broke our long silence.

"You know, these females... These girls... You know, I mean, all these pretty little bitches. If only they knew what I could do for them, given half a chance. I've read Burton's Kama Sutra and Castaneda's The Teachings of Don Juan. If they only knew…"

He trailed off, shook his head, and pushed a barbell above his head. It was like he wasn't talking to me, he was simply declaring it, to anyone or anything who might hear him.

I was stuck at the time in the Nautilus overhead shoulder press. I couldn't muster anything to say except, "Yes… Of course. I mean, they wouldn't stand a chance."

He put the weights down and walked over to me. He poked me in the chest.

"I've been watching you, Livingston. I've been watching you *carefully*. You're a clown. But… You really did a number on Arges. Hell, I like you! You don't play by the rules! You got that little monkey *good*! Have you seen him wandering around the halls lately? It looks like you ripped his soul right out of his fucking body!" Without another word, he walked out.

I didn't think much about Dolbeck after that. I was too busy with school. In English, we'd finished *Julius Caesar*. Ms. Buchwald announced one day that she'd graded our class essays, and the mark would be worth an enormous percentage of our final grade. As we sat at our tiny school desks, I was the only one paying attention to her. I loved the play. I worked my ass off on my essay. I was looking forward to getting the results back. Papadopoulos sat next to me, again. He wrapped his hands backward around his ears, inverted his thumbs, and pushed his nose up.

"Mr. Papadopoulos!" Ms. Buchwald shouted.

Papadopoulos dropped his hands to his sides. Ms. Buchwald walked around the class, dropping our graded essays on our desks, one by one. She read out the result.

"Fitzgerald... C+."

"Papadopoulos... F."

Jesus, I thought, *poor Papadopoulos*. His parents couldn't even speak English. How was a guy like that supposed to get a passing grade on a Shakespeare paper?

"Gibson... B."

She walked over and dropped my essay onto my desk. On the cover page:

> *"The Fearful Symmetry of Mark Antony in*
> *William Shakespeare's Julius Caesar"*
> By Andrew Livingston

An *A+* was stamped on it. Ms. Buchwald raised an eyebrow.

"Andrew Livingston... A+ Well *done*. Nice work."

Something clicked in me. That paper hadn't been hard for me to write, in fact, it had been easy. *Wow!* I thought, *maybe I could be a writer... How hard could it be?* All a guy had to do was sit around all day, thinking and writing. The most important thing was not to try to con your readers by making up lies about stuff you'd never done or seen or lived through. An honest field report. That's what people wanted.

I looked around. There was no reaction to my A+. Papadopoulos tapped me on the shoulder. He made his face again, opening his mouth wide with his fingers this time so I could see inside. Streams of cavity fillings ran up each side. I looked at the sheet of paper on the desk in front of him. On it, he'd drawn a full-page picture of Batman's Joker. Across the Joker's face was a huge grin. It was a great rendering—original, creepy, colourful, as good or even better than the Marvel comic book. The bell rang.

37

The Birdman

Dolbeck spotted me at my locker. He was wearing his black trench coat. A giant cello case was strapped onto his back.

"There you are! I've been looking all over this godforsaken penal colony for you!" He grinned and leaned his shoulder up against Heather's locker.

"Listen up. Harrison and I are holding a conference in the library at 2:00 this afternoon. Can you make it?"

"Ah, I think so."

Heather and Ferriera appeared. Heather tried to get into her locker, bumping Dolbeck.

"Er, can I help you?" Dolbeck asked, towering over her. Ferriera jumped between them.

"She's trying to get into her locker and get to class. Do you need glasses, Narbo?" With raptorial speed, Dolbeck slammed Ferreira against the wall, putting his large, sharp nose only inches from Ferriera's.

"Do I need *glasses*? Is that what you asked me? Meathead? 'If you gaze long enough into an abyss, the abyss will gaze back into you.' That's what I see when I look at you, golem. Nothing. 'Ferriera'—that's what, Portuguese? You're a Catholic, then?"

The bell rang.

"That's all right, Portuguese. I was on my way to class anyway. Livingston, I'll see you at two." I looked over at Ferriera, but he wouldn't meet my eyes, the pussy.

That afternoon, wandering the halls, waiting for two o'clock to arrive, I felt like an egg on the conveyor belt at the old Livingston Produce warehouse, carried along with a whole bunch of other unwashed eggs, waiting to get cleaned up, graded, and packaged into a box. Magee wasn't a school. It was a processing plant.

I found the library, opened the door, and walked in. It was empty, unsurprisingly, except for the librarian, a middle aged woman. She smiled at me. There was no sign of Dolbeck, so I killed time looking at book spines in the stacks. In the literature section, I found a copy of the Beowulf by Howell D. Chickering, a dual-language edition, published in 1977. I sat down at an empty table and opened it up.

I lost track of time. I looked up from *Beowulf* and Harrison was sitting across from me. *How long had he been there?* Like Dolbeck, he was tall. He had a narrow face, very light blue eyes, and badly cut, unwashed hair. He put a book down on the table and leaned in close to me and said, in a lowered voice, "So what'chu think kicked it off between you and Arges? Did you insult him? Did you screw his girlfriend?" Not waiting for an answer, he continued, "I think you got him real good, like when you ground his head into the sidewalk at the end."

"Ya, that was a swell touch," added Dolbeck, arriving, and sitting down.

"Well," said Harrison, "the short story is we *like* you. We've got some capers planned and we want you to help us out. Are you interested?"

I thought about it for a moment. "Well, sure. Sounds good. What did you have in mind?"

"Capers?" What were we anyway? Gangsters from the 1930's? Who even talks like that?

After exchanging glances, and smiling, Dolbeck spoke up.

"We're going to get the Birdman. We need you to drive the getaway car."

"The Birdman?" I asked.

"Mr. Rothstein, you idiot. Our chemistry teacher. Who else?"

The librarian walked by our table. We looked suspicious; the two guys across from me both wore black trench coats and lace-up boots. Harrison's book, on the table in front of him, was Shirer's *The Rise and Fall of the Third Reich*, a black swastika on the cover.

"Good afternoon, Ms. Lawrence," Dolbeck said.

We didn't speak again until she sat down behind her desk.

Dolbeck smirked. "We're going to tar and feather the Birdman after school next Wednesday." He pushed a piece of paper toward me across the table, on it was drawn a crude map of the school and grounds. In the parking lot, at the stairwell fire exit, was a giant X. He put his finger on it.

"Right here. Right here is where we hit him!"

"Great," I replied. "I do have one question, though. Why Rothstein? I mean, he's so…meek. He looks like he wouldn't hurt anybody. I guess if anything, he probably wants to be liked by the kids in his class a bit too much, like he has an inferiority complex or something."

"That's exactly why we need to hit him," Dolbeck replied.

"OK. I guess I can help you out. But I need something from you guys. I have to do an English assignment for Ms. Buchwald on *Beowulf*." I lifted my copy of Chickering and pushed it across the table to Harrison. "I want to do something totally different. Have you heard of a camcorder? It's a handheld camera. I want to film the demon Grendel's death scene. I found a swamp in the UBC Endowment Lands. We can use it as a shooting location."

"Beowulf?" asked Harrison, picking up Chickering, and leafing through the pages. He read line 559 aloud, badly.

Swa mec gelome   *lado-gereonan*
Preatedon pearle;   *ic him penode*
Deoran sweorde,   *swa hiut gedefe waes*

"OK, OK. Very funny. Hand it over. It's an epic poem—it's famous. It's pagan. The King of the Danes is being attacked by a monster named Grendel. A hero of the Geats, Beowulf, comes to his aid and kills Grendel. Grendel's mom freaks and Beowulf kills her, too."

Dolbek looked at me and said, "*Beowulf*... Beowulf. I know the story—it's full of a bunch of Christian bullshit. Like, Grendel is descended from Cain or something. As if. Grendel and his mom had every right to tear those Danish pricks limb from limb."

"Well, Harrison, fuck it. We need to get the Birdman, so it's a deal. Let's stack it." He put out his hand. Dolbeck put his overtop. They looked at me expectantly.

"Well, what are you waiting for? Stack it!" commanded Harrison.

I put my hand on top of theirs.

"It's done. Let's bounce." Dolbeck grabbed his map off the table, crumpled it into a small ball in his fist, put it in his mouth, and swallowed.

When the day of the Birdman hit arrived, or Tar & Feather A High School Teacher Day, I convinced the Old Man I needed the Firebird so I could run some errands. He sat in his chair and simply nodded; I guessed he was in mute mode. He was talking less now. He seemed to have accepted his fate. Instead of yelling, striding, laughing, and telling everybody what to do, he lurched and doddered, floundered and staggered. He drank, he ate, he smoked; he worked on the grass.

To me, he acted like a guy with a hand gripping his throat all the time, 24/7. The only thing that released that grip was booze. Maybe Grandpa Earl strapped his ass every day when he was a kid; maybe his best friend lit a cigarette on the deck of a merchant ship in the war in the middle of the night and got his head shot off. Who knows? When he had a buzz on, it was the only time he felt any good. When he woke up with a hangover, the only thing he could do to feel any better was to have a drink. He was caught in a trap and couldn't get out. One thing was for sure: if he had a secret, he wasn't letting on. He resented the things that helped living people live. *He was Grendel.*

I drove to Magee, parked, and met Dolbeck, behind one of the playing fields. He was smoking a cigarette. On the pitch, the Senior A Rugby squad was running drills: the evasion hot box, two plus one versus two, wrap and finish.

"Would you look at these morons?" said Dolbeck, shaking his head. He offered me a cigarette. "You better take it, it's my last one. It's my wish-butt." It was upside down in the pack. "You're supposed to make a wish before you light it." He held up his lighter and fired it up for me. He smiled. "What did'ya wish for?"

"Somebody else's life."

He smirked. "Let's get out of here. It's time to hit the Birdman!"

We walked a few blocks down the street to where I'd parked the Firebird. As Dolbeck stood at the car door, he pulled a black Balaclava out of his coat pocket and put it on.

"Can you please take that thing off your head?" I implored him.

"Ha!" he howled. "I knew it. You're all hat and no cattle; all foam, no beer."

"Look, I'm not afraid. I want to be smart and not get busted. Where the hell's Harrison, by the way?"

"Oh, he'll be here, don't you worry."

We got into the car and slammed the doors shut. I turned on the radio. Outside, an old blue hair crossed the street in flesh-coloured stockings. Dolbeck shook his head.

"Such a waste of space. I fucking hate old people."

"Jesus. Don't you have any grandparents?"

"Nah, they were both killed in a car accident."

"Oh man, I'm sorry." I said, backtracking.

"Don't be."

A loud *thud* came from the trunk. It was Harrison, throwing his large duffel onto the back of the car. "Hey, let's get this thing open and get this party started!" he hollered at us.

I jumped out, fumbled with the key, and opened it. Harrison spread out his supplies.

"OK, first, we have two big, sticky cans of molasses. Next, maybe a dozen bags of fake goose feathers in bright, neon colours—red, yellow, bright blue, green."

Dolbeck nodded. "Those colours are a nice touch. Let's rock 'n roll!"

Harrison packed up, walked around to the side of the car, and jumped into the front seat, forcing Dolbeck into the back. He hit eject on the cassette player and popped out the tape; it was the Old Man's favourite, the Stan Kenton Orchestra. He laughed and threw it over his shoulder.

"Ha. Stuff this up your ass, Dolbeck."

He pulled out his own cassette tape from one of his ten pockets, put it into the tape deck, and turned up the volume. It was called "Burn in Hell." A maelstrom of drum beats, screaming guitar, and demonic vocals filled the car. I turned it down. We had some time to wait until Rothstein made his way out into the teacher's parking lot after class.

"I've been watching this clown for weeks," said Harrison. "He's like clockwork. He packs up his stuff and makes his way to his car coffin at 3:15 exactly every day. He's never late. He doesn't even bother to stay after school to tutor anybody or anything. I pretended to adjust the rearview. Dolbeck grunted; he looked distracted. He mumbled something.

"What's that Dolbeck? Speak up!" Harrison said.

Dolbeck was looking out the window, watching some kids throwing a frisbee around on the grass. "Look at those assholes. They have no idea who or what they really are. Ya know, someday I'd really like to blow this place up. D'ya know what I mean? Just *BOOM*, and it's hee-haw, hee-haw!"

I was starting to have second thoughts. These two were nuts; what with their heavy plans and schemes—attacking people, threatening to blow stuff up, their not-so-petty hatreds. *I might have to find another Grendel and Beowulf.*

Dolbeck's hand came down on my shoulder. "Livingston let's go. My watch says 3:14!"

I turned the ignition and eased the Firebird into traffic on West 49th. I made a left-hand turn into the teacher's parking lot. It was half-empty. We were lucky—Rothstein was there, standing next to an old Datsun as I pulled over.

Dolbeck pushed the passenger seat forward and jumped out. He popped open the trunk and grabbed one of the big cans of molasses. He slipped on the pavement as he sprinted toward the Birdman. Harrison leapt out next with the bag of feathers and ran after Harrison.

"Birdman! *CAW CAW CAW!!*" Hearing this, Dolbeck squawked back. "*Cacacaw! Cacacacaw!!*"

Dolbeck struck first. He hit Rothstein clean, smothering his head and shoulders with molasses. Harrison was up next, deciding at the last minute not to shake the feathers out of the bag but to hit Rothstein as hard as he could with the whole bag, which, on impact, exploded.

Dolbeck jumped back into the Firebird; Harrison followed. I had a good look at the Birdman. He was standing next to his car, fully feathered. He looked like a man in a nightmare, standing on a bridge, alone. His glasses had been knocked off his head.

I stepped on the gas.

"Woo-hoo!" Dolbeck laughed. "We hit that sucker good!"

We sped down the quiet streets of Kerrisdale, across Southwest Marine Drive and down to the bank of the Fraser River where Chinsky and I used to ride bikes and smash concrete bricks. We dumped the balaclavas and extra cans of molasses in a bush.

That night, laying on my bed in the dark and listening to AM radio ("Eye of the Tiger" "Hold Me" "Ebony and Ivory") I couldn't figure out why Dolbeck and Harrison would carry out an attack like that. It didn't make any sense. It was more than a cheap thrill for them. What they, *what we*, had done, was evil.

Amazingly, there were zero repercussions from the hit. Rothstein didn't file a complaint or call the police, or even tell anyone. Maybe he was too humiliated. Dolbeck and Harrison had read him correctly.

38

America!

Mom got the idea that the Old Man and I should spend some quality time together—get out of the house, get out of the country, and experience the world together. Or, she may have got the idea that she needed a break from the two of us for the sake of her sanity. Who could blame her? Either way, she made arrangements for the Old Man and me to take the train to Seattle the following weekend.

On an overcast Saturday morning, we dusted off two old suitcases and packed for an overnight trip. I put on a Hang Ten long-sleeved shirt, jeans, and my Nikes. Dad wore his favourite brown suede jacket. Tidied up, with combed grey hair (the silver fox!) and big leather shoes, he might have passed for a local politician or lawyer.

A MacLures taxi pulled up in front of the house. "Serving Vancouver Since 1911" the logo, on each side door, proudly announced. We dumped the luggage in the trunk and slid onto the black vinyl seats in the back. Mom stood outside the house on our radioactive lawn (emerald green) in the rain, getting pissed on, as usual, and waved goodbye.

On the way to the train station, I checked Dad's pocket to make sure he had our passports. "Relax. There's no need to keep bothering me," he said, swatting my hand away. When we arrived, we got out of the cab, grabbed our suitcases, walked into the station, and found the boarding lounge.

An old timer sat across from us. He was a real Fraser Valley character. Unlike me, he looked like he'd lived a real life. A life with meaning; a life of purpose. It was all there on his weathered face: tragedy, joy, wind, rain, love, ocean, work. It had all passed through him and now he was on the other side of it, sitting there waiting for a train, looking cool as a cucumber. I would have liked to talk to him.

I played with my fingers, curling the pinkie over my ring finger, curling my ring finger over the middle finger, and curling my middle finger over my index finger. It's a nervous habit, I guess. I couldn't stop myself. Over the loudspeakers, the Seattle train was announced. "Bellingham, Aberdeen... *Seeeaayytttlle!*" I looked again for the old timer, but his seat was empty.

While the Old Man was in the bathroom, I reached into his jacket pocket and found a half-finished mickey of Smirnoff vodka. I held it for a minute, staring at the bright red shield and logo, "Purveyor to the Russian Court." I imagined horse-drawn carriages in the snow, squat-dancing, Russian kicks, and spirited countesses. Without much thought, I took the cap off and took a big swig. "Take that, you son of a bitch." I said under my breath.

We boarded the train and found our seats. I took the window seat. The Old Man sat down and cracked open the Vancouver Province newspaper. The headline: "Squamish Five Sentenced for Red Hot Video Firebombing." A few minutes after we pulled out of downtown Vancouver, I felt incredibly tired. I closed my eyes and fell asleep.

When I woke up, my head throbbed. I could feel the wheels rolling beneath the car. We were really moving, man. Outside, field workers in bright tunics hunched over bright green rows of strawberry plants. The Old Man couldn't help himself.

"Look at those Pakis, wouldya? Picking berries."

I ignored him. He was trying to get me started. A bald businessman made his way down the aisle, tripped, and knocked the hat off some guy's head. The Old Man kept quiet. He read a dog-eared copy of a true crime book about a Los Angeles serial killer. He slept. We ate some soggy sandwiches from the porter's cart. The train crossed over an old wooden railway bridge. Two kids threw a baseball across an irrigation ditch next to a wooden house with a busted window.

We crossed into the United States of America.

Rich cousin, old friend, *America!* It's not a country, it's a world. Home to NASA, nuclear warheads, Brooks Brothers, Penthouse Pets, Hershey Kisses, and my crush, Tatum O'Neal. At our final destination, the Seattle Space Needle, built for the 1962 World's Fair. I reached into the Old Man's pocket to check our passports another time. They were exactly where he'd left them. The Smirnoff bottle was gone, though. He'd polished it off in the bathroom when I was sleeping. I looked out the window and saw Mount Baker, a real live volcano, rising so high in the sky it cast a shadow on the clouds. We rolled past Ferndale, Bellingham, Marysville, Everett, and finally arrived in Seattle at dusk.

We disembarked onto the platform of the station, and the Old Man stumbled on the stairs. *He can't already be plastered, can he?*

He laughed and cursed at the same time. "Jesus H. Christ!" he cried out, pushing me forward.

Outside, I was blasted by the smell of sweat, sweet American tobacco, and copper coins. Rain plastered old King Street. I tried to hail a taxi the way I had seen it done in the movies; arm held high in the air. The Old Man sat on his suitcase and lit up one of his Lucky Strikes. I flagged down a yellow cab. I soaked one of my runners when I stepped onto the street to open the rear passenger door. The driver, some kind of aged hippie, in a bead headband, peered back at me from the driver's seat. *Oh boy, the Old Man better behave himself.* The driver waved us in. I slid across the vinyl seat. The Old Man sat next to me.

"How are you doing, son?" he asked, kindly.

"Oh, I'm OK, thank you."

"The Camlin Hotel!" The Old Man barked out with surprising authority.

The driver smiled, looked ahead, and put the car in drive.

"Yes, sir!"

As we pulled out into traffic, I caught the Old Man smirking to himself, in an odd way. It was childish. I was travelling with a child in a fully grown, man's body. On the dash, next to the metre (already reading one dollar and twenty cents American!) was a red drinking bird in a blue top hat. It was designed to pitch its beak down into a glass of water when propelled. It must have bowed down and came back again a dozen times during the ride. Our cabbie looked at me in his rearview.

"Where are you boys from, anyhows?"

"Vancouver," I answered.

"Canada! What a country! Hah, ya know, Canadians burned

down the White House one time. Imagine that!" He chuckled. "I got me a sister who lives in Canada, but she can't stand the place. It's too cold! She hates living in an igloo and chewing on seal skin for breakfast!" He turned, winked at me, and sang, "'Oh Canada, glorious and free. Oh Canada! We stand on guard for thee!'"

39

Dragon Bones

Our hotel, The Camlin, in downtown Seattle, was about ten stories tall with a huge green sign on the roof in medieval lettering. We had a room reserved for one night. The Old Man paid in cash and asked for two room keys. We made it to our room on the fifth floor after a couple of wrong turns in the hallway. The Old Man was not in a good mood. He let out a loud belch as soon as we opened the hotel door.

"Jesus, Dad, what the heck?"

In our room, 501, were two single beds and an armchair.

The Old Man took off his jacket and threw it on one of the two single beds in the room. He opened his suitcase and pulled out a big bottle of vodka.

"Go down to the ice machine and fill this thing up for me, wouldya?" he said, waving the ice bucket at me. When I got back to our room, he poured himself a stiff drink. He turned the armchair around, sat in front of the window, and began to drink.

I was too excited to sit around and do nothing with the old boozer; I grabbed my room key and ran outside to explore. I wasn't

204

going to sit around all day in a lousy hotel room with the Old Man. I was in America! I rode the elevator all the way to the top floor of the hotel and rode it back down again to the lobby. A middle-aged man and a pretty girl stepped in on the seventh floor. He looked at the call buttons and looked at me. I'd pressed them all. I smiled at him and shrugged. It was a little embarrassing, to tell you the truth.

"The thing is, honey pie, I can't make it work," he said to the elevator door.

"You damn well could if you wanted to. You don't want to, that's all," the pretty girl answered, looking at him. It was awkward. The man wore a dark grey hat. He gave me a cool, sidelong glance, before answering her.

"That's a foolish thing to say, and you don't mean it."

It took a long time for the elevator to get to the first floor. As we rode it down, I figured I could write a good story about these two. They were good looking, well-dressed, and unhappy as hell. That's a good start. *Well, if you gave her a gun, maybe things could get interesting...*

By the time the elevator doors opened, I'd given them new names. I ran out, looked back, waved at them, and said, "Good day, Austin! Good morrow, Eve!" Eve looked at Austin, and frowned. They stepped out of the elevator and into the lobby.

I was excited. I'd only ever been on a vacation once before when Darlene came along with Mom and Dad, and we spent the weekend in an old cabin at the Harrison Hot Springs Resort on Harrison Lake. Here, I was breathing *American air!* and hearing *American voices!*

I ran out through the revolving doors but got stuck. I had to wait for the bellhop to see me, come over, and push the door so I could get out. When I was free, I ran all the way down to the waterfront—more than ten city blocks.

A hot dog vendor on the street called out, "Hot dogs! Hot dogs! Get your dogs here!"

My stomach groaned. I wondered what the Old Man was going to do about dinner, if anything. I had about ten dollars Mom had put in my pocket, and some more money in my jacket back in the room. I bought three hot dogs, smothered them with ketchup, onions, pickles, and sauerkraut, and ate all three, one after the other. Sitting on a park bench, I belched and farted. An American burp. A freedom fart.

I wandered for twenty minutes, passed a convenience store, and went inside. To my astonishment, the aisles were packed, row after row, tower after tower, with giant bottles of Coca Cola, Dr. Pepper, Mountain Dew, Pepsi —you name it, they had it. Junk food was everywhere. On bright, multicoloured, packages: "New, Fresh, Vanilla-Flavoured, They're G-R-R-Reat! 100% Daily Value Vitamin C, 3 Pops in One! Free Prize Inside! Alive with Flavour!" It's a good thing Chow didn't have to compete with this place. He wouldn't have stood a chance.

I grabbed a Coke, a bag of Bugles, a giant pack of mini M&Ms, a pink styrofoam cowboy hat, a ping pong paddle, a plastic tie with piano keys, a Mr. Frosty Slush Master, and 3D glasses, and carried them all over to the refrigerator at the back, my true purpose. There I found cases of cold beer stacked high on shelves: Olympia, Miller, Coors, Coors Light, Budweiser, Pabst Blue Ribbon. I grabbed a six pack of Olympia and walked casually over to the cash register.

Next to the counter, was a newspaper with the headline

"Headless Body in Topless Bar." It was the kind of thing the Old Man liked, I grabbed a copy. I dropped everything on the counter in front of the checkout girl. She was chewing gum the same way the pugs ate peanut butter. She reached into my pile and pulled out the beer. She smirked.

"Aw, hun, I don't think so."

"What?"

A couple of people had lined up behind me. My stomach turned.

"You look so young, is all."

I tried to appear as old as possible. I *willed* age onto my face. A big Black guy behind us laughed, and hollered at her.

"Aw, come on! Give the kid a break, baby, and let's all get out of here!"

She rang it up. I headed straight for the doors. I'd only been in America for a couple hours and had already broken the law. *To hell with it*, I thought. I was on holiday.

Feeling swell, I went down to Pike Place to see if I could find a bench where I could drink my beer without anybody bothering me. When I arrived at the market, it was deserted except for two punks sitting on a bench, drinking out of paper bags. The dude's hair was a giant rainbow mohawk, and he had chains with razor blades around his neck. The girl, sitting next to him, looked Asian. It was tough to tell. I walked past them and the girl pulled out a plastic bag from inside her jacket and put it over her nose. *Huffers!* I said to myself. She closed her eyes. Her head bobbed slowly, fell forward for a few seconds, then popped back up. *The bobbing bird from the taxi!* It spooked me. The face on an old fashioned street clock showed ten o'clock. I sat down and drank a few beers looking out over the water in the harbour.

I headed back to the hotel.

Back at the room, I found the Old Man passed out in the big chair. A cigarette was still burning in the ashtray. I put it out after taking a hit. I pulled him up and dragged him over to his bed. I didn't bother taking off his shirt or his pants; I let him lay there, face-down, like he'd been murdered. It served him right. I turned off the lights and went to bed.

In the morning, the apricot light of the dawn woke me up. I'd forgotten to pull the shade down over the window the night before. I got up and stepped over to the Old Man's bed. I shook him by the shoulders. His eyes looked like two crater-lake calderas. Worse still, he smelled bad.

He'd shit his pants.

Well, there it is. It doesn't get any worse than this. We've hit rock bottom.

You might think I'd be angry, but I wasn't, I was sad; I pitied him. It was going to be up to me to get us home! I lifted him up and pushed him into the bathroom. I helped him get undressed. I put his pants and underwear into my grocery bag, tied the handles into a knot, and stuffed it to the bottom of the hotel trash can. I turned on the shower. Warm steam filled the bathroom and fogged the mirror. As the Old Man showered, I wrote on the bathroom mirror with my finger: *Handy Andy was Here!*

After he dried off and dressed, we went down to the hotel cafeteria and ate some scrambled eggs, bacon, sausage, toast, and bananas. The Old Man was oddly polite, mannerly, and cordial. He asked me how things were going at school, if Fozzy had been arrested yet, if I'd seen Chinsky's dad lately, if I had a girlfriend. We took the elevator back up to the room and packed up our bags.

All the excitement I felt from the day before was gone. We never did make it to a Mariners game. We didn't even try to get tickets. We took a taxi to the train station and boarded our two o'clock train home, back to Canada, back to the land of snow and igloos.

With Dad sleeping next to me, I watched the same fields roll past that I'd seen on the way down. Mount Baker stood on the horizon getting ready to blast its guts of magma and dragon bones all over Cascadia some day. I guess I should have been angry or upset, but I wasn't, really.

When Dad woke up, we spent a fair amount of time getting the story we were going to tell Mom, straight, like how we visited the Space Needle and Pike Place, and how the Old Man ate three hot dogs and I ate four. By the time the train rolled into the station in Vancouver, we were cracking jokes. I think it started when he asked me, maybe too politely, if I had to go to the bathroom. I told him I didn't. I asked him, also politely, if he had to go instead. But added, "Well, Dad, why go to all that trouble? Why don't you take one right there in your seat? Go full Grendel."

"Full what?"

"Well, he's... Ah, nevermind."

40

Beowulf

The long ride home on the train gave me time to think about my *Beowulf* project. Ms. Buchwald was trying to get everybody interested in what she considered "the greatest Anglo-Saxon poem."

The last time I saw the Old Man's drinking buddy, Mueller, he was playing around with a new Sony Betamax camera. I asked him if I could have a look at it, but what I really meant was I wanted to try my hand at it. When I discovered you could play back what you had filmed only a few seconds before, it blew my mind. I asked Ms. Buchwald if I could film a *Beowulf* movie instead of writing an essay, and she agreed.

The other end of the deal I had negotiated with Harrison and Dolbeck was if I drove the getaway car in the Birdman hit, they would play parts in my movie. I spent two weeks getting supplies for the shoot and writing the script. I wanted to capture the scene after Grendel, demon son and scourge, fatally loses a fight to the Danish hero in King Hrothgar's mead hall, his arm out at the socket. Grendel drags himself back to an underwater cave filled with treasure in a swamp, where he lives with the aglæca-wif, his demon mother, and dies. Dolbek was to play Grendel, and Harrison, the aglæca-wif.

I picked Dolbek and Harrison up at school and we drove out to the UBC Endowment Lands. It took a long time to find a good place to park, and we spent over an hour moving equipment and supplies—two crazy wigs and fake blood from a costume supply store in Chinatown—into the forest.

"OK. Dolbek!" I shouted. "Put on Grendel's swamp suit and crawl toward the edge of the water. Harrison will come out of the water to help you."

"All right!" he agreed.

"Harrison, put on your wig and get into the water. Hold your breath until you see Grendel come over to the side."

Harrison put on the wig and dropped into the swamp. We put fake blood all over Dolbeck—in his hair, on his body, and all over his face. We tied one arm behind his back using a rope. He didn't mind at all; in fact, threw himself into the role.

When everything was ready, I shouted, "OK. Action!"

I turned on the camera. Dolbeck whimpered as he crawled across the forest floor. He stopped, rolled on his back, and looked up at the twilight sky. I pranced up to him, attempting to capture the moment and film the tortured expression, of ignominious defeat, of impending death, on his face. It was incredible.

At that moment, Harrison splashed up out of the water, his costume covered in disgusting slime, and crawled along the forest floor over to Grendel. He (she) pulled his body onto her lap and cupped Dolbeck's face in his hands. He (she) moaned and cried out softly in unintelligible Old English. *Where did he learn that?*

Harrison lifted Dolbeck's body high up over his head with his strong arms and walked slowly back into the water until they both disappeared into the murk. The last frame of the film was of the reflection of tree branches and a shimmering moon across the water. We packed up. All the way home, I congratulated myself. It was *magnificent*. My film would be famous. Like Beowulf himself, I would live forever in the hearts and minds of men. My light, like Beowulf's, would never go out.

Monday morning, I took it to class and screened it for Ms. Buchwald. We sat in the dark in her classroom. I had trouble keeping a smile off my face. When it was over, I turned on the classroom lights and sat down.

"Andy, can you answer me one question? Why did you choose those two to act in your film?" *That's an odd question*, I thought to myself. "The entire thing is a mess. You can't tell who's who. It's incoherent." She shook her head. "They look like maniacs, running around in the woods, screaming, covered in—what was that ketchup? Forget it. Nevermind." She sighed. "Anyway, I do, however, appreciate the effort you put into making it, Andrew. That's why I'm giving you a C+."

"What! A C+? You've got to be kidding me! That thing took me hours to film and edit. we could have all died from exposure!"

Unmoved, she sat expressionless, her arms folded across her chest. As I packed up the projector, I thought to myself, *that's all right. That's fine*. Obviously, Ms. Buchwald was narrow minded. It's quite common. I was going to have to learn to face that as an artist. *You can't give people the eyes to see*, I reasoned.

I ran into Dolbeck a couple days later in the hallway.

"Listen up," he said. "We're going to get them again. I need you to drive us to a hardware store on the east side."

"For what?"

He lowered his voice. "Oh, there's a music recital next week. We're going to—get this—drop a Nazi flag onto the stage. We're going to get it set up by remote control. I'm going to push a button from over two hundred yards away. It's going to be massive. Everybody's going to be there, parents, teachers, all of them." I didn't say anything. "Well, are you in?" He asked me, expectantly.

"Am I in? No, I am not in. Ah, thanks and everything, but it's not for me."

"What? What do you mean 'it's not for me?' What does that mean?"

"Just that, Dolbeck. Like I said. It's a bad idea. All your ideas are bad. And who's this 'everybody' you are trying to get? What did someone like Lisa Cheung or her parents ever do to you? I mean, *Nazis?*" I scoffed. "You can't be serious. It's cruel and it doesn't make any sense."

This took him by surprise. "I knew it. You're a crow left of the murder. You're just like the humans in that stupid poem. You're a measure maker, a counter." He spat his insults at me. "You're not real. I tried to tell Harrison, but he wouldn't listen."

"Listen carefully to me. I'm done." I walked away. He watched me go, thank Christ. You never knew how a maniac like that might react to bad news.

41

A Precious Jewel

After I fell out with the two sociopaths, time passed. I got tangled up again with Chinsky. He played basketball every day after school with Piero. One afternoon, Peiro threw me the ball when I was passing by the court on my way home and that was it. From that day forward, if you walked past the court after school, you'd see me out there, passing the ball, calling for shots, and trying to make baskets.

Despite our early scrapes as kids, Piero and I, over time, had come full circle and were now friends. He was failing English, and Ms. Buchwald was at the end of her rope with him. He was in real danger of failing and not graduating. He showed me one of his failed assignments. It was so marked up, crossed out, and commented upon, it looked like an abstract painting. When he asked me to help him out, I agreed.

We met on the swing set in Riverview Park. His assignment was another Shakespeare play, *As You Like It*. Piero couldn't get his head around any of it. He stuck out his feet and launched himself high into the air while I sat on a bench and read over his notes on the duke's adversity speech.

Sweet are the uses of adversity,
Which, like the toad, ugly and venomous,
Wears yet a precious jewel in his head.

"Well, you know, Piero, the point is that when your life is going badly—you know, when things get rotten or hard, or both, it's a great chance to learn. Learning is valuable like a precious jewel. Maybe even more valuable."

"Jewel?" he asked me, launching himself higher into the air.

"Ya, you know, like a diamond or a ruby."

"So. He could get money and buy food if he was hungry?" he asked as he jumped down off the swing and landed on the sand.

"No, not like that. More like he discovers he doesn't really need money in exile in the woods. He discovers hunting and fishing, and he realizes he doesn't need a kitchen or cooks or anybody, or a royal court and courtiers, to be happy. It's like that knowledge or that discovery held tremendous value for him, more value, more than a precious jewel, more value than you or I could imagine, and he gets to keep it. No one can ever take it away from him." He stared at me with the bored gaze of a parking lot attendant. "OK, so the toad symbolizes a painful reality…" We got nowhere. I gave up and wrote the essay for him.

I guess you'd call me, Chinsky, and Piero "nerds." If you wanted, you could also include a new arrival: Fak Assaf, originally from Abidjan on the Ivory Coast in Africa. Fak was short, had black curly hair, a big nose, and a five o'clock shadow. He looked like he might have been twenty-five years old. Fak had come on the nerd scene like me; he picked up the basketball and started playing after school on the court one day, and that was it.

"Livingston, send him the ball, you bull-duster," Fak called out one afternoon on the court. Laughing, I stopped bouncing the ball and asked what he meant. He seemed confused. "Bull-duster? Well, what is the word? You are a liar, no?"

"What? No. Not a liar," I shook my head.

"He says to me that you are a liar; therefore, you are a bull-duster."

Chinsky burst out laughing. "Fak! Goddamn it, you can't call him a bull-duster, you call him a bullshitter!"

"Ah, OK," Fak nodded.

Our graduating class had over 180 kids. We had preps, burnouts, jocks, nerds, punks, and the strays. The preps held it all together at the top. The most popular guy in the whole school—well, both loved and feared, like all the best leaders—was Teddy Sullivan. He was charismatic, intelligent, and funny. Teddy cruised all over the streets of Kerrisdale, his turf, in a vintage MGB roadster convertible, his sexy girlfriend, Zoe Fisher, along for the ride in the passenger seat.

Teddy told me he was once offered a job at the Pacific National Exhibition as a carnie running one of the booths. He was excited about it—he would have made his own money, received first-hand experience in trade and deception, and had an opportunity to study the lower classes, first hand. It would have been a building-block experience. When he told his dad about the job, he wouldn't let Teddy do it. It was beneath a young man of Teddy's station, he said. He asked Teddy how much money he was going to make that summer, and when Teddy told him, his dad dropped a cheque onto his bed for the entire amount. Teddy didn't work that summer, or any other summer ever again, for that matter.

42

Café Bourgeois

The gas guzzling Firebird was nearly out of gas. Again. I needed money—I was dead broke. At this point, both the Old Man and I were technically unemployed.

When I saw a "Help Wanted" sign for a dishwasher in the window of the Cafe Bourgeois restaurant on Granville Street in Marpole, a few blocks from my house, I jumped on it. I made my mom type out my resume at work. I quit our regular after-school basketball game early, playing terribly as usual, and hopped on my bike.

The Café Bourgeois sat next to a gas station. I parked my bike and nervously paced back and forth on the sidewalk in front of the place for fifteen minutes. It's not as easy as you think to apply for a job. In fact, it was torture, in case you're interested. I walked inside.

The cafe had sixteen tables. On the wall was a variety of art—fruit in a bowl, flowers in a vase, a lap dog that looked like a woman's purse. I walked up to the only employee standing at the back; a tall, good-looking guy in his mid thirties with a dark face and sharp features. He wore a crisp, white dress shirt and black pants.

I cleared my throat. "I was wondering about the sign in the window?"

"Oh—well, what do we have here? How can I help you, sir?" He laid down a fistful of cutlery on the table and folded a towel over his arm.

"Um, well, about the work—I mean the job?"

"A job, huh. Now why would you want to get a job and ruin your life?"

"I don't have any money."

"I see. Why are you worried about that? The universe is a banquet hall and will supply you with everything you need. All you have to do is open your hand, like this." He put his arm forward and extended an open palm. I wasn't sure what to do next, so I pulled out my resume, enclosed in a neatly folded envelope, and set it onto his hand. We stared at it, my life-to-date on paper, held aloft in the space between us.

"Oh, don't worry about it too much, I'm just having some fun with you! The owner's name is Victoria, and I'll make sure she gets this right away." He pulled out a pen from his breast pocket, put the envelope down on a small table near the cash register, and wrote 'THE BIG BOSS LADY' in black letters across the front. He stuck it on a bulletin board above the waiter's station.

"You see? Now that won't get lost."

I smiled. "Well thanks, I guess."

"My name's Nicolas, but most people, mostly friends, call me The Cos." He flashed his hands up as if he was presenting his name on a billboard. "It's short for 'Cosmic.'"

"OK. Well, thanks. Cos."

I turned, walked out of the restaurant, and jumped back on my bike.

A few days later, the Old Man hollered down the stairs as I was organizing my small book collection for the millionth time.

"*ANDREW!*" he shouted. "Get up here and answer the goddamn phone!"

He probably thought swearing in front of potential employers was funny. His new mantra was, "I *like* to be disliked." It was annoying.

Victoria from the Bourgeois was at the end of the line. "Hello, Andrew?"

"Yeah?"

"Are you looking for a dishwashing job?"

"Is it looking for me?"

"Sorry?"

"Nevermind. Yes, yes. I am. Very much"

"Well, it's $6 an hour."

"OK."

"OK, see you Friday night at 6 p.m. Don't be late please."

Jesus, I thought, hanging up the phone. *Six o'clock? Every night? That's going to really put a dent in my non-existent social life.*

On Friday, I showed up on time and hung my jacket on a peg on the wall in the back. Victoria was sitting at a table across from the kitchen. She stood up, looked me up and down, and shook my hand.

"Well, good news Andy. You're on time. In fact, you're early. C'mon then. Let me show you around."

The kitchen of the Cafe Bourgeois was tiny. It had a single ridiculous electric stove with only four burners, the same size as the one we had in my house at home. She pointed as we moved through the restaurant. "This is where you get the glasses, and this is where you put the soap when you turn on the dishwasher."

We walked out to the back where there was a trailer. "This is the dry pantry. This is the garbage." She continued pointing at various spots. "This is where we keep toilet paper and paper towels." We passed an unlocked shelving unit on the way back into the restaurant packed with beer: Labatt Blue, Heineken, Tuborg, Dos Equis XX.

She introduced me to the chef, Franz, a German immigrant with a severe crew cut. He could have been in his thirties or his fifties, it was hard to tell. Next, she introduced me to the bartender, Dave, a balding stoner from Vancouver Island. After a busy dinner rush, Franz cracked open a Heineken out of the beer fridge and poured it into a tall amber glass. A few hours and a few more Heinekens later, he was cracked. He laughed to himself about nothing, he muttered, he cursed. He even threw sharp knives into my sink. It was tough to stay out his way, especially with my hands full of dishes.

Around eleven, the restaurant was empty. Dave asked me if I could help him take out the garbage. We pulled out all the trash bags in the place and headed out to the back. After launching them off the stairwell into a dumpster, Dave pulled out a joint, fired it up, and inhaled deeply. He croaked, trying to keep the weed smoke in his lungs, "I think...you're...going to work out fine... Keep your head down... Do what Victoria says." He coughed. "She thinks she's a hippie. Ya know, all that free love and come together and 'screw the man?' All that stuff. Actually, she and all her friends are rich white people from Ontario with nothing better to do." He exhaled, clearing what was left in his lungs. Blue smoke shot out of his open mouth and into my face.

He offered me a hit. I took it. *Well*, I thought, *what's the worst that could happen?*

We went back inside and began closing protocols. The Cos punched a mixtape into the cassette player and turned up the volume. "Solsbury Hill" by Peter Gabriel was the first song on the playlist. I felt good. Really good.

I went back to my sink and filled it with hot, soapy water. I put my hands down deep and rinsed the dinner plates. I pulled each one out carefully and placed them in even rows on the dishwasher tray, poured some pink soap into the soap holder, closed the door, and turned on the machine. Next, I grabbed a wet dish towel, shot some soap onto it, and ran it under warm water. I ran the cloth across the steel of the dish sink, down its legs, and across the burners on the kitchen stove.

Once I started, I couldn't stop. I went across all the counters and made wide, soapy circles. I cleaned all the cabinet drawers. I cleaned the dirty hinges. I was in my final year of high school and had my whole life in front of me! My mind was racing with plans, ideas, and schemes.

After I'd finished washing and polishing the entire kitchen, Franz—obviously impressed with my energy, my dedication to my work—and being very drunk, flash-fried a house special for me: a Cajun burger with a shotgun blast of hot mustard, medium rare beef, sharp cheese, and Creole spice. It might have been the best goddamned hamburger I'd ever eaten. My eyes glassed over as I chewed. I felt like I was staring into an ancient fire.

Polishing off my plate, I looked at the clock on the wall: five minutes left until the end of my shift. "Hey, new kid!" Franz called out from his kitchen station. "Take this pot of green pea zoup and put it in the fridge!"

"Sure, Franz, old boy, no problemo."

I grabbed the heavy pot from him, filled to the brim with thick green soup. I lumbered into the hallway. I navigated carefully past the Cos, who was heading out to set the tables with fresh cutlery for the lunch shift the following day. Tom Waits' "Rain Dogs" poured out of the two small speakers above the register. As I walked down the back hallway, I lost my balance, tilted the pot, and spilled all of the soup into Franz's motorcycle boots.

43

A Piece of Cake

Renting a house on Laburnum Street, in South Granville, allowed Fak to enrol as a student at Magee. Fak's older brother, Jasar, went to the University of British Columbia, where he studied business. At the same time, the family also rented a house in Seattle, where a couple of Fak and Jasar's cousins went to Bellevue College to study nursing and information technology.

Originally from Lebanon, the Assaf family immigrated to the Cote d'Ivoire in West Africa when Lebanon exploded in a civil war in the 1970s. In Abidjan, they owned local businesses; a travel agency, a T-shirt manufacturing company, an exotic flower nursery. All the kids were sent abroad to be educated at schools in major cities in stable, first-world, democracies: Paris, London, Seattle, Vancouver. The risk, of course, was that on top of acquiring a first-class, Western education, they also learned how to smoke dope, fuck, and drink.

In November, when the rain came —Vancouver's lower mainland is a temperate coastal rainforest— and refused to leave, Fak's parents left instead, back home to warm west Africa, leaving Jasar in charge.

It was a lucky break. Fak settled into a routine of going to school, playing basketball after school, smoking massive amounts of weed, using a giant Yoda quad-tube water bong, and listening to Pink Floyd, Yes, and Peter Gabriel, in no particular order.

Fak and Jasar were excellent, straight-A students. They didn't just make it look easy; it *was* easy for them. They spoke English, Arabic, and French, often switching between all three in a single conversation. You could end up with a headache listening to them. If I wanted an explanation of what they were talking about, Fak would smile at me, condescendingly, and translate very slowly in English, as if he were speaking to a small child or a moron. In return, I dropped idiom bombs on him.

"Oh Fak, hah! Well, I'm not one to beat around the bush," or, "You know Fak, it takes two to tango," or even, "Listen Fak, I don't want to be the one to shoot the messenger, but…"

His bearded, forty-year-old-looking man's face would go blank.

"Whatiszis this bush you beat? Why would a man hit a bush?" or, "Why would you take ze measurement of a thumb?" or maybe, "What is this piece of cake? You want to eat cake? Now? We don't have any cake here."

I fired up Yoda's head, inhaled deeply, and held it out to Fak, who was staring out the big front window of the house on Laburnum, listening to the pitapat of the rain falling outside on the trees.

I sat next to him and daydreamed. I was a fat kid sitting on an overturned picnic bench wearing a red cowboy hat. My mom was in the kitchen, washing Mesozoic-sized fruit in the sink: bright red raspberries, strawberries, and cherries. The Old Man, sweating, swearing, pushed his hand-powered mower, driving it hard across the front lawn.

The big front window of the house became a giant magnifying glass, refracting shards of light, fragments of branches, and glimpses of clouds. The wind washed over the branches of the trees. Their needles moved like fur on a dog's coat. The light changed.

"Hey, great bullshitter!" Fak snapped at me. "Ça va bien? Gaz?" He looked at me with worried, hooded, falcon eyes.

"*Oui, oui, ça va bien, bien—merci, mon ami.* Dude, chill!"

The back door of the house slammed shut. It was Jasar's girlfriend. Fak and I had nicknamed her Terrible Tracy. I heard her loud steps in the hallway long before she landed on us in the front room.

"Jasar, I'm almost out of gas, can you take my car... Oh, it's *you* two. Are you having a nice afternoon? Are youse? Sitting around, enjoying yourselves?" She scoffed. "Like I says, Jasar, can you take my car and fill it up with gas? I swear I filled it up, but the red light is on, and I got to get to the library later and..."

She went on and on, like water running in the tank of a toilet. Tracy was awful. She'd cut her hair short like a boy and wore the same ugly, faded blue dockers every day. She hated Fak and me.

"Let's get out of here and go over and see Bob," said Fak. Inexplicably, Fak and the Old Man were friends. More than once, I came home and I found them relaxing in the study, smoking, drinking, shooting the shit, and having a grand old time: generations, races, education, languages, you name it, apart.

44

Rick the Dick

The Gooch heard about my getting a dishwashing job at the Café Bourgeois. It got stuck in the murky fish pond of her mind, and she wouldn't let it go until Chinsky got a job as a kitchen helper at a terrible restaurant called Mr. Mike's Steakhouse, up the street, in Marpole.

It sat, like a stepped-on box, at the corner of Granville and Southwest Marine Drive. Sometimes, I'd go down there after closing the Bourgeois and hang out with him while he closed the place at the end of his shift. I figured, why not? What else was I going to do? We weren't getting invited to any big parties with the cool kids, being an oddball collection of nerds and geeks, so weekend nights we worked or tried to kill time the best we could.

"C'mon, forget about the stove oil tonight and let's get out of here," I barked at Chinsky. I was sitting in the gloomy dark at the back of the steakhouse, drinking mixed fountain drinks from a machine behind the register. The place closed at eleven o'clock and it was after midnight. Chinsky, disagreeable and disorganized, ran around trying to finish up the closing protocols his manager, Rick, had written out for him in an embarrassingly detailed list and taped to the side of the meat refrigerator.

BY ORDER OF
RICK MOODY
ASSISTANT MANAGER
MR. MIKE'S STEAKHOUSE
ALL ITEMS ON THIS LIST REQUIRE
GETTING DOING
WASH AND TAKE OUT BOTTLES
TIE UP GARBAGE BAGS AND REMOVE TO
DUMPSTER
CLEAN AND WASH GRILL
REMOVE GRILL OIL
TAKE OIL THER
WASH FLOR USING WARM WATER

Rick wore a small black moustache he couldn't grow out properly. It looked like grass growing on a rock. If you had the bad luck to work for him, you'd probably have hated him as much as we did. "Hey, are you sure Rick's gone home for the night?" I called out to Chinsky as he scraped out a huge fire pit grill with a giant steel brush.

"Yeah. Yeah, he's gone."

"Well, does that mean he went home? I think I heard a noise from the storage room downstairs."

"Relax. Anyway, I'm almost finished."

"OK, bitchin'." I stared at the floor. "Chinsky, what are you going to do next year when we graduate?"

"Oh, I don't know. I hafta go to BCIT and get a diploma in surveying. It's unionized."

"What does that mean? Like what do you do, surveying? Do you give people questionnaires?"

"No. You examine and record an area and its features so as to construct a map or plan."

"What does that mean?"

"I don't even really know. I read it in the school catalog."

As he was talking, I walked over to the beer fridge, opened it, and pulled out a couple of cold Canadians.

"Hey, what are you doing?" he asked, glancing at me.

"Grabbing a couple of cold ones. 'Betcha no one even counts them."

"Like hell. Rick is always walking around with a clipboard, taking inventory counts."

I drank the beer as Chinsky moved down his to-do list. He ran hot water into a big yellow mop bucket and poured soap into it. I walked over to the bar and poked around. I found a big bottle of Crown Royal inside a closed cabinet. I twisted off the cap and poured two huge glasses, taking one over to where Chinsky was now squeezing soapy water out of a mop head.

"You've got to be kidding me." He took the glass and polished it off in one giant gulp, and I did the same. It felt good. I walked over to the fridge and opened it. Inside were dozens of marbled steaks stacked atop one another, labelled and packed in cellophane. I pulled out a couple of juicy ones and tossed them on the counter, moving to go fire up the grill. Chinsky was mopping the back area and couldn't see me as I looped back around to the bar for another shot.

"Hey! What are you going to do next year?" he hollered.

"I don't know. I was thinking about becoming a professional gambler. You know, I could work the circuit starting here at Exhibition Park. In the fall, I could head down to Longacres in Washington, keep moving south down to Golden Gate Fields, and maybe finish off at Santa Anita."

I put the steaks on the grill, and dusted them with some special Mr. Mike's steak seasoning I found above the stove. Chinsky finished mopping the floor and walked the dirty water-filled bucket over to the sink. He spotted me, whiskey bottle in one hand, grilling tongs in the other.

"Man, what the hell are you doing?" he moaned. "You're going to get me fired!"

"Oh, relax, you big baby," I sneered. With a flourish, I poured the whiskey over the steaks. Within seconds, there was a loud bang, and a huge flame rose up from the grill, engulfing the cooking pit all the way up to the stainless hood. A red fire claw swirled around my head as I screamed, burning off part of one of my eyebrows.

Unsurprisingly, Rick materialized. He'd come up the stairs from the basement storage room. "What are you doing?!" he screamed. "Just what the *hell* do you think you're doing?!"

I dropped everything and made a run for the door, howling over my shoulder,

"Fuck you, Rick!"

Chinsky was fast on my heels. I sobered up on the outside. We got lucky; the Old Man had let me take the Firebird to work; it sat in the empty lot like a horse hitched to a post in an old Western. I could hear Chinsky behind me, breathing hard. I flung open the driver door, fumbled for my keys, and fired up the big engine. I reached over to open Chinsky's door. He was still wearing his cleaning apron, and I motioned for him to take it off as he slid into the seat. Rick burst out of the restaurant doors and came running as fast as he could toward the car.

I'd left a cassette in the car stereo. "Shake Some Action" by the Flamin' Groovies blasted out of the side door speakers. It was a fucking great song. It wasn't mine—someone had snuck a mixtape into my backpack at school when I left it on the grass, unattended. It had all kinds of great music on it: David Bowie covering John Lennon's "Mother," Midnight Oil covering "Instant Karma," "Is it Like Today?" by World Party. Whoever put it together sure knew their stuff. But why sneak around like that? Why not just hand it to me?

The Firebird rocketed out onto Granville Street. The steering was terrible; the brakes worse. I veered right, then left. We hit a speed bump on the way out. Sparks flew out from under the rear axle. Rick chased the car for at least two city blocks—he even ran through a red light, maniacally waving Chinsky's white apron above his head. Chinsky rolled down his window, stuck out his hand, and gave Rick the finger.

"Fuck you, Rick!" He sat back down in his seat, shook his head, and muttered. "What a dick."

45

The Right Image

The Café Bourgeois turned out to be much more than the sum of its parts: an espresso machine, an electric stove, a stereo system, a dishwasher, cutlery and plates, pots and pans, tables and chairs, glasses and cups.

A fair number of freaks and dropouts hung out, worked at, and patronized the restaurant, including but not limited to: Fast Freddie, a gambling addict and recreational cokehead from New Brunswick; Sad Sylvie, a thirty-something divorcee whose locally famous jazz musician husband left her for a groupie; Mad Michael, a middle-aged Greek hipster with bug-eye glasses; Lousy Lorraine, a thin-haired, overweight cook who liked threesomes; and Randy Richard, a young gay waiter with a thin moustache who once gave me a book of photographs by Ansel Adams for my birthday.

Victoria told me she wanted to see me when my shift ended. Over the course of the next few hours, no matter how hard I tried, I couldn't think of a reason why she might want to talk to me. Maybe Victoria wanted to congratulate me on the good work I was doing and give me a raise? I pulled the cutlery out of the dishwasher basket and wiped off each knife, spoon, and fork, then put them away in a flatware rack on the opposite side of the kitchen counter so the waiters could grab them easily when setting tables.

Victoria sat at a table across from the kitchen working on the company books using an old-fashioned adding machine. Whenever she hit the enter button, a receipt spilled out the top and she'd tear it off and staple it to a daily sales summary. It was probably tough to reconcile the books. Even though I'd only been working at Bourgeois a short time, I felt I could've told her a few things about running a restaurant.

The first thing would have been to put a lock on the booze inventory so Franz and the Cos and everyone else couldn't just grab a beer anytime they felt like it. Franz and everybody else got cracked on restaurant inventory beer, and not cheap Labatt Blue or Canadians either. Amber Dos Equis and cold Heinekens were Franz and Cos's choice almost every night. Next, I would have set up some checks and balances to police the waiters. When Victoria wasn't around—which was often—I watched the Cos in action. If a customer wanted to pay cash and the bill was small, he'd tell them the total instead of issuing an invoice. He'd make change right at the table from money he kept in his pocket. The Bourgeois never saw the order and the Cos kept all the money for himself, including the tip.

Maybe Victoria is going to make me a waiter! I could easily have handled the job. In fact, *I might even put in some protocols to stop staff theft and make Victoria some money.*

"Goddammit to fucking hell!" screamed Franz, snapping me out of my reverie. "I can't cook on this fucking toy stove!"

Heavy cream spilled out onto the small stovetop and seeped

down and into the electric element buckets. He walked over to the bar fridge, pulled out a Heineken, and popped off the top. "Andy, clean up zis mess!"

There was no use arguing with Franz, especially when he was half-cracked. I picked up a towel, wiped off the top of the stove, and dismantled each element. I washed, rinsed, and dried each one, and carefully set them back in place on the stove.

When I finished, I worked on my other closing duties, including taking the three trash bins and the recycling out to the back lane. While I was there, Franz strutted out, dressed in his black leather motorcycle suit and boots. I watched him put on his helmet, unsteadily straddle his Ducati racing bike, turn the throttle, and roar down the lane. It looked like a lot of fun, all that power between your legs—not to mention all that booze firing in your brain, telling you that you're going to live forever, and if not, what would it matter if at least you went out in a Mad Maxian blaze of glory?

I trudged back inside, filled a bucket with water and industrial soap from the storage closet, and mopped the kitchen while the Cos went to work vacuuming the floor of the restaurant. After I finished, I went to the bathroom to wash up, and gave myself a long look in the mirror before I came back out. If I got a promotion to waiter, it would mean more hourly wages and tips. I'd have to remember to ask the Cos how much he made on a good night. There's not a chance they'd give me a Saturday night shift. I'd need a lot of training and experience for that. *Well, who knows? Maybe, I'm a natural.*

I made my way to the front of the restaurant, and found Victoria at a table, working on a ledger. "Victoria, you wanted to see me?"

"Ah, yes, Andy—sit down."

It looked like she was trying to balance entries without any luck. *Good luck with that*, I thought as I watched her try and try again. Frustrated, she put her pencil down.

"Andy, let me get right to the point. It's about the way you dress."

"Huh?"

"Yes. You should consider buying a new pair of pants and a shirt. Your jeans are torn, your shirt is dirty, and your running shoes are finished."

I glanced down at my feet. She did have a point there—a large tear had opened at the top of my right runner. I wiggled my toe.

"Why don't you dress more like the Cos," she said, "or Franz, or any of the other guys? We're trying to project the right image here at the Bourgeois."

"Well, I… I don't know. I mean, sure. Sorry."

"OK. It's settled. Here's your paycheque." She handed me a personal cheque. The amount: sixty-nine dollars and eighteen cents. I thanked her as I rose from the table and went to grab my jacket.

"And one more thing, Andy."

"Yeah?"

"Don't cash that for a few days. I mean, wait until Wednesday at least, OK?"

46

Fuck Nut

I was looking forward to graduation in June. The idea began to take on more and more clarity, as if you were pointing a camera lens at an object, and by turning the lens, the plane of focus sharpens.

You might think the life I led in my final year of high school was carefree. Living in the basement at home, going to class, eating junk food lunches in the cafeteria, smoking weed with Fak and listening to Pink Floyd in his basement in the dark, playing basketball, and working with the Cos at the Bourgeois? Well, it might sound great except, what if I told you there were dragon eggs all around us, waiting to crack open, and grow into supersized, bat-winged, fire-breathing, scaly lizards?

Front and centre was Mean Boland. He had somehow gone from an oversized boy to a huge man in the space of months. He was acting up again, this time teasing Fak about his accent and the way he dressed. At lunch, in the cafeteria, I overheard him blabbering away to a cluster of Neanderthals. He wore thick rings on his fingers, sharp rings, rings designed to cause harm to people.

"Look at that fucking loser Livingston and his new camel

jockey buddy. Who does he think he's kidding? You know he fucked his mom's vacuum cleaner?"

Fak either pretended he didn't hear it, or he didn't care. Stuff that bugged me, didn't bug him. He existed in a parallel universe: alien, advanced, rich in music, mathematics, language. Maybe that's what I liked about him. Soon, he was going to graduate with top grades, enroll at UBC, obtain an advanced business degree, fly back home to Africa, and apprentice in a bunch of businesses for his family—a Lebanese Michael Corleone, without the guns and tragedy. My future, on the other hand, was not as clear. I didn't have any idea what the future held for me.

On top of Mean Boland's brewing antagonism, tough guys from Vancouver's east side—some still in school, some not; big, hairy knuckle draggers—were showing up at Magee at lunch and after school in wild packs, jumping guys for kicks. Just a few days earlier, Teddy Sullivan got torn out of his convertible and beaten up badly in front of his howling girlfriend. Fozzy, always on the lookout for criminal accomplices, befriended a few of them, the traitor. He told me at lunch about one night when he'd gone out roaming with one of the leaders, a bogeyman named Doolin, and a few of his baboon buddies: Keith Moraine, Daniel Herrington, and a guy everybody just called "Fuck Nut."

"So, we was driving in the car, and man, it was beautiful—we had the Judas Priest blasting, and then Doolin sees this cunt rambling down the sidewalk minding hisself, so he jumps out and fucking starts whaling on his face, I mean fucking *really* whacking him out, until this old fucker folds up on the ground like a piece of toilet paper."

"Jesus," I whistled through my teeth. "And then what happened?"

"Well, Moraine—nah wait, it was Fuck Nut—well, he jumped out and put the boots into this old, crumpled ball, laid out on the grass. He busted him up in the face, in the guts, everywhere."

At this point in the story, Fozzy was so excited he kicked a trash can, he jumped up and down, he howled, hell, he even tried to kick me in the shins.

"Fozzy, that's some crazy, fucked-up shit. Don't ever tell me anything like that again."

I meant it, too. I even went home that night and checked the *Kerrisdale Courier* to see if anyone had been beaten up or if there was some kind of Crime Stoppers report on criminal assaults in the neighbourhood. I found nothing.

The next morning, I decided we were going to need some protection to see us through to the end of the school year. I sized up this big loner for the job, Hans Smit. Hans always ate his lunch at school alone and wandered the hallways like a hunted animal even though he was over 6'5" and at least 240 pounds.

I felt sorry for him. A couple of the younger kids called him "Ugly Hans." One afternoon, as he walked past the basketball court after school, I shot the ball over to him. It bounced a couple of times and rolled past his feet, stopping still on the grass. He stopped walking to stare at it, but he didn't pick it up.

"Aw, c'mon Hans, grab it and come over and play. It might even be fun. What've you got to lose?" I asked.

I picked up the ball and bounced it up and down. *Boom! Boom! Boom!*

"Leave me alone," he said.

I bounced the ball again. *Boom! Boom! Boom!*

On the third bounce, I pushed it too hard. When it bounced

back up, I missed it, and it hit me square in the face. Hans chuckled. Everybody on the court killed themselves laughing except for me. Fak saw the whole thing. He picked up the ball and placed it gently into Hans's giant hands and said,

"Ah, c'mon Hans! What have you got to lose?" Then, in French, "*Vous serez la bienvenue!*"

Hans hesitated for a moment and walked onto the court with the ball. He made a run for the hoop and leapt, ball outstretched atop his palm, at the correct moment, he turned his wrist and slammed it through the hoop, a slam dunk!

We cheered. Hans was in. We had our own muscle.

47

Moon Walk

I was still a virgin—a greenhorn, a sex stooge, unsullied (if you will) at seventeen. I mean, there are only so many beautiful naked women in glossy skin mags you could call your own. The nurse, the girl-next-door, the lady of the manor, the cheerleader—and aren't they, really, everybody's?

If you've had enough wanks—hunched over magazine pages, splayed-out under bed covers, coiled up on toilet seats—you'll know it requires plenty of effort, imagination, variety, preparation, and *privacy*. Another problem was I didn't have much to work with. I didn't have enough material. I only had four or five old porn mags hidden between the beams of my bedroom ceiling.

What I needed was a real girl.

Fak, bless his Arab, pimping heart, took pity on me. We were eating lunch together in the cafeteria. He wore a white Guayabera shirt and Italian loafers without socks. He asked me, casually, "What are you doing this weekend?"

"Same as usual."

"Masturbating alone in your basement bedroom? Watching

239

game shows on TV with Bob?"

"Hah. Good one. Probably working, unlike you. Some people have to work, you know." I told him this knowing full well he was insecure about the private income given to him by his dad, Abu-Jasar, a serious Muslim and an unapologetically, old-school family patriarch.

"Well, take some time off. I've invited my curvy friend Shannon and her friend Cheryl from Seattle this weekend. We are all going to enjoy ourselves at my place."

"Shannon? Washington State Shannon? *That* Shannon?" I was curious. "Doesn't she have a boyfriend, Jim? Did you invite him?"

"Don't flip your hair."

"'Your wig.'"

"Ah, OK. Don't flip your wig," he repeated, slowly.

"No. No Jim."

"Wow."

I had to work the next night at the Bourgeois. When I showed up for my shift, Victoria was sitting at the manager's table, clearly in a bad mood. She looked at my torn jeans, Clash T-shirt, dirty runners, and frowned. The Cos, on the other hand, was in a great mood. He was grinning and chatting up customers as he took out his plates and cups and saucers.

"Hey man, what's happening? What's the buzz?" he asked me, walking me into the kitchen.

"I have a date tonight after work, so don't mess around at close."

"Who's the lucky girl?"

"Oh, some American girl from Seattle. Her name's Shannon."

He passed me a giant tray of dirty glasses, plates, and cutlery. I dumped them in the sink, rinsed them in hot water, and put them in the dishwasher.

Franz was cursing at the stove again. "Victoria! This is *bullsheet*!" he hollered out toward the manager's table. "How can you expect anything from me? I can't cook on this suburban housewife's stove. If you don't get a gas oven in here, you are going to need another chef, and this is the last time I tell you!"

Frazzled, he walked over to the bar fridge and popped open a Heineken. I watched him settle down by way of guzzling six more before we closed for the night. The whole night, the restaurant was busy. From the time anybody walked in right up to the time they left, at least a dozen things, all designed to make them happy, had to happen. At close, when the Cos finally went up to the front to lock the door, a couple was still lingering over Irish coffees, mooning into each other's eyes, and driving me crazy.

"Cos, for Christ's sake, have you given those guys their bill yet? I must get out of here! It's practically an emergency."

"Hold on, now hold on, *relax*." He slowly lowered his hands in a calming gesture. "It's cool. Be late. You don't want to show up looking like you've been sitting around waiting for them like a dog. What else have you got to do, anyway?"

"Uh, I have to put those coffee cups into the dishwasher, run it, take out the garbage, and wipe down the two bathrooms."

"No problemo, man. Get lost and I will take care of all of that for you."

"Really?! You can?"

"Sure. You are what you do, not what you say you'll do."

What a relief. "Great! Thanks!"

I took off my apron, threw it into a corner bin, and went to the back to get my jacket and bike lock. The Cos followed a few seconds after and popped his head around the corner.

"Oh, Andy, one more thing before you get going—I think there's a lightbulb that needs changing in the men's bathroom"

"Oh, all right." I went into the supply closet and pulled out a fresh 40W light bulb. I walked over to the bathroom, opened the door, and stood up on the toilet seat, high enough where I could reach an upper shelf, beyond which was the light socket. I screwed in the new bulb and the bathroom filled with light. On a small, amber salad plate on the top shelf were four two-inch lines of flaky, crystal-white cocaine next to a rolled-up ten-dollar bill.

My mind immediately went to work. *Well, the Cos must have put them there for me, obviously. Also, he's much older than me, and he looks like he's having a good time most of the time. He wouldn't send me down the wrong road. Would he? Anyway, I could probably use a confidence boost. Why not try some Bolivian marching powder? Heck, the Cos might even be from Bolivia himself, originally.*

I snorted each line in turn, stepped down off the toilet, took off my apron, and blasted off to Fak's place on my bike; my head a waltz—a twist, a floss, a moonwalk, an electric slide.

48

It Ain't You

Rolling down Laburnum Street, palms off the handle bars, coasting freestyle, I saw warm light flooding out of the big front window of Fak's house. His big staff car, with velour seating and a radar detector, was parked out front. It meant he—they, Shannon and what's her name—all safely made it through the Canada-US border at Peace Arch Park.

It was always touch-and-go with Fak and law enforcement. In Africa, the police officers knew their place. Fak told me they sat on the lower rungs of society, one level above criminals, appropriately. Before you were pulled over by a cop in Abidjan, you had to move sunglasses and lighters—anything valuable, really—from the dash into the glove compartment or else a cop would reach inside and steal it. Here, cops acted like celebrities. Fak could never get his head around it. Any time he was pulled over by the cops (which was often) or at a border crossing kiosk, it began.

"Good afternoon, sir. Driver's licence and registration?"

"*Comment? Je ne comprends pas.*"

I walked up the front steps, running my hand through my hair.

243

I stood at the front door, pausing, and looked back down the street. I could see my house a block and a half away. My parents would be asleep, although, seeing as it was a Friday night, the Old Man might have been on his bed, smoking gaspers and staring at the ceiling, thinking about God knows what. I pushed open the door.

Inside, two Puma bags and two pairs of shoes sat on the floor in the hallway. I kicked my own shoes off next to them, just to be safe, and made my way into the living room. Two teenage girls, about the same age, stretched out over the floor atop a brightly coloured mat. One of them, the prettier one, was on all fours, and the second was underneath her, giggling. They were playing Twister.

Fak sat on the couch, grinning. Jasar's giant Yoda pipe was on the centre of the coffee table, its four giant hoses flying out in all directions.

"If it isn't the great bull-duster himself!" Fak called out, seeing me.

"Funny, Fak." I rolled my eyes, then looked at the Twister mat. "Hello. My name is Andrew."

"Hiya." The giggling girl smiled at me, waving back. "My name's Cheryl. This here's Shannon," she said, pointing to her friend. "She's come all the way from Issaquack, Washington to see you."

"'Issaquah,' silly fool," Shannon snipped. "It's nice to meet you," she said to the wall, still on all fours, her back to me.

"I can't hold on anymore Cheryl, I'm gonna go bust!"

She dropped to the ground, laughing. She stood up and grabbed a half-empty bottle of Old Castle wine off the table.

"It's better to be full of wine than full of shit!" she proclaimed and sat down on the couch. "Come on, Cheryl, it's lonely over here."

I watched the girls and their lovely American faces. It was sweet they both wore makeup, like grown-ups, as if the whole weekend away was a special event like a wedding, or an adult dinner party.

"Why are you so late?" Fak asked me. "Have you been slaving at your dishes like an old peasant woman again?"

He was an awful snob and terrible rich kid. He had no idea what it was like to have only five bucks in your bank account and how that can telescope your opportunities down to zero.

"Why are *you* so late, Fakhead?" I glared at him. "Problems at the border again? Canada doesn't want any more terrorists blowing up our parliament buildings?"

"Is that supposed to be a joke?"

"If the shoe fits, wear it."

He looked at me, puzzled. "Why would I put on my shoes? I don't understand." He looked at his feet. "I'm not wearing shoes right now. Why would you say that?"

"You guys are boring," Shannon said, standing up from the couch. "Andy, can I get you a beer from the fridge?" She went into the kitchen and brought out a six-pack. I grabbed one, popped it open, and took a deep swig. I was thirsty as hell.

"Shannon, where are you going to sleep? Did you find a bedroom yet? There are at least five or six," asked Fak. He was enjoying himself.

"Not yet," Shannon answered. "I thought I'd play it by ear."

"We're sharing one of the bedrooms, heh," Cheryl chimed in, nervous. "Let's go check it out right now, Shannon."

Cheryl got up from the mat and I had a good look at both of them. Shannon was the better-looking of the two; she was shorter, with a fuller, more mature body. She wore her dirty blonde hair long, down her back. Cheryl was the taller of the two. A thin brunette. Shannon shrugged and went to the front door to grab her bag. Outside, the weeping willow on the lawn, right in front of the window, shuddered. "Looks like there's a thunder banger coming tonight," I said.

"What gave you the clue, Sherlock?" Shannon snickered, adding to Cheryl, "Come on, let's check out this big ol' haunted house."

Fak and I watched them saunter up the stairs together.

"What's going on?" I yell-whispered at Fak. "There's no way we're getting lucky with these two. Shannon doesn't even like me, I can tell you that right now."

"Shannon might take pity on a poor, sexually frustrated celibate like you. You never know. She's American, so..." He smirked. "She has a boyfriend, but you never can tell—it's an away game for her, a foreign country. American girls, generally, can't really help themselves, at least before marriage, and then, well, even after..."

A full, sly grin formed across the lower half of his face.

"Hmmm." I considered this, thinking about the two of them upstairs. "Well, I guess. You might be right. But, still, don't you think they're kind of...trashy?"

"Are zey trashy?"

"Sure, you know."

"Ah, don't you think that maybe it's you? That you're the one who's trashy? *Zut Alors!*"

"One man's trash is another's man's treasure."

"Wait, what?"

"Beggars can't be choosers."

"Oh, for Christ's sake!"

"Don't throw pearls before swine."

"Oh my God!" he huffed.

"Fak, forget about it. Fill up that goddamn hookah!"

While the girls were upstairs doing God-knows-what, Fak and I killed time. We smoked some weed and lit a crackling fire. After twenty minutes of staring into the fireplace, a dancing abyss, I started a swashbuckling fight with Fak using an iron poker. I won, of course. It ended with a wrestling match on the carpet: the legendary Train Wrecker versus the Golden Sheikh.

We heard a massive crack of thunder; followed seconds later, by a distant white flash across the night sky. Screams rained down on us from the second floor. Cheryl and Shannon bounced down the stairs, loud as falling paint cans, as the power went out.

"Oh my gosh, that last banger was so loud I almost peed my pants!" squealed Cheryl. By firelight, I saw her grab a long scarf hanging off a hook by the front door; she danced around the room. She stood in front of me, swaying. In the next instant, she bolted out the back door. Another loud thunderclap shook the house. In the backyard, Cheryl danced barefoot on the grass, surrounded by ominous green hedges.

"Let's go!" cried Shannon.

We all ran barefoot onto the lawn as the rain fell. In the sky in the distance, white yellow veins of lightning flashed against the black sky, illuminating massive, menacing, clouds.

Sometime later—well, it was later. Aw, who knows? Later, I was trying to get my wet pants off in the small laundry room in the basement. One leg of my skinny jeans got stuck on my foot, and I couldn't bend it properly to slip over my ankle and get my leg out. Shannon was with me, sitting on top of the big, white dryer.

We were alone.

"This darn thing's so wet," she drawled. Her eyelids were heavy, and her makeup had run down her face in the rain. She was washed out. She pulled off her top. She reached out to me with both arms. We kissed. She wrapped her legs around my back. It was freezing cold in the basement, and we were both soaking wet, but I couldn't feel anything other than Shannon's lips on my mouth and my hands on her shoulders. She pulled away, sounding stone cold sober and deadly serious,

"Let's go upstairs." We slinked up the stairs in the dark, our hands against the wall.

"Helloooo? Helloooo up there..." Shannon called out.. She giggled and called out again, in a louder, deeper, voice. "Virgin alert! Alert, Staff Sergeant, we have a bona fide virgin coming up these here stairs!"

"Fuck *off*, Shannon! And *shhhhh!*" I said and put my finger to my lips.

We tumbled into Jasar's room. I fell back on the futon as Shannon disappeared into the bathroom. I found a big bottle of Drakkar Noir on the bedside stand and pressed the nozzle. The bed smelled like a hot forest. I was waving a pillow madly when the bathroom door opened. Shannon—who found the whole thing funny, and maybe thought I was crazy—ran, jumped into bed, and pulled the covers over her head. My erect penis, single and long-suffering, was, at last, to be liberated from years of autocratic rule, abuse, suffering, and neglect by an American nymphomaniac.

When it was over, my eyes were glassy, like I'd been hit on the head with a heavy stick. It was no vulgar attack; it was a good-luck whammy. A whammy of pale, ripe fruit, offered and taken in tenderness. She sat on the far edge of the bed and began to cry, softly. After a moment, she began sobbing in waves she couldn't control. It was terrible. *Oh my God! I must be some kind of monster! What have I done?!* I reached across the bed and lay my hand on her shoulder.

"Don't. Don't, please." She said, and pulled away.

"It ain't you."

49

The Twin Sisters

"Hey man, do you want to go to Wreck Beach tomorrow?" the Cos asked me at the end of my shift at the Bourgeois.

"Cos, seriously? A nudist beach? It's not even warm outside. Are you going to make me go naked?"

"Relax. You can wear your bathing suit! And don't worry, it's one of the grooviest places around." I thought this over. Groovy was good.

"Sure… Why not?"

In the morning, I grabbed my towel and swimming trunks, no easy feat to find, trust me. I took three buses to get to UBC. We'd arranged to meet at the Wreck Beach trail entrance, on South West Marine Drive. The Cos was going to drive up from Kitsilano. I got off the bus, sat on the curb, and waited. A long line of dirty hippies, university students, and families were waiting to descend single file down a steep cliff path to the ocean below.

A loud horn sounded. It was the Cos. He was wearing drug-dealer sunglasses and drove a beat-up old Volvo with expired plates. He parked, jumped out, and grabbed a canvas backpack from his trunk. He greeted me, smiling, his pearly whites glistening in the late morning light. "What's the buzz, man?"

I shrugged.

We joined the parade of West Coast freaks hiking down the trail. I was behind a guy with no shirt, brown Rasta locks, and bare feet. "I've had this backpack since I was your age, man," the Cos said, making conversation. "It was with me in Nogales, it was with me in L.A., it was with me in Whistler, and I still have it now." We were halfway down when we passed an older couple, each of them wearing ugly Birkenstocks, who had stopped to catch their breath. "I can tell you, man, I've been around man, I've been around," he continued.

"So why did you leave Los Angeles?"

"It was the war, man, the war. It was crazy." He shuddered slightly. "They were shooting babies in Vietnam. They were raping people. They were feeding us kill ratios and body counts. Westmoreland, Nixon, McNamara... Lying, bloodthirsty beasts. That's not my scene. Is it yours?" I shook my head. "And the funny thing is, man, the thing that people still don't get is that we *lost* that fucking war. Giap was a military genius. These white-bread, West-Point, corn-fed assholes had more than met their match, man. This guy Giap lived in a fucking cave, built a revolutionary army from nothing, and the whole time he had a fucking Vichy gun to his head." I must admit, I didn't really know what he was talking about. When we reached the bottom of the trail, he clapped me on the back. "Here we are, safe and sound in our own little piece of paradise!"

Wreck Beach was at the tip of the peninsula where the Fraser finally fucked the Pacific Ocean, after a long journey down from Fraser Pass in the Rockies. To the north was Squamish, Powell

River, and Bella Bella, where my cousins grew up, and if you went further north, Alaska.

The Cos stopped and took off his sandals, sticking his toes in the sand and wiggling them. To our right was a short, middle-aged dude with a crew cut. He wore white running shoes and tall black socks. The Cos nudged me in the ribs and whispered, "That guy's a narc. You can always tell. It's the socks."

The beach was half-littered with people lying on the sand or wading slowly into the cool, lazy, waves of Georgia Strait. Lying on towels, mats, and under umbrellas were the local lotus-eaters, killing time, free of cares, letting the sound of the water, the warm sun, and the smell of the forest turn time upside down and inside out. Beyond them, past the sea-wood, ocean-battered logs, stood the massive mountains of the north shore, white snow capping their peaks like winter toques.

I wanted to find a spot against a log where I could rest my back and keep my eyes on the scene. We kept walking, trying to look cool; well, as cool as you might expect given we were non-nudists at a nudist beach. In the end, we simply laid our towels down in the best spot we could find. I reached into my backpack, and fished around.

"Damnit, Cos! I forgot my suntan lotion!"

"Well, don't look at me."

I looked at him. He was a deep brown from head to toe, the Spanish Mexican American bastard. Further down the beach, a Black guy splashed around in the water, having fun with a couple of girls.

"Now you don't see that every day."

"Aw, come on, man," said the Cos.

"No, really, I haven't seen a Black guy in this town in over a year. It's like they don't exist in Vancouver."

"Well, that's about right." He smiled. "Why would anybody move to this heavenly hell hole? It's a racist paradise. Time you wised up a bit. OK, amigo?" I didn't answer him. An out of shape, middle-aged couple, hardcore nudists, de-camped behind us. Between his legs, he had a tiny salt and pepper nest with what looked like a small, exhausted bird at rest in the middle. She looked like her body was slowly melting into the sand, an ice cream cone caught in the sun. I reached into my bag again and checked my wallet. I had twenty bucks in total. Plenty for hippie-veggie lunch and, with any luck, maybe a couple of cold beers.

After about an hour of daydreaming on the sand—restless, bored, repeat—I turned to the Cos, sitting quietly next to me, probably committing the size and shape of every tit on the beach to memory in his sick, American mind. "Hey Cos, how long did you live in Whistler?"

"Oh man, I don't know. I lost track of time."

"Aw c'mon. Give me a break. I'm bored as all hell. I hate the beach."

"OK, OK, let me think about it... It was probably around 1971, up 'til about five years ago. Señor, a golden age."

"How did you make money? What did you do?"

"I did what I do best. I worked the lifts. I was also a waiter. I had plenty of side hustles all the time, this and that, here and there, you know." He waved his hand. "And the women—the women were off the charts, beautiful and sexy. It was one of the greatest places in the world. The guys working on the lifts, the restaurant workers, millionaires, department store owners—anybody could hang out anywhere with anyone. Let me tell you, if you ever find a place like that in the world, where everybody agrees to rules decided by something bigger and more beautiful than themselves, stay there. Can you dig it?"

I dug it. "Well, I knew plenty of guys who died on the Sea-to-Sky Highway."

"I'm sure you did."

"At least two guys from my school this year. One of them, a guy everybody was in love with, got clipped by a pickup truck and dragged for a mile in front of all his friends."

"Well, I'm sorry about that. Mountains are dangerous, in general."

"Did you ski?"

"Hell no, man. I hate the snow."

A nude beach vendor, bearded and thin, dragged a cooler across the sand in front of us.

"Hell yeah, brother!" The Cos reached into his knapsack, and pulled out his crumpled tip money—or the money he'd ripped off in his chit scam at the cafe. In the end, it was all the same, I guess.

The nudebeachpreneur, engaged now, interested, smiled wide and sat down on his cooler. "Well, OK then! What can I get for you two fellers? I've got sandwiches and beer, mostly."

He stood up, lifted the lid of his cooler, and peered inside. His balls swung casually between his legs. The rays of the mid-afternoon sun hit his sack and a long shadow crossed our bodies and extended all the way back to the nudists ten metres behind us. Two crows flew down and landed on the rim of his cooler. They looked at us, then inside the cooler, and back again.

"Jesus Christ! Fuck off!" our friend hollered, shooing them off. "Goddamn shit-hawks!"

He reached into the cooler, pulled out two avocado and alfalfa sprout sandwiches, two bottles of beer, and handed them to us. The Cos paid him and immediately our beach vendor fumbled for change—a scam, a gambit so obvious, it was comical. The Cos fell for it, despite the miles on him, the years of dodgy situations, all his life experience.

"Ah, forget it," he said, waving him off with a smile. "No big deal."

He thanked us, packed up, and moved on. We devoured the big sandwiches and downed the beers. As soon as mine was gone, I wanted another. When we'd finished eating, the Cos looked around the beach.

"Hey, check this out, man." He reached into his backpack and pulled out a sheet of blotter paper. On it, were printed row upon row of identical Mr Smiley Face images.

"What are those?" I asked him.

"It's time to take a trip, man. Tear one off. It's your ticket"

"My ticket?"

"Acid, man. 'Buy the ticket, take the ride,' as the man said."

"Well, I don't know. I… I've never…"

"Andy. Relax." He tore one off for me. "Now, stick out your tongue." I had no choice. *Buy a ticket, take the ride.* I swallowed. The Cos smiled, satisfied.

"Hey man, what happened to your eyebrow?"

"Aw, that?" I touched it self-consciously. "Oh, this guy named Rick—I mean, I was cooking some steaks and this guy… Ah, nevermind. I burned it off by mistake."

"It looks freaky, man."

"Ya, I know."

I lay down on my towel and closed my eyes. I listened to the seagulls, the wind, and the water. A kid cried out; there was laughter; a game of beach volleyball broke out a few hundred metres down the beach. After about forty-five minutes, I poked the Cos in the ribs.

"Hey, Cos. Cos? I think I know those guys back there."

"What guys?"

"Back there." He looked over. It was Henry Tunselman and his pals from Magee. One of them, Gus Brown maybe, lay on his back with a towel carefully tented over his head. Inside the towel tent, or tent towel, he was hotboxing a giant bong. Tunselman, short, in a bright red and white bathing suit, beer in one hand, pulled out his penis. A long stream of piss formed a parabolic arc—aw heck, essentially, he took a piss on Brown's back. Brown laughed at first, thinking maybe it was water or warm beer. When the truth hit him, he yelled, leapt up, and started swinging. Laughing, Tunselman pushed him aside, and put his dick back into his swim trunks.

"Aw c'mon man. Are those guys your friends?"

"Well, they're in my grade at school. They're not my friends."

I rested on my elbows and looked across Burrard Inlet. In the distance, from behind the mountains of the north shore, rose an enormous reticular cloud, fuchsia at the bottom, salmon pink at the top. It floated toward me, toward Wreck Beach, moving slowly across the water. It came to a stop above me. It looked to be spinning and transforming at the same time. Its edges whorled and spun, increasing in both size and magnitude. Suddenly, it opened, and out of its sweet brume, two phantasms appeared in the sky. They were identical females, and beautiful. I heard the slow beating of a drum that didn't exactly sound like a drum. It sounded like a baby crying, the wings of an eagle, the sound of a ball hitting a tennis racket, and a fire burning. All of it was one sound.

The girls danced in the sky above me. I could see their faces. They were Coast Salish. The Twin Sisters! They smiled, winked at me, and vanished into nothing. I looked over at the Cos. He was asleep. I closed my eyes. When I opened them again, the sky above me was clear and blue. My magic cloud was gone. I closed my eyes, again. When I opened them up again, this time, something or someone blocked the sun.

"Hey, Andy? Is that you? Andrew Livingston?"

"Yah?" I stood up. Molly Murphy stood in front of me.

"Oh, hey there. You," I stammered. "I'm sorry, I mean, I didn't recognize you—ya know, it's so bright and everything."

The Cos jumped up and dusted himself off. Instantly, he was engaged, chatty, and charming. "Cos, this is my friend Molly, and…" Molly turned and introduced us to her friends.

"Jennifer, Rachel, and Queenie. Well, Queenie's name is really Sandra, but we all call her Queenie because she acts like… Aw, never mind." Queenie did a body ripple. Each girl wore a bright neon bikini. They looked like they'd just washed up on the beach, pink and fully formed, inside giant oyster shells. I pointed to the Cos.

"The Cos and I work together at a restaurant. We're pals."

"Do you guys have any beer?" asked Rachel.

"Well, sure," the Cos answered. "I think I can be of assistance. Why don't you take a walk with me?"

"Ya, OK. Why don't you guys take a walk and I'll watch our stuff?" I said, still reeling from the acid, although what only a few moments ago felt like a surging storm were now ripples on a pond.

"OK, see you later, gator," said the Cos. I lay down on my towel and looked up at the sky. The clouds, what few were left, behaved like clouds again. I closed my eyes and fell asleep. When I woke up, the sun was going down and the Cos was resting on his elbows next to me.

"I like your friends," he said.

"I bet." I propped myself up, stretching. "They're sixteen years old, Cos. You could teach them to drive."

"Are you sure?"

"I'm sure."

"OK, OK," he laughed. "Lighten up. Give me a break. We're on Wreck Beach, man, anything can happen down here. It's magic, like Narnia. One of those girls, your friend, Molly? Her dad died."

"What?"

"Ya man, it was a freak accident. The one with the funny tooth told me."

"Jesus."

I walked down to the water where Molly was sitting by herself, holding her knees, watching the waves wash up over her toes. I settled down on the sand next to her.

"Molly, I... I'm not sure what to say," I mustered. "The Cos told me about your dad. I'm really sorry." I dragged my fingers through the sand, making a trench for the water to make its way back to the ocean. "I mean, I know we don't know each other very well, but I mean, jeez, I'm sorry and everything, I guess."

"Thanks." She looked at me, then back out over the water. After a minute, she went on, "He was heli-logging for Mac Blo, and a fog came in on him. He was good... He was a great pilot. Everybody says so. The company says he lost 'spatial orientation,' whatever that means... But that doesn't sound right to me. I think his tail rotor fell off because the company didn't want to pay to get it fixed. Or, at least, that's what my mom and my brother said. Something wasn't right about it. He was a good pilot. A great pilot…"

She trailed off for a moment before clearing her throat. "Hey, you!" She punched me lightly on the arm and smiled. "You're graduating soon. What are you going to do?"

"Me? Ha! I don't really know." I looked around, the beach was almost empty now.

"Hey, did you get my tape?"

"What tape?"

"The mixtape I made for you and put in your backpack?"

"You? That was you?"

"Sure."

I let out a whistle. I didn't know what to tell her. "That is one bitchin' mixtape, young lady."

A couple of big Chinese freighters were anchored on the water in the middle of the strait. A cruise ship, probably on its way to Alaska, moved up the coast in the distance. Three windsurfers shot past us, grappling hard with their sails. A scream came down from the trees.

"What was that?" Molly turned around, confused.

"I guess we should pack up and get going." I said.

I walked her back up to where the Cos was now holding court with Rachel and Queenie, all sitting in a semicircle. The Cos was reclining back on his elbows, picking at his teeth with a reed. "Karma is basically energy. You need to pay attention to your thoughts, because thoughts can create karma." A second scream interrupted him.

"Cos! Was that a scream?" I asked.

"Oh, that? Forget about it. It was either a bad drug deal, or a rent-boy stabbed, or got stabbed by, one of his johns. It happens all the time. They moved over from the Granville Mall last year. They like it down here because they can do whatever they want. The hike is too much hassle for the cops, you dig?"

"No, I don't dig! Look. Can we get going? It's getting dark and we've got to make it all the way back up the hill."

We said goodbye to Molly and her friends, bumming out the Cos, and walked back up the hill to his car. "What were you thinking Cos? Molly's friends are less than half your age!"

"Are you kidding me? Those girls have been around. You don't know anything, man. Jesus, sometimes I think you're missing a few buttons on your remote control." As we hiked back up the steep incline, one foot after the other, almost 300 steps in total, I concluded he was probably right. I was probably a few buttons short on my remote control.

50

Doolin's Mellow

Chinsky and I walked along the tracks to his house. We hopped across the rails, jumped over the oil-streaked planks, and pulled blackberries off the bushes running along the either side. At the 57th and Angus intersection, we saw Fozzy walking in the distance. Simply out of habit, I guess, Chinsky bent down and fingered some good-sized rocks.

"Don't even think about it! Jesus Christ, Chinsky." When we caught up with Fozzy, something was on his mind. He began a couple of times, stopped, and began again. He pronounced triumphantly.

"A vagina is indestructible."

"Aha," said Chinsky.

"Think about it. It bleeds, it pees, it can take everything in sight, no problem: fingers, dicks, vibrators, bottles, whatever. Finally, giant fucking babies take the biggest ride of their lives inside of them. Vaginas are the source of all human life. I'm telling you. It's not a joke. You guys better start taking them more seriously."

When we arrived at Chinsky's house, emboldened by truth, we found Fak and Hans waiting outside. The stench of old carpet and the Gooch's cigarette butts hit me in the face as soon as I walked in the front door. I quickly bolted down the stairs.

In Chinsky's rec room, there was a ping pong table and some ancient couches. The springs in the couches were so far gone that if you sat down, you had to move around some to avoid getting a spring up your ass. A battered dart board was on the back of the door. A poster of Michael Jackson hung above the fireplace. On the poster was some kind of poem.

> *I'm going to search for my star until I find it.*
> *It's hidden in the drawer of innocence,*
> *wrapped in a scarf of wonder.*

"Jesus Christ. Where did you get that?" I asked Chinsky.

"Fuck off, Andy. My mom gave it to me for my birthday."

Fak bounced a ping pong ball, up and down, again and again, on the table.

"OK." I stood up and addressed everybody. "So, ya know, I'm hosting the after-grad party at my house. I haven't told my parents yet, but I talked to Geoff Lister from the graduation committee yesterday."

"And? What did he say?" asked Fak.

"He told me my house was too small, but nobody else had volunteered, so they didn't have any choice but to accept."

"He has a point," Chinsky pointed out. "There are nearly 200 students in our class, and your house is, what, around 1,200 square feet? So..."

"Don't try to trip me up on the details, Chinsky. Let me worry about that."

"Well, OK," Fak started, "but if we can't use your parents' bedrooms or the storage area…"

"What are you going to do about your dad?" asked Fozzy. "Are you going to send him to a hotel or something?"

"Nah. He'll be fine."

No he won't. I hadn't considered what to do about the Old Man. He didn't have a lock on his door. Maybe we could jam it or angle a chair against the handle and confine him somehow.

"What about all those East Van assholes?" asked Chinsky. "Aren't they bound to hear about it and show up and start whaling on everybody?"

We all looked over at Hans. He smiled.

"Don't worry about it. I'll make a deal with Doolin," Fozzy volunteered. "I'll get him to bring Bignault. Maybe we can pay them, like security guards or something."

"Bignault! Bignault? You've got to be kidding me!" Chinsky cried. "I heard he gave some poor guy a Smilin' Buddha! He split his head open like an acorn. He's got an attempted murder charge hanging over his head! He's locked up in the BC Penitentiary in New Westminster!"

"No, he got out," Fozzy added, unhelpfully.

"What do you mean—Doolin's good to go and Bignault's out?" I asked.

"Stop worrying. Doolin's mellow now."

"Oh well, that's probably fine." I surveyed them. "Hans? Fak? Sure." I rolled my eyes. "Doolin's mellow. That's great. What could go wrong?"

A door slammed upstairs.

"Is that Karla?" Fozzy asked, looking up at the ceiling.

"Nah. She moved out. She lives with a friend in Marpole," Chinsky said.

"Well, who was it then?" I asked. "The Gooch?"

"Relax. She won't be home for hours." Chinsky jumped up off the couch. He moved his chair to a corner. He stood up on the seat, put his hands on a ceiling tile, and pushed it aside. He reached up into the hole in the ceiling and pulled down a blue, velvet Seagram's bag. He put the bag between his legs, replaced the ceiling tile, and jumped down off the chair and onto the floor. He reached into the bag and pulled out a dozen Olympic Games, Montreal 1976, coins in five and ten-dollar denominations each with an engraving of the stadium, or athletes running, or cyclists, or map of Canada, or an Olympic wreath. We passed them around.

"Jeez, some of these are really beautiful," I said.

"That's right, Andy, they *are* beautiful. There are fourteen ten-dollar face value coins that each contain 1.44 troy ounces of pure silver, and fourteen five-dollar face value coins each containing 0.72 troy ounces," he boasted.

"Did your aunt or uncle or somebody give them to you for your birthday?" asked Fak.

"Heck no, fool! Fozzy here stole them by busting into the Cunningham's place when they were on vacation! I've been holding them for him."

"Way to go Chinsky. Now we're all fucked," said Fozzy.

"Jesus, Fozzy, I thought you quit all that," I said.

"Screw you, Livingston. The Cunninghams are assholes. Remember when old man Cunningham took his belt to Piero when he hit his car with an ice ball on 57th?" He had a point. Old man Cunningham was an asshole.

"Where's all the booze, Chinsky?" asked Fozzy.

"Oh yeah, I almost forgot. They're on the windowsill behind the curtain. Hans, go get them." Hans stood up, went to the window, pulled back the curtain, and revealed two big bottles of Peach Schnapps.

"What the hell are those?" I asked.

"It's a kind of booze, idiot. We pulled them from the Cunninghams' liquor cabinet," said Fozzy. Chinsky grabbed one, popped off the top, took a massive swig, and passed it over. Hans turned the bottle around and around in his hand, admiring it. He put it to his mouth and took a huge swig.

"Jesus, Hans, what are you doing?" Chinskey gawked.

"Screw it. Way to go, Hans! Hand it over." I commanded.

Hans gave me the bottle. I took a drink. I felt a sickly sweet, burning sensation in my throat. I handed the bottle over to Fozzy, who finished it. After a while, Fozzy didn't look so good. He stood up, staggered out the door, and stumbled into the bathroom.

"Well, he's spent," said Chinsky, laughing. I picked up some darts and started hucking them one by one at the dartboard. I took a drink from the other bottle before passing it over to Hans.

"Is that you down there, Richard?" called out a muffled voice from the top of the stairs. It was the Gooch. Chinsky rushed to the door, opened it, and yelled up the stairs.

"Ya, it's me and a few of the guys. We're playing some darts!"

"Is Andrew Livingston with you?"

"Nah."

"Are you sure? I thought I heard his voice."

"No, Gooch," Chinsky lied.

"Ah, OK. Do you want some juice and cookies?"

"No. Thanks, Gooch!"

"Alright. Don't bother me. I'm going into my bedroom to take a nap."

"OK!"

Chinsky grabbed the other schnapps bottle from Hans. He took a huge drink and picked up one of the copper darts off the floor. He closed the door, backed up several feet, and took aim. Just as he released the copper missile, the door swung open. Fozzy stepped back into the room.

"Hey guys, I've got to get…" The dart sunk halfway into his temple.

"Mark! *Mon Dieu*, your *head*!" cried Fak.

Fozzy grabbed the dart, pulled it out slowly, turned, and stuck the tip into the bull's-eye of the dart board.

"Listen, I've got to get going," he said, as if nothing happened. "I'm supposed to play golf with my dad down at Marine Drive." With that, he walked back out the door and up the stairs. We finished off the rest of the booze. We laughed for no reason, tripped over chairs, and played ping-pong, badly. I pulled Michael Jackson off the wall and tore him to pieces.

Chinsky grabbed me by the shoulders. "Andy. Andrew! You've got to pull yourself together. Get control of yourself!"

"'Get myself together?' Get myself together?! You're the one who looks like you're going to die!"

He took the news like a punch. He clutched his stomach and collapsed on the floor. I grabbed him by the arms and dragged him to the bathroom. He attacked the toilet seat. Gripping the sides of the bowl with both hands, he stuck his head deep inside, and retched. The sound was terrible. If you didn't know what was happening you might think a poltergeist was sucking him into the bowels of the house. When he finished, he collapsed on the floor and rolled onto his back. Fak and I pushed him back over onto his stomach and got the hell out of there.

We staggered up the stairs and out the side door. We walked to Riverview Park and sat down, each one of us at either end of the teeter-totter. Fak pulled out a golden cigarette case from his jacket pocket. He pulled out a beautifully rolled cone, lit a match, and fired it up. He smoked as we teetered and tottered, see'd and sawed.

"Andrew, my friend, you great bull-duster, I want you to fly to the Cote d'Ivoire with me this summer."

"What?"

"Of course. After that, we can fly to Monaco and Paris. I have cousins all over France. We must get a travel visa for you in New York city first, however."

"Wait, what? There's no way I can afford it."

"Don't worry about it. Abu-Jasar has agreed to pay for the trip, and your mom is going to pay him back when we get back at the end of the summer."

"She agreed to that already?"

"It's been settled. We leave after graduation."

I never would have thought my parents would go for something like that. I had a little money saved up; I was still working at the Bourgeois three nights a week, but it was chump change if you compared it to what a trip like that would cost.

To hell with it, I said to myself.

After Fak and I said goodbye, I lumbered home. I sat down in the kitchen. Mom stood at the sink, looking out the window, while she washed dishes. After some time, she pulled off her gloves and set them down on the counter beside her. Her eyes on the back yard, she asked me a question. "So, what are your plans after high school?"

"How's that?"

"Where are you going to go to school?" I thought this over for a while before answering. "Oh. Well, forget all that. I'm going to be a writer!" I announced. "You don't need to go to school for that. You only need the school of life!"

"That's not a plan, being a writer. It isn't a plan."

"Listen, Mom, I'm not some party crasher in the Temple of Literature. I know my way around. There's a seat waiting there for me. I have an invitation!" I said to her back.

She turned, came over to the counter and sat down next to me. Looking at me for the first time, she said, "Sure, you do Hemingway. You're going to go to university. You'll be the first in the family to get a degree. You can apply now and be accepted in an arts program for the fall semester. It's been agreed upon."

"Agreed upon? By whom?"

"Abu-Jasar and I spoke at length this morning. He thinks it's a good idea. Your father and I also agree. The trip is off if you decide to ignore our advice." So, there it was: a set-up. If I wanted to go on an adventure to Africa and Europe with Fak, I was going to have to go to UBC.

"And by the way, you're going to have to pay for school yourself. Your father and I haven't saved any money, so you better get busy washing dishes or whatever it is you do at that restaurant."

51

Ave Atque Vale

The colossal day, high school graduation day, finally arrived in mid-June like the warm sun breaking through a heavy jacket of ugly, black, acid-wash-denim cloud. At school, in the exit melee, trash cans were turned upside down, water fountains overflowed, hugs extended, hands shook, fives were highed, and backs, slapped. I emptied my locker and slammed the door shut for the last time.

I said goodbye to Ms. Buchwald, my favourite teacher, and she wished me luck. I began the long walk home from school, for the last time, along the railway tracks. I skipped, leaped and bounded over the planks, tie to tie. It felt like I was moving back in time and not forward, as I should, into the future. On the way, an old dog confronted me at the 49th Street crossing. He barked—a long, truncated, wheeze. I clapped my hands. It was an old routine for us, begun years before, when I was a boy and he, an energetic adolescent.

I made it to the front door at 4:05 p.m. I had only a few hours to get the house ready for the *Spirit of '83* after-graduation party. The party committee had been desperate; they couldn't find anybody stupid or reckless enough to host until I volunteered. *Sure, we can have it at my place. No problem.* I'm still not sure what came over me. If I thought about it, maybe, I felt I had one final shot to show the kids at school I was more than a hallway ghost; that I *mattered.*

I lied and told mom and the Old Man I was only going to have a few friends over to watch a movie on the Betamax. What I didn't tell them was the entire, jacked-up, ready-to-party, Magee class of 1983, was set to drop like a thermobaric bomb on the house in only a few hours.

I hid in my basement bathroom and worked on my look in the mirror. I ran a brush through my hair. First, I went straight over the top and across the sides. Next, I misted the sides and front with a can of Aussie hairspray I stole from Darlene and kept hidden in a drawer for eight months. My goal? Hair blown by unseen, celestial, winds.

I went into my bedroom and pulled out a pair of pants. I reached into my closet and grabbed a shirt. I changed my pants. I changed my shirt. I changed my pants again. I changed my shirt again. I called Fozzy on the phone to make sure he was bringing Doolin as security.

"Fozzy, what's the buzz? Is Doolin coming? What time will you be here? Do you have any weed or booze?"

"Ah, er... Yes?" Obviously, I'd asked him too many questions.

"OK. Great. Well, what time are you guys coming over?"

"We'll be there at around ten o'clock. And remember, Doolin's mellow." I didn't laugh.

"OK. OK. See ya later."

I went back into the bathroom and I stared at my reflection in the mirror for a long time. I tried on some faces for myself:

surprised, disdainful, delighted, flattered, insulted. I heard loud steps on the stairs to the basement. *Who could that be? The Old Man...? He never comes downstairs into my room. Ever.*

"Oh, come on!" I shouted out from behind the bathroom door. It was him.

"Are you having a nice time in there all by yourself?"

"Dad, I don't have time for this. I need to get ready."

The doorknob turned and he opened the door. He was plastered. He stepped forward and pushed me, so I pushed him back, harder. He stumbled backward and fell on his ass. He got back up and lunged at me. I lost my balance, fell backward, and hit my head against the bathroom sink. I roared back at him, my arm a fisted windmill. I slugged him as hard as I could, deep into his gut. He crumpled. As he went down, on his face was a strange smile, like he was thinking of something funny. He got back up. I grabbed his arm, found his wrist, and locked his hand in mine which, in turn, locked his arm. I tightened my grip.

"Argghhh! For Christ's sake, let me go!" He yelled. He cried out. I dropped his wrist and made a run for it. *The bastard.* I blubbered my way up the stairs. Oh yeah, well, you try to fight your dad without crying. It's tougher than you think. Behind me, I heard the Old Man swear, "Jesus Christ!"

What I needed was fresh air, trees, space. I pulled my school yearbook out of my backpack, raced out the front door, and crossed the street into the park. I ran up the hill and sat down on the grass. With one eye on the door of my house, I leafed through the pages of the "*Magee Spirit of '83*" yearbook. It didn't take me long to discover it had been autographed, handsomely signed, and childishly vandalized. On the very first page,

To Magee's 70th Grad Class, bold in spirit, confident in manner,
fragile inside, riding off into an uncertain future . . . with heartfelt
thanks to the teachers and staff who have guided us so well through
these growing years: ave atque vale . . . hale and farewell!

On the second page, a pencil drawing of a knight on horseback jumping off a cliff into the unknown. An abyss? The future? Who knows? On page three, in elegant handwriting, next to a half a dozen black-and-white student snapshots,

Mon Cher, Andy, you Great Bull-Duster! Are you glad now I invited
Shannon and her friend to Vancouver for the weekend? You have been
a challenging friend. I will continue my work on you abroad in New
York, U.S.A., Abidjan, Cote'd'Ivoire, Nice, and Paris. Dude—you are
a bird of rare plumage! Ha Ha.
Allons y!
Fak

On the fourth page, almost illegible, beneath a black-and-white photo of himself giving a junior student "a noogie":
Andy, you are a good freind.
It's been swell knowing you. I
hope you have a happy life.
HANS

I fast forwarded to the inside back cover where I found a photograph of a classroom filled with students. On its opposite page was the same photograph, except, the classroom was empty. I discovered a giant message from Chinsky.

Andy, You're an ASSHOLE
Chinsky

Underneath, in the right hand corner, in smaller print, was another message alongside a crudely drawn picture of a burning marijuana cigarette:

Andy, let's twist one up and get real blitzed—soon.
PSYCHE!
Fozzy.

Next to that, a short, blunt, message, its meaning unclear,

Andy,
EXCRETION
Henry Tunselman

I skipped back a few pages and found, under a half-page photo of the U.N. Club:

The future's uncertain but the end is always near!
Cheers, Sully

A few more pages back, scribbled across a photo of a dozen kids (I barely recognized) on the Student Council,

Throw me to the wolves and I will return leading the pack.
John Dolbeck

Opposite, over the top of a photo of the female bantam volleyball team,

Madness is the Emergency Exit! Ha. Ha.
See you on the other side!
Tom Papadopoulos

In a section dedicated to the students of the eleventh grade, written in careful print underneath a black and white photo of Molly Murphy,

Dear Andy, it was fun getting to know you better this year. You are a schweet guy (Ha Ha). I will always remember playing box hockey with you and wiggling our toes in the sand on Wreck Beach! I am stuck here for another year, so you know where to find me—
if I don't find you first.
XOXOXO
MARVELLOUS Molly

I turned back to the front and found a page with a class dedication, written by Principal McLintock.

The Class of 1983 has maintained and enhanced the shining tradition of Magee. It has established an admirable standard of excellence in the fields of academic achievement, service, fine arts, and athletics. I wish each member of the class, health, happiness, and success. I am confident that your years at Magee will have provided you with the resources to make a meaningful contribution to your profession, your community, and your country.

A black-and-white photograph of McLintock accompanied it. He sat in a chair, smiling, his hands folded at his crotch. An ejaculating penis had been drawn coming out of his pants; in a text bubble, at his mouth, "Ahh."

I closed the book, stood up, and walked back home. Once inside, I set up the stereo turntable in the living room. I put two large speakers adjacent to one another, one pointing back to the rear deck, and the other pointing out toward the front door. On the turntable: The Tubes, *Outside Inside*.

A low, buzzsaw rumble drifted into the living room from outside on the street. I looked out the window, the pugs flanking me. Henry Tunselman, wearing tight white pants, British aviator goggles, and a red helmet, sat astride on a Japanese moped. When he saw me in the window, he revved the engine. The front wheel sat on top of the curb, pointing toward the door of the house. The pugs, excited, began to bark.

Tunselman kicked the clutch and roared forward onto the lawn. He headed for the door at a dangerous speed. At the last minute, he steered his front wheel into one of my mom's large terra-cotta planters. At impact, the planter shot back a couple of feet, wobbled, cracked, and split in half. Black dirt, stalk, and petals lay scattered on the landing, murdered in cold blood by Tunselman and his machine. Both bike and rider collapsed in a wreck on the lawn. A minute later, he got up, straightened himself, regained his focus, walked up to the door, and knocked. I opened it. We greeted one another, cordially.

"Hello, Andy."

He stepped inside.

"Hello, Henry."

A stream of kids flooded the front, back, and side doors of the house at an alarming rate, carrying six-packs, cases, two-fours, 26ers, and bottles of Black Tower wine.

Within half an hour, the house was so full, grads had gathered outside in groups on the back lawn and on the porch above the carport. Chris Kaholo passed me in the hallway, gave me a Shaka, and called out, "Hang Loose!"

"Kaholo! What's happening with the Hot Nuts? Have you got any gigs?" I asked him.

"Nah, nothing. Zilch." He told me, shaking his head. "We don't have anyone who can play a Moog—hey, wait a minute. What about you?"

"A Moog?"

"An electric synthesizer. We don't have the sound people want to hear now. To tell you the truth, I only did it to get girls."

"Did it work?"

"Hell yes, it worked."

"Well, O.K.!"

He handed me a large joint, expertly rolled into the shape of a scorpion. I smoked one of the front pincers and passed it back to him. Gus Brown passed us in the hall. He paused and said, "Hey, now that it's dark, we're going out into the park to light a candle for the fallen. Do you guys want to join us?"

"The fallen?" I asked him.

"Yah, you know, your fallen classmates. People in our class who should be here but aren't because they're dead?" I nodded. I could recall a few—two accidents on the Sea-to-Sky highway, an early morning joyride with a tragic ending in Kerrisdale, a Katimavik wilderness program accident, and a Hawaiian riptide.

"Gus, thanks. I'd really like to but I can't. I've got too much happening here."

"Kaholo, what about you?"

"You bet. I'm coming."

I grabbed a candle from one of the drawers in the kitchen and handed it to Gus and watched them go. I swallowed the last of my third beer. I smoked my twenty-fifth cigarette of the day, Player's Navy Cut, and crumpled up the pack in my hand. I tossed it into a trash can. I walked back into the living room. I found and unsheathed *Regatta de Blanc* by The Police and put it carefully on the turntable. With Sting singing in the background, I went in to each room of the house, over and over, to make sure nobody was fucking or stealing, or both. I discovered somebody had locked themselves in the bathroom on the main floor, next to the Old Man's bedroom, and wouldn't come out. I knocked on the door. "Is everything OK in there? Hello??" I received no reply. Guests couldn't fix their hair, piss, shit, or vomit because they couldn't get into the bathroom. Becoming hostile, a few had tried the door next to the bathroom —the Old Man's bedroom door. I heard the door open and close, again, this time, with a warning,

"Watch it, man. Don't go in there. There's an old dead guy laying on the bed."

I checked my watch. It was 9:30. There was still no sign of Fozzy and Doolin. I shotgunned my fourth beer and lit another cigarette. I scrambled downstairs, navigating a bowling alley of beer cans on each step. I picked up the receiver of the phone, put it next to my head, and dialed the Fozzy with my finger. The phone rang a dozen times. Nobody answered.

Two guys dressed like surfers in long shorts and Vans sat talking on the couch.

"So, I was riding one of these new Jap mopeds on the U.B.C highway, right?"

"Right."

"And I had this bright red helmet on my head, right, and this goddamn hawk or eagle or something swoops down, like, out of the fucking sky, and starts pecking at my head, right? I think the stupid bastard thought I was a giant berry!"

"Gnarly!"

"Whose house we at, anyhow?"

"Who the fuck knows? It's some guy named Levingstoun. He's some kind of a Farmer Ted. Ya know, like, the 'King of the Nerds' or 'Nerd King' or whatever. I heard he fucked a vacuum cleaner in elementary school."

I squeezed my way into the kitchen. *Jeez, could it get any more crowded…?* Abraham Huang —enjoying himself—laid an enthusiastic high five and congratulations on me. "Skookum party, Andy!" The kitchen was surly. A surly, hurly burly. I was clapped on the back by complete strangers who yelled, inches from my face, "Bitchin' bash!" I hadn't seen my mom for over two hours. Earlier, she was running around in an old housecoat, emptying cigarette butts out of aluminium McDonald's ashtrays.

I opened the fridge door. Inside, it was empty except for a cling-filmed bowl of orange macaroni from Darlene's last visit. I pulled it out and carried it over to the microwave. When I opened the door, inside, quivering, her two eyes bugged out even bigger than usual, was one of the pugs: Franny. She hadn't been microwaved, yet, but some sicko was getting ready to go for it. Getting ready to push the button on HIGH.

What a freak show! It's a good thing I came along when I did.

I reached in and gently lifted her out. "EAT ME" was written across her stomach in giant black letters. A crowd formed around us. One moron to chant,

"Eat me! Eat me! Eat me!" There was no escape. "Eat me! Eat me! Eat me!" got picked up by almost everyone inside and rippled out the front door, over the back patio, and into the street. "Eat me! Eat me! Eat me!" I held Franny to my chest and ran outside. Out of breath, I put her down on the grass. I hadn't seen the other pug, Zooey, for hours. "Eat me! Eat me! Eat me!" still rang in my ears.

I saw Fak. He was sitting, legs crossed, on an old folding aluminium chair, smoking one of his over 50 daily butts—actually, you know what? Why don't you just imagine Fak smoking all the time, and you'll be right more times than you're wrong. It'll be easier that way.

"Jesus, Fak, look what they did to Franny." I grabbed the dog, lifted her up, and showed Fak her vandalized underbelly.

"Astonishing," he answered me, not surprised.

"And look—look! The foundation of the house is coming apart! *Look*!"

"Oh, that," he muses. "It is merely a *tour de l'œil*."

"Fak, really, I'm not in the mood."

"A trick of the eye."

"Hey, why are you sitting back here all by yourself?"

"Ah, well. I received some bad news tonight, I'm afraid. My uncle Toufic was murdered, only yesterday."

"Murdered?!"

"*C'est vrai*. He was delivering the payroll to the workers at an exotic flower orchard we have." He told me, nonchalantly. "You know, we sell them to the grand hotels of Europe. Anyway, he was walking down a path and the bandits jumped him, clubbed him, and took the money. They didn't even ask him to hand it over. They 'shoot first and ask questions later?' Is that it?"

"No, yes. Jesus, I am so sorry. That's terrible. Does that kind of thing happen a lot in Abidjan?"

"Ah, not so much in Abidjan, but in the Côte d'Ivoire, yes."

"Does that mean we're still going?"

"But of course," he answered. Two long plumes of blue smoke shoot out of his nostrils. We sat in silence.

A bright light struck the carport, illuminating the silhouette of a guy between the legs of a girl, her knees up, feet out, on the hood of the Firebird. A black muscle car—a Plymouth Barracuda? — pulled into the driveway. Fozzy jumped out and opened the passenger door. A large black Dayton motorcycle boot stepped out on the pavement. It was Doolin.

"Good evening, gentlemen," Fak said as they approached us.

"OK, so how's it going, what's happening, where are the babes?" Fozzy asked me, blistering with excitement.

"Well, they put one of my dogs in the microwave, for one thing."

"They didn't!"

"They did."

"Those *animals!*"

Doolin stood there, smiling. He didn't look the way I expected. He was short, stocky, with a thick face and a weak moustache.

"Well, let's get this party started!" Fozzy cried out. He howled. *Aww Ooooooooo!*

I walked Doolin and Fozzy around the side of the house. As we made our way down the path, I called out over my shoulder,

"So, what happened to Bignault?"

"Oh, he couldn't make it. He had to go see a movie with his mom at the Richmond Cineplex. He has to do it once a week and tonight was the night," Doolin told me. Incredibly, for a guy with a murderer's rep, his voice was a thin falsetto. It took everything I had to stop myself from bursting out laughing. As we continued down the path, a warm stream hit the back of my neck and ran down my back, soaking my shirt. *What the heck...? Why would someone shoot me with a water gun? Filled with warm water?*

I looked up. Tom Papadopoulos was standing high up on the porch railing, like a musketeer or a pirate, swaying, penis in hand.

"Jesus Christ, Papadopoulos! What the hell are you doing?! You pissed on me! You could have hit Doolin!"

"And what would that matter? What does anything matter?" he yelled back, drunk as hell.

We hurried down the path and I parked Doolin and Fozzy at the front door.

I drank a beer and went back inside. By now, a good number of the graduating class of 1983 has either stumbled home, coupled up, or passed out like spent fireworks. Only the stalwarts remained, the deep-dyed, the campaigners.

Some Cro-Magnon played "Safety Dance" by Men Without Hats three times in a row. I reached for the album *War* by U2. It was time for a change. It was time for Dublin, Ireland. It was time for "Sunday Bloody Sunday!" I air guitared the long introduction before the chorus kicked in. I saw Chinsky in the corner, swaying on his heels. I walked over.

"What's up, Chinsky?"

"Terrific, just terrific, just fine, I'm fine."

My mom passed us, scowling, our vacuum cleaner in her hands.

She was cleaning the house! She plugged it in and turned it on. The sound of the engine filled the room.

"Hey," Chinsky slurred. "Doesn't that turn you on? Seeing your old flame? I mean, your first love? Was that the same vacuum cleaner you made it with in elementary school?"

"Oh my God! Chinsky! You made my life a living hell! You were supposed to be my best friend. How could you have done something like that? Shout something like that out in front of our entire class! How did you find out?"

Chinsky put both hands out and flipped his fingers back and forth, like a duck paddling in the water. "You're like a fucking duck, man. Everything's cool. It's all smooth, just gliding along—nice and easy—on the water's surface, but man, oh man, those little duck feet of yours are paddling as fast as they possibly can under the water." He scoffs, sways, and seems to remember what he was going to say. "OK, OK. I'll tell you." He put both of his hands onto my shoulders. "Well, your mommy," he says, nodding in the direction of the hallway, "used to telephone the Gooch practically every other night. God knows why. On one very special night, she let it slip that you—that you, you know, ah, liked to 'do the nasty' with her vacuum cleaner. She said she and Darlene walked in on you while you were getting it on. She was very worried. She thought you should see a psychiatrist."

"Jesus. Of course. Of *course*. The Gooch! It was *The Gooch* who told you. I knew it. She's always had it in for me." I shook my head and for a minute felt sorry for my younger self. "I had to transfer schools."

"Aw, screw you, Andy," Chinsky snapped. "You're an asshole. I get it, though—you're like that because you had to survive. Now, I

want you to pay attention to me. For once. Grow up! You made it!
"And do you want to know what? You're boring. You're the lead in
your own one act play, the unsympathetic hero of your own, stupid,
sad, story. To top it off, you're a narcissist".

"What? Uh, er, . . . OK?" I stumbled. He scoffed.

"That's right. You have no idea what I'm talking about. Do you?
And, for the record . Let me ask you a question: when was the last
time you asked me how I was doing and meant it?"

"What? Uh, er... OK?" I stumbled.

"Let me help you out." He said, sarcastically. "Hi Rick, how are
you doing?"

Pause.

"How are your mom and dad?"

Pause.

"Wanna spend some time together?" He scoffed. "And, for the
record, life's been no picnic for me. You deserted me in elementary
school—without saying a word—and went to that swanky private
school in Dunbar. You didn't talk to me for over two years until you
needed me to save your ass before your fight with Arges. You fooled
around with Karla behind my back and you got me fired from Mr.
Mike's Steakhouse." I stared into his sad, drunk face. I felt bad.

"Oh, wow..." I exhaled. "That was heavy, Chinsky. Really, heavy.
Maybe too heavy? OK. I am so sorry. I really mean it." I put my
hands on his shoulders. "But right now... I've really got to go."

I lurched into the living room, still reeling. I guess some of what
Chinsky said was true, but me? A narcissist? Grandiosity? Need
for attention? Lack of empathy? No way. He must be crazy. And
honestly, how dare he speak to me like that, especially after all I'd
done for him.

I turned up the volume on the stereo. I felt the party needed new life—amplification, acceleration. I put on "Sweet Dreams (Are Made of This)" by the Eurythmics. Who was I to disagree? I drank two more beers, one right after the other, and smoked three more cigarettes.

Teddy Sullivan, wearing a tie and blue blazer, sat on the floor, legs crossed, my albums in front of him: AC/DC, Supertramp, Queen, Roxy Music, The Clash, Duran Duran. Some were in their record sleeves, others were not. He had headphones around his neck with a long cable attached to a small black case on his belt, a Sony Walkman.

"Ha, Livingston! Just the man I've been looking for. Super. Great party! Skookum, skookum!"

"Hi, Sully."

"What are your plans for the future? What's next then, old boy?" he asked me.

"Oh, I'm going to travel with Fak this summer and after that, well, I'm not sure. I think I want to be a writer . . ."

"A writer! Of course! The curse of creativity, eh? Well, I think a writer would be a fine thing to be, maybe one of the finest. More noble than medicine!"

"Ah, thanks, Sully, you're a good friend." I smiled. "Well, what are you going to do?"

"Oh, I'm going to be a billionaire entrepreneur and own an '85 Monk McQueen."

"A what?"

"A McQueen. It's a motor-yacht." He stood up, winked, and put his headphones over his ears. He clicked a button on the Sony player attached to his belt and walked out of the room. I found

Queen's *News of the World*, pulled the album out of the record sleeve (with a giant robot on the cover), and dropped it down, somewhat unsteadily, onto the turntable. The opening lines—barren, yearning—of "Bohemian Rhapsody" filled the room: "Is this the real life?"

I thought about Fak. I was worried about him. I hadn't seen him for a long time. He was a terrible drinker. He pretended to like beer, trying to fit in, to be *Canadian*, but it was forced. He was a faker, Fak, a Fakker—he couldn't fool me. I found Fozzy behind the stupid fake Tiki bar in Darlene's old room in the basement, serving drinks. In front of him was an ancient bottle of yellow Galliano liqueur. A bunch of yellow shots were lined up on the bar. Standing in front of them were a large group of eleventh-grade designated drivers with "Stay Alive, Don't Drink and Drive." lanyards around their necks. I struggled to get Fozzy's attention. "Fozzy, goddamn it. What are you doing? These guys have to drive tonight!"

"Relax. It's cool. They're going to be fine. Everybody just needs to fucking loosen up a bit."

The shots quickly disappeared and appeared again, refilled by Fozzy. I pushed one of the designated drivers out of the way and drank one. It was revolting. I did another. Fozzy was arse holed. His hands rested flat on the bar, an attempt to maintain equilibrium.

"Hey! Great party, Andy." He looked at me; his eyes, stagnant ponds. "A real train wrecker—I mean, it's a real train wreck."

"What? Why would you say that? I mean, what made you think of that?"

"Well, look around you, for once." I looked around. I had to admit—he had a point.

"Fozzy, have you seen Fak? I need to find him."

"Sure, I saw that little sand monkey outside on the front lawn."

"Fozzy! Seriously? C'mon, Fak's my friend."

"You're right. You're absolutely right." Up came his hands in mock defence. "I'm sorry. I saw him out front a while ago. He was fumbling with his car keys." I ran upstairs and out the front door and nearly tripped over the pugs. *Zooey was alive!* I saw Tunselman's moped lying on its side. The clutch pedal had left a huge wound on the Old Man's lawn. Fak's car was gone. The street was empty.

On the front steps of the house, Doolin, and Ugly Hans, my new security detail, were laughing and patting each other on the back. "Under Pressure" played *loud* on the stereo. Hans wore a bright Lacoste polo, turned up at the collar, and leather boat shoes. Doolin was in a black leather jacket and motorcycle boots.

"What a goddamn fake preppy you are, Hans," Doolin said. "All of you guys are phoneys." Doolin, the murderous sociopath, was enjoying himself. Heck, it looked like he was having a great time. *Jesus*, I thought to myself, *So that's all there was to it? All these tough guys wanted was to be invited to the party like everybody else. Who would have guessed? Could it really be that simple?* I sat down on the couch.

I closed my eyes and fell asleep. When I woke up, I saw dawn fire up like the burning cherry at the end of one of the Gooch's cigarette butts. New Order's "Blue Monday" spun on the turntable, the needle tracking dead wax on the run-out area, resulting in a fuzzy, constant, low-level surface noise. I walked over to the sink to get some water. I turned on the tap. A sudden torrent of water hit the kitchen window and fanned out in a terrifying skein across the windowpane.

I ran out onto the back deck. In the morning light, the Old Man stood on the grass, barefoot, a garden hose in his hands. He was spraying water on anybody in range, both conscious and unconscious. It was a masterstroke. Patterson, Brown, Gerber, Dickinson, and a couple of unrecognizable girls, screaming, scattered. Papadopoulos, caught behind, on his knees, begged for mercy. The Old Man shot him in the face. It was only minutes before the backyard and deck were clear. Remaining, alongside a few empty beer cans, a wine bottle, a girl's wrap sweater, and a high top running shoe, was the Old Man, standing on the grass, watering his flowerbeds. The Old Man abideth.

I went back inside. I could barely move my arms and legs. I'd been running around for twenty hours straight, drunk buckets of beer, chain-smoked dozens of butts, and flash-guzzled Galiano shots. Oh yeah—I almost forgot— I beat up my dad. On the way down the hall, I peeked into Mom's room. Henry Tunselman lay passed out on her bed. He was still wearing his aviator glasses. Across his crotch was a large, asymmetrical, piss stain. I quietly closed the door, crept down the stairs, careered into my room and stood in front of the bed. I abandoned my clothes and planked down onto the mattress.

I surrendered to sleep.

52

Big Bird in the Sky

Where am I? What happened last night at the party? What party? The grad party? There's been a catastrophe, a falling out, a tragedy... Oh head, my poor head.

I opened my eyes. My head felt like a holocaust helmet. A winding crack was visible on the ceiling next to the light fixture. I heard birds singing in the trees in the backyard. A couple of houses over, Rex Wilson's lawn mower threshed blades of green grass in the morning sun.

I lifted my right hand. The inside tips of my index and middle fingers were nicotine stained an ugly, piss-water yellow. I felt bad. I rested my hand at my side again. A *tap, tap, tap* on my bedroom door cracked the still gloom of the bedroom. I ignored it.

After a few more minutes came a second series, this time, louder: *knock, knock, knock.* Could it be the Old Man? He wouldn't *knock.* He'd have put one of his big imperial Brogues on the door and sent it out of its frame with a booming crack, followed by an explosion of wood and nails. In fact, I was surprised he hadn't come down already.

I waded across the floor to the door. I reached for the handle, turned the knob, and opened it. On the other side, an embarrassed smile on her face, stood Molly Murphy in an awesome *Frankie Says Relax* T-shirt. Her bright eyes, spring rainbows encircling black suns.

"Molly!" I blurted out. "Molly? Hiya—I mean, hello. Ah, what are you doing here? Is everything alright?"

"Oh, you know, I was… Ya know, in the neighbourhood."

She stepped forward and kissed me. And do you want to know something? She threw her whole beautiful heart into it.

A couple days later, Mom came out onto the back patio where I was suntanning and handed me a white envelope.

"What's this?"

"Open it."

I tore it open. "What is this? What? C'mon. An invoice?"

"Mom. That's all the money I have."

"Tough. We can come up with a repayment plan, and amortize the interest. Oh yes, and by the way—after the events of the past week, Abu-Jasar nearly called your trip off. I've never heard anyone so angry and disappointed. Fak is lucky." She clicked her tongue. "So are you, buster."

Jeez, well, I forgot to mention: Fak really messed up on the night of the party. After smoking an ounce of weed and shooting Galliano shots all night with "the morons of the inferno," as he put it, he'd gotten behind the wheel of his Oldsmobile and driven home. On the way, he side-swiped a neighbour's car and rear-ended a second, pushing it onto the lawn of another neighbour, a retired BC Supreme Court Justice. He abandoned his car on the grass, somehow made it home, and went to bed.

In the middle of the night, the cops broke into his house, woke him up, and arrested him. Abu-Jasar forbade us from seeing each other until it was time to board our plane for New York. The whole thing was outrageous. I looked closely at Mom's invoice again. She'd put her bed sheets on there, the planter, the house speakers, even the disgusting bottle of Galliano liqueur. At the bottom, before the total, was an insane "administrative penalty."

On the day of our flight, Mom and the Old Man drove me to the Vancouver International Airport. We took the AMC Eagle, fresh out of the repair shop, again, passed Bobby Jobby's grandparents' place, down Angus Drive to Southwest Marine Drive, and passed in front of the house where Mark Robinson blew his head off with a shotgun when he didn't get into medical school. We passed by the Fraser Arms Hotel, where the Old Man got his ass kicked, passed Brown's Auto, where Gus Brown's old man repaired cars, crossed into Marpole, where we got off South West Marine Drive and took the Arthur Laing bridge into Richmond.

Molly and Rachel came out to see us off. Mom and the Old Man had a great time, laughing and kidding around with the girls. At one point, it even felt like Molly might have come out to see them off on a trip instead of me. I kissed Molly, waved goodbye to the Old Man, and hugged Mom. Fak and I walked over to the baggage check. Fak dropped his crocodile duffel onto the conveyor belt and I followed with my MEC backpack. When it looked like it was going to disappear into a square hole in the wall, I jumped onto the belt and tried to get it back. Fak, embarrassed, reassured me the airline would load it into the belly of the plane and I'd get it back in New York.

I'd never been on an airplane, obviously; I behaved badly, like a giant baby. I was forced to follow all of Fak's instructions from check-in through security, until we finally boarded our plane and sat down in our seats. "Jesus, Fak, look at that!" An enormous, bright orange, Hawaiian Air 747, was taxiing out onto a runway, next to our plane.

"Ah, you see, it's an orange colour in order for the marine search party to be able to identify it under the water." Fak pushed down his armrest, popped open the ashtray, and lit a cigarette. He blew a bouquet of blue smoke across two rows of seats.

"Man, you can even hit those sticks on a plane?" After taking another deep drag, he said,

"But of course." I pulled my itinerary out of my pocket and read it over again:

Vancouver YVR to New York JFK
New York JFK to Félix-Houphouët-Boigny International
Airport Abidjan ABJ
Félix-Houphouët-Boigny International Airport Abidjan ABJ to
Paris CDG
Paris CDG to Vancouver YVR

We taxied onto the runway and waited. The engines roared to life. The giant blades spun. Expanding gases jetted out the rear of the airplane's engines, producing thrust. The nose of the big bird lifted and we ascended into the sky. She—we—passed through a grey band of cloud and broke free into the stratosphere.

As we began our journey east, over the lakes, the forests, and the mountains of Canada, my soul swung as I caught sight, through my porthole on the rear horizon, of the two snow-capped peaks I left behind, the Twin Sisters, soaring high over all the spirits of that rough-hewn and verdant valley of my youth.

Made in the USA
Las Vegas, NV
08 March 2024

86872605R00173